Gossip
Can Be
Murder

Charlie Parker Mystery #11

Connie Shelton

Secret Staircase Books

Gossip Can Be Murder
Published by Secret Staircase Books, an imprint of
Columbine Publishing Group

Printed and bound in the United States of America

This book is a work of fiction. Names, characters, places and
incidents are either the product of the author's imagination or are
used fictitiously. Any resemblance to actual events or locales or
persons, living or dead, is entirely coincidental.

Book layout and design by Secret Staircase Books
Cover image © KCPhotos, Cover silhouette © Ayutaka

Publisher's Cataloging-in-Publication Data

Shelton, Connie
Gossip can be murder / by Connie Shelton.
p. cm.
ISBN 978-1945422119 (paperback)

1. Parker, Charlie (Fictitious character)--Fiction. 2. Women
private investigators--New Mexico--Fiction. 3. Santa Fe, New
Mexico--Fiction. 4. Women accountants--Fiction. 5. Women dog
owners. I. Title.

Charlie Parker Mystery Series : Book #11.
Shelton, Connie, Charlie Parker mysteries.
BISAC : FICTION / Mystery & Detective.

813'.54

Gossip
Can Be
Murder

Connie Shelton

Books by Connie Shelton
THE CHARLIE PARKER SERIES
Deadly Gamble
Vacations Can Be Murder
Partnerships Can Be Murder
Small Towns Can Be Murder
Memories Can Be Murder
Honeymoons Can Be Murder
Reunions Can Be Murder
Competition Can Be Murder
Balloons Can Be Murder
Obsessions Can Be Murder
Gossip Can Be Murder
Stardom Can Be Murder
Phantoms Can Be Murder
Buried Secrets Can Be Murder
Legends Can Be Murder
Weddings Can Be Murder
Holidays Can Be Murder - a Christmas novella

THE SAMANTHA SWEET SERIES
Sweet Masterpiece
Sweet's Sweets
Sweet Holidays
Sweet Hearts
Bitter Sweet
Sweets Galore
Sweets, Begorra
Sweet Payback
Sweet Somethings
Sweets Fogotten
The Woodcarver's Secret

NON-FICTION
Show, Don't Tell
Novel In A Weekend (writing course)

CHILDREN'S BOOKS
Daisy and Maisie and the Great Lizard Hunt
Daisy and Maisie and the Lost Kitten

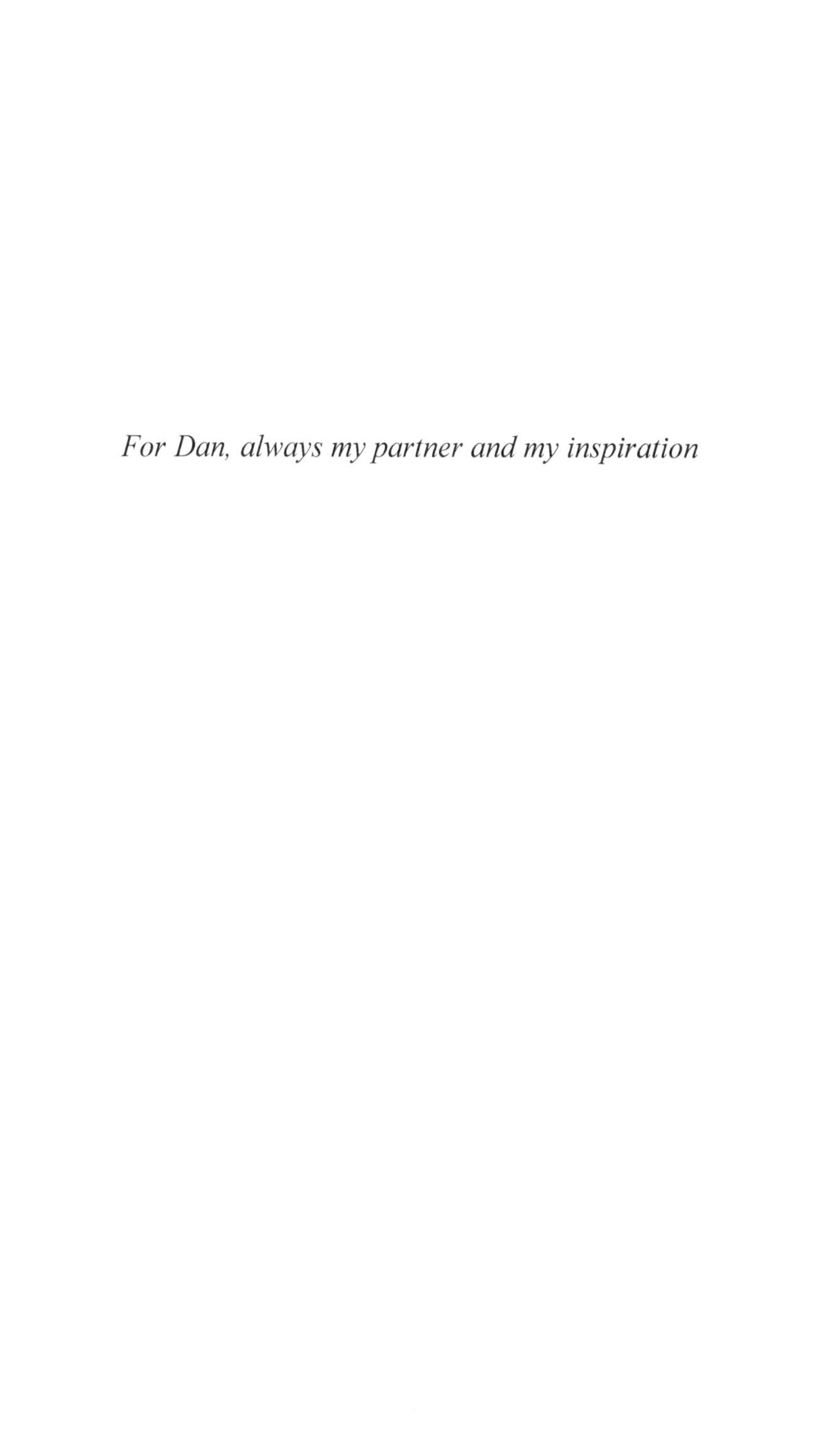

For Dan, always my partner and my inspiration

Chapter 1

Drake's voice came through my headset. "You're less than fifty feet above treetop," he cautioned.

"I know," I said. "I'm setting up for the L.Z. at my ten o'clock." I continued easing left pedal and watching my airspeed. Keeping an eye on the tiny field less than a quarter mile ahead of the Eurocopter A-Star I was flying today.

"Watch it, watch it."

"I *am* watching it," I snapped. Even though I had less than a hundred hours in this aircraft, he didn't need to coach me through every single step, for god's sake.

My eyes scanned the instruments. Normal, normal . . . oh, no. The rotor RPM had dropped below the red line so fast I'd not noticed. The low rotor horn suddenly blared, right beside my head. I jammed the collective down as fast as I could. It helped a little but the RPM continued to decay.

"Drake!" I felt the scream rise in my throat.

"Flare!"

"Yes! I'm starting to. I *am* flaring!"

Outside the windows, treetops flashed by. My heart pounded and my palms felt like glazed ice cubes.

"Bring the nose up more!" he yelled.

I yanked the cyclic back and the nose came up.

"I've lost the engine," I screamed. "I've got no engine RPM. Engine horn is on!"

"You're going in."

The ground rose sickeningly. There was a shudder as the rotor blades struck trees. The cyclic jerked in my hand. I could feel my eyes grow wide as the earth came toward me, little details like pebbles and wildflowers coming into sharp focus, then blurring. I pulled up on the collective for all it was worth. I squeezed my eyes shut, waiting for the impact.

An electronic boom caused me to open them again and the screen in front of me was now solid blue. YOU CRASHED. The words in bright white on the simulator screen slammed my ego. A crash—even a simulated one— the worst thing a pilot could experience. My pent-up breath rushed out.

My husband stuck his head in through the cabin door, a grim little smile on his face. "It worked."

I took three more breaths. "Yeah, it sure did."

"This gives me the evidence I need." He reached over to unfasten my harness and realized I was shaking. "Hon, you did exactly what you should have, exactly what even an experienced pilot like Mike Walters would have done. I'm proud of you."

Tears welled but I blinked them back. "Really?"

"You helped make my case for me." He offered a hand to help me out of the simulator cockpit.

I stepped out and gave him a gentle jab to the ribs. "Next time, you're the pilot who crashes and I'm the one who gets to loosen the thingamajig and cause your engine to fail."

"Deal." He kissed me solidly. "Let's go check out that wine festival now."

Two hours later, Drake and I were finally relaxing, having snagged a table at one of the more popular wine-tasting events in the city. Although this morning's crash had not been real, the adrenalin charge certainly was. I willed the tightness from my shoulders and put my feet up on an adjoining empty chair, a glass of pinot noir nearby.

I took a deep breath of September. I love the crisp air, the late-blooming roses, the purple and gold chrysanthemums, the way the State of New Mexico celebrates with cultural and festive events. We seem to pack a lot of art shows in alongside the State Fair and Balloon Fiesta. We're reveling in cool mornings and glowing afternoons, when you can drive up to the mountains to witness the turning leaves and come back to the city by mid-afternoon to sit at an outdoor café with the sun warming your back.

So much had happened to us in the past year—we'd thought we might become parents, only to have that possibility taken away; I'd gone through a blue winter, guilting over my role in the loss. Our chance at a getaway vacation for two last spring had somehow morphed into my taking a new case in the northern part of the state while Drake rushed off to start an early fire season with his helicopter business. The summer brought so much flight work we could hardly keep up with it; after several years of drought the state had become a tinderbox and Drake continually stayed busy with one fire contract after the other. I'd gone along on a few of the jobs, getting additional qualifications for flying difficult water bucket drops and a bit of long-line work. But those weeks and months didn't exactly provide quality time as a couple. Bone tired and caked with soot at the end of each day, we were doing well to manage a quick shower and goodnight kiss before dropping off into exhausted slumber.

I looked over at Drake and noticed the strain around his eyes. This crash investigation has turned into more than he bargained for. But he's coping.

He reached for my hand and gave it a squeeze. When our eyes met, I knew that he'd divined all the thoughts that had just run through my head. "It's okay," he said. "We'll get past the bad stuff. I'll take some time off this winter. Promise."

I blinked a couple of times, smiled and stroked his jaw. "I know."

"We're going to make the most of that second honeymoon," he promised, referring to an upcoming trip we'd booked to Kauai for November.

A flash vision of some of the moments from our first honeymoon zipped through my head. I couldn't help sending him a rather naughty grin.

"Charlie! Hey, Charlie!" A female voice grabbed my attention and I stood up and turned around.

"Linda—wow, imagine the odds of running into someone you know in this mob." We hugged. I reintroduced Drake to Linda Casper, my close friend since elementary school, now also my physician. He offered to get Linda a glass of wine, princely guy that he is, and she accepted. I think he simply found standing in line preferable to listening to ten minutes of girl-babble.

"I was planning to call you the minute I got home," Linda said after he'd gone.

"We're due for our monthly lunch, aren't we?" Considering I'd skipped them the past two months, I should have been the one calling her. "I've gotta tell you about the summer and gosh it seems like there's tons to catch up on."

"How about if we take a whole week to do just that? This week?" Her blond curls bounced when she talked and the blue eyes held the same sparkle as when we'd met in the fifth grade. She was still a full six inches shorter than I, her growth having moved in an outward rather than upward direction. Today she wore pink, a summer flowered top and capris that showed off the curve of her calves.

In college, our paths had diverged with mine going toward accounting and a CPA certificate, while she finished med school in record time and started her own practice a few years ago. Our schedules were equally erratic and it was rare that we found more than an hour at a time for each other.

"A week? What've you got in mind?" My mind flashed back over the promises I'd made to my brother Ron about spending some time at RJP, the investigation business we own together. But with Drake leaving tomorrow for a Fish and Game job the prospect of sitting home alone every evening wasn't all that appealing.

"How about a week at the plushest spa in Santa Fe . . ." she paused for effect. "Huge rooms with views toward the ski slopes, meals by a staff of gourmet chefs, massages every day, yoga classes, peace and quiet."

"What's the catch?" Something this good always has a catch.

"Okay, honestly?" She fiddled with the clasp on her watchband. "Alex was going with me but he got an emergency call from the folks back home and had to cancel." Freckles popped through her light makeup; it happens when she's embarrassed. "I didn't mean to make it sound like you were second choice . . ."

"But I am." I laughed. "So? Since when has that ever mattered between us? I've canceled lunch with you a dozen times since Drake came along. It took both of us forever to meet our Mr. Rights, so we adjust, right?"

"Well, it's not just a trip purely for pampering. That's the other thing." She fidgeted with the watch again.

"Uh-oh. What *other thing?*"

"I'm taking classes in Eastern medicine." She held up one hand. "No kidding—it's really fascinating. Makes so much more sense than a lot of the stuff we learn in traditional Western medicine. I've been studying quite a lot and I want to learn more about it, see if I can incorporate some of these ideas about diet and treatments with my current patients."

"And I figure into this, how?"

"Alex and I had planned to each attend some of the sessions, then share notes afterward. He wants to put it to use in his practice, too."

"Oh, Linda, I'm not qualified. I wouldn't know what they were talking about when it comes to anything medical."

"Yeah, you will." The blue eyes sparkled again. "I've looked through the course schedule. Anyone can attend the basic classes in nutrition and meditation. And there's a lot of philosophy. I think you'll love those. I'll take the sessions for medical professionals. Mainly, I need someone to pick up the handouts and take notes, get the materials that each instructor provides—two copies, if possible. Please, Charlie."

"And the massages—"

"Every day. Different techniques for different conditions, so of course I'll need you to experience each one and report to me. All the spa facilities are open to attendees, so . . . mineral baths, hot tubs, lounge chairs around a pool . . ."

"Wow, you make it sound pretty tough." I had to laugh at her sales pitch. "It's this week, though?"

"Sunday evening, a reception. Monday morning, the classes start. I know, it's short notice and I'm really sorry. But you'd really be helping me out."

Drake walked up with two new glasses of wine. He gave Linda one and lifted the other, indicating it was for me. She quickly filled him in on her request.

He glanced at me, gauging my enthusiasm for it. "Whatever you want," he said. "I'll have to stay over at the jobsite, anyway, the government being too cheap to pay ferry time for me to fly home and back each day."

"I'll need to clear a few things at the office with Ron, but if you don't mind my not being at home . . ." I knew better. Drake's always good with nearly anything I want to do.

"Let me just—" I pulled my cell phone out of my jacket pocket and punched in Ron's cell number. It rang four times before his voice came on.

"One second, please," he said. I heard fumbling and kid voices in the background. A full minute went by. "Thanks for holding. Ron Parker here."

"Did I catch you in bad traffic?" I asked. He and his new lady, Victoria, had taken his three boys to the State Fair and I'd teased him about how much fun they would have eating a ton of junk food and riding the carnival rides until they puked. And if Ron didn't go quite that far, it was a cinch one of the boys would.

"Uh, no, we got out of the fairgrounds okay. We're pulled over at a gas station on Lomas."

I didn't want to visualize what was going on, but I knew it involved one of the kids in the bathroom. "Okay, I won't keep you long. Just wanted to let you know that something's come up and I'm planning to go to Santa Fe for a few days. You've got the situation with Graham and Valdez under control at this point, don't you?" Our wrongful-death helicopter case.

"Charlie, what is it this time?" he demanded. "You're always roaring off somewhere!"

"Excuse me?" I turned away from Linda and Drake and walked toward the back of a vendor tent. "What—"

"You know what I mean. We're partners. And you're always finding something to do outside the office."

A grain of truth in that, but where on earth did this *outburst* come from? "Ron, that's ridic—"

He cut me off. "No, it's not. Between helicopter jobs with Drake and whatever other fun things you come up with . . ."

"Fun? I'm usually snagged into doing things that bring money into this company. I lost—" My throat tightened.

Silence on his end.

I took a deep breath. "Ron, despite all this *goofing off* you think I'm doing I haven't missed a payroll, I've never been late with a tax return or any other stupid-ass government report that's been required of me." I straightened my shoulders. "I'll be in the office this evening. I'll be there tomorrow. I don't need to be in Santa Fe until Monday morning. But you'll have to plan on my being gone for the week. I'll have my cell if there's a *real* reason to reach me."

"Fine. Oh, great—Jason! Get . . ." His voice trailed off and I lost the connection.

I waited a minute to see if he would call back then dropped the silent phone into my pocket. I was *not* going to beg his permission to take a personal week off.

"All set." I walked back to Linda. "I better plan to take my own car, just in case something drastic happens." I didn't elaborate and she didn't seem to notice. Drake, on the other hand, gave me a quizzical look.

Linda beamed. "Thanks, Charlie. This is gonna be so much fun!" Her dimples went deep. "Here's a map to Casa de Tranquilidad. I've already switched the room from a king bed to two doubles, so that's set. I'm driving up this afternoon to get a head start, but you come along whenever." She gave a little wiggle, her bosomy chest shaking like a gelatin mold. "Gotta go pack. I'm *really* looking forward to this!" She drained her glass and practically skipped as she headed out of the park.

Drake smiled. "She's got the enthusiasm of a cheerleader, doesn't she?"

"Used to be one, in junior high."

He gave me another close look. "Problem with Ron?"

"It'll be okay." I sipped from the glass he'd handed me. "You sure you don't mind my going off for a week?"

"To Santa Fe? Heck no. In fact, since I'll be working up there in the Pecos area, maybe we can both break away and meet somewhere for dinner in town."

We finished our wine and decided we better get home and pack for our respective journeys. Something about the way his eyes gleamed told me that we were going to make the most of our last night at home.

Chapter 2

Eager as we were to get home, I convinced Drake to stop by my office at RJP Investigations on the way. I'd left some of the files for the Graham and Valdez case, *Walters et al versus Starland Helicopter Manufacturing and S-Jet Engines*, on my desk and decided it would be safer if I put them in the locked file cabinet. Ron's and my little business enterprise is located in a converted Victorian house in what's now a combination residential/office neighborhood near downtown. Although we've never had a security problem, I've always taken reasonable precautions about leaving sensitive information out in plain sight. I'd originally planned to come back here this evening to organize paperwork, and type up some of Ron's notes. Considering his attitude today, I decided screw him. I'd rather spend the evening with Drake. I would get him on his way in the early morning, then I could come back to the office to wrap up a few things Sunday morning and leave for Santa Fe when I was finished.

"Do you want to look over the file on the engine data?" I asked Drake as we climbed the stairs to my second floor office.

I didn't hear his response as I hit the light switch and I turned to look at him. He shook his head. "Not now."

"Sorry. I know this is hard for you."

"It's just that Mike Walters and I worked together several fire seasons. He was a good pilot. I can't stand the idea that all these lawyers are trying to place blame with him, and I just can't believe the accident was his fault."

"I know. And it wasn't. Didn't our simulated crash this morning prove mechanical failure? Isn't that enough to clear him?" I sat down at my desk, opened the file and picked up the printout of our test data. "Or almost enough?"

"What we did today proves that a loose nut would cause that particular engine failure. I still have to prove *that* exact nut failed in *this* accident." And Ron continued to put pressure on Drake to hurry the investigation.

I watched his profile and saw the jaw muscle flexing. This was the first instance where the firm's work had caused friction between my husband and my brother. "It's okay. Let's put this out of our minds and deal with it later."

After a minute or so he blew out a long breath. The jaw muscle relaxed and his military-sharp posture loosened up.

"Look, there's nothing here I can't do tomorrow morning." I said. "Let's grab some dinner." I gathered the folders quickly and took them to the fireproof file cabinet in Ron's office.

"Pedro's?" I asked, knowing he'd hear the hopeful tone.

"Sure."

A couple minutes later I'd locked the drawers and switched out the light.

Drake rubbed the back of my neck as we walked down the hall toward the kitchen together, a silent apology for his testy attitude earlier. I slipped my arm around his waist and pulled closer to him.

We locked the back door and drove in Drake's pickup truck the few blocks to Pedro's Mexican restaurant near Old Town. By the time we walked in and got our first whiff of green chile and tortilla chips, the earlier conversation had receded to the back of my mind. When Pedro brought our customary margaritas with extra salt, my stomach began to growl.

"No Rusty tonight?" Concha, Pedro's wife, waitress and chief cook, asked as she set plates of steaming green chile chicken enchiladas in front of us.

Our rust-brown Lab is a fixture here, as much as we are. He normally takes a spot in the corner beside our table and manages to catch any loose, unwanted tortilla chips that fall his way. Pedro always brings a heaping basket of them, just to cover that situation.

"No, we've been out all day. He would have gotten bored at the wine festival, I'm afraid," I told her. "But he'll be jealous that we came here without him." I knew we'd get a huge sniff-over from the dog the minute we walked in the house and he'd know exactly where we'd been.

She set the hot plates down and scanned the table. "Just a minute."

About the time I'd blown the steam off my first bite and put it into my mouth she came back with a basket of fresh sopapillas—three of them. "Here's a spare napkin.

Take Rusty one of these and the extra chips. So he won't be angry with me."

Drake laughed as she walked away. "Good thing that dog isn't spoiled."

I pulled one corner off my little pillow-shaped pastry and let the steam billow out. As I poured honey into the hollow interior I told Drake, "Well, I'm not performing this part of the routine for the dog. Can you imagine what a mess he'd make? He'll just have to eat his sopa without the sweet."

Thirty minutes later we made our way to the truck, carrying our little bundle of doggie goodies. An hour after that, with two duffle bags packed and waiting near the front door, we fell into bed. Drake reached for me hungrily.

"I hate time apart," he said, nuzzling into my neck.

We spent the next forty-five minutes relieving that sadness before we fell into a deep sleep. The alarm went off way too quickly as the first light of Sunday's dawn began to gray the windows. I rolled over, planning to snuggle into Drake's warmth, only to find that he was already wide awake staring at the ceiling. My little whimpery sounds got his attention and he pulled his hands out from behind his head and wrapped me in a cozy embrace. That lasted about three minutes before I could tell he was antsy to get moving. First day of a new job.

We grabbed a quick breakfast of cereal and I stuck the bowls in the dishwasher while he walked Rusty over to Elsa Higgins's house next door. Bless her heart, she's always a willing sitter even on a moment's notice. When I'd called her as we were leaving the wine festival she'd even offered to come over and pick up the pooch right then. I felt guilty that my requests had become so routine that she assumed the need was immediate. I vowed to bring her something from Santa Fe and to manage to spend more time with her. Our times together are becoming precious, as she is approaching ninety. She's an amazing lady, putting up with me all these years, and now caring for my dog as well.

Drake came back with a baggie full of homemade chocolate chip cookies, picked up his duffle, and we both walked out to our vehicles. He watched me as I started my Jeep, asked me if I'd checked the oil and topped off with fuel (the answer to both of these was that I was going to stop at the first station I came to), then he kissed me so well that I wanted to switch off the engine and take my husband and our bags back inside. With a reluctant smile I backed out of the driveway and watched him do the same. He turned left at Central, heading out to the airport on the west side of town, while I aimed for that promised gas station. I even remembered to check my tires' air pressure while I was at it. Marriage to a pilot. He'd done a good job of training me in the wisdom of being prepared.

At the office I pulled out the files on the crash case and reread the notes. I felt a pang of sadness that Drake and Ron were at odds over the case. More so that I'd had words with my brother yesterday. Normally, we work together really well. I pushed the thoughts aside, resolving to keep doing my best for the business, but not to let Ron's wishes take over my life. He's got his own set of problems.

Turning back to the file I saw that, in a phone message from Graham and Valdez, Rick Valdez had requested copies of several of the documents Ron had obtained, along with Drake's informal notes. Soon, Drake would be required to give an official deposition—something he was looking forward to like a case of the flu—but for now Valdez simply wanted to review the initial findings. I stacked the pages and started the fax machine. Once they'd gone through I re-inserted them into the files in the correct order and noted the date and time the faxed pages had been sent.

I typed letters to a couple of other important clients, paid some upcoming bills and entered monthly statements into the computer before I realized that most of the day had slipped away and I really ought to be heading north. I locked the files away again, making sure to leave Ron one of our loosely coded messages telling him what I'd done with them. I scanned the rest of the office to be sure I hadn't left anything terribly crucial undone. I couldn't imagine having a whole week—especially spur of the moment as it was—to myself. There was always some little crisis that brought me back into the office but I would leave things in good shape for now.

Downstairs, in the reception room, I left my outgoing mail and jotted a note for Sally including the name of Casa Tranquilidad and the central phone number, just in case my cell didn't quite connect there in the mountains. I also reminded her that Ron had an optometry appointment mid-week and that he probably wouldn't go unless someone nudged him. Sometimes I feel like everyone's mom.

I snacked on a granola bar that had probably been in the console of my car for at least six months and managed to hit a bunch of the weekend traffic on I-25 heading toward Santa Fe. By the time I reached the edge of town I felt more than ready for some classes on how to relax.

Chapter 3

They don't call Santa Fe the City Different for no reason. The street layout follows no sort of grid but is instead a meandering maze of twists and turns that can lead a driver in circles. I know it's historic, I know you can't redesign a city that's been around since before 1600, but moving around this place is a pain in the ass. I absolutely hate getting entangled anywhere around the plaza or government offices so I took the St. Francis Road exit and made my way north.

Gradually I left the commercial areas behind, then the smaller residential streets. Following Linda's map, I drove a winding dirt road north of the city, into foothills dotted with piñon trees and juniper. In the higher elevations near the ski area, distant aspens had already begun to turn, and their myriad shades of gold, yellow and celadon painted the hills in a palette of autumn. The contrast with the pure blue sky felt almost startling. This is the sky for which the Spanish *azul celeste* surely must have been invented. I began to relax at the sight.

As I rounded the final curve at the top of the hill, I got glimpses of Casa de Tranquilidad between stands of piñon and ponderosa pine. A winding adobe structure, it seemed designed to fit the hills like a boa draping a woman's shoulders. Late afternoon sun burnished the various buildings in rose-gold. The drive was paved in slate tiles, which curved around a circular entrance and framed a planter of brilliant purple petunias. I pulled my Jeep to the front entry under a wide, shady portico.

A valet, uniformed in green and gold, met me and offered to park the car but I told him I'd rather do it myself. It's just a quirk of mine. He directed me to a small, discreet lot on the north side of the building, behind an adobe wall. I grabbed my duffle bag and walked back to the front of the building.

A woman was pulling two large trays from the back of a small SUV parked under the portico. The trays, stacked high with homemade cookies that smelled like they'd come from the oven minutes earlier, looked like they were about to get the better of her.

"Can I give you a hand with those?" I asked, dropping my duffle beside her vehicle.

"Oh, sweetie, you sure can." She lifted one tray toward me, leaving the other one balanced a little precariously on the edge of the vehicle's cargo space. I reached out and caught mine just as she had to let it go and make a grab for the other. "Whoa, that was a little too close."

We stood there, frozen in a little 'what's next?' moment in time. I have to admit that it was tempting to make a run for it, keeping five dozen elegantly decorated butter cookies all for my very own.

"I've got to get these to one of the conference rooms," she said. "Could you spare a second out of your way?"

"Sure." I followed her lead. We walked through a lobby filled with heavy, hand-carved furniture and Two Gray Hills rugs. Enormous arrangements of fresh flowers topped a table in the center of the room and several side tables. Down a corridor and past a dining room, doors to a meeting room stood open and a jacketed waiter was setting up a large coffee service. He tilted his head toward an empty stretch of table and we deposited our treasures there.

"Whew! Thanks so much!" The woman turned to me and held out her hand. "Samantha Sweet."

I introduced myself. She was a stocky woman in her late fifties, short graying hair in a shaggy cut, smile wrinkles at the eyes and mouth. She had that jovial, open friendliness that reminded me of the actress Kathy Bates.

"I don't know why I tried to handle both of those at once. I know better. Just get myself in a hurry sometimes."

"Hey, no problem." We walked back outside where I retrieved my duffle.

"If you ever need customized, homemade baked goodies, that's what I do," she told me, reaching into the pocket of her white slacks and pulling out a business card. "Sweet's Sweets." She rummaged into a large paper sack in the car and came out with a baggie that held four exquisite little cookies. "There you go—a sample."

I swear that my salivary glands went into overdrive just looking at them.

"Thanks, Samantha. Nice meeting you." Knowing about this great lady might give me the excuse to hold an office party at Christmas this year.

She thanked me again and climbed into the SUV, waving through her open window as she pulled away. I hefted the duffle again and headed inside.

The front desk was made of golden pine, topped with hammered copper. An extremely polite young lady greeted me, tapped my name into the computer and scrunched her eyebrows slightly.

"I don't seem to have your reservation, Ms. Parker," she said.

"Sorry. I'm rooming with Linda Casper."

"Ah, yes. Dr. Casper arrived earlier. I have you in Room 12, a very nice double just beyond the garden." She finished clicking the computer keys and shuffling papers then handed me a tiny folder with a plastic key card in it. "Just out this way, take a right through those double doors."

By the time I'd made my way through shady cloisters beside lush gardens of autumn flowers to Room 12, I was suitably impressed.

"Hey, you came this afternoon after all!" Linda greeted me with her usual dimples and a hug.

"Afraid I might not be great company for the evening," I said. "It was a very early morning and the traffic up here was a mess." I eyed the undisturbed bed on the far side of the room as I set my bag on the floor beside a desk carved with Mexican designs. "A quick little nap would feel so good."

She didn't pick up on my hint. Just bustled over to the desk and handed me a folder with an Eastern-looking emblem on it and the words "Lightness in Living."

The daylight through our gauzy drapes had faded to deep lavender and I guessed it must be around six o'clock. I sat down on the polished cotton spread on my bed and flipped open the folder.

"Save that," she said. "Let's freshen up and check out the dining room. Bring your folder with you, and later I can show you around."

I quickly unpacked my meager wardrobe of jeans, sweaters, and five sets of clean undies. Linda had told me to expect casual-comfortable wear, and I'd brought one broomstick skirt and tunic, in case there was a dress-up dinner at some point. Unfortunately, I'm not one of those women who's ready with a chic outfit for every occasion. If I couldn't attend a nutrition class in jeans, well, too bad.

I almost regretted that stance when I saw the dining room. It was one of those with a black-tie maitre d', real linen, and three goblets at each place setting. After I noticed that most of the other patrons were also dressed very casually I relaxed a little. The menu was about ninety-percent vegetarian, with a couple of fish dishes thrown in to pacify us rabid carnivores. Luckily, I love veggies too and we were both able to quickly choose dishes that sounded wonderful.

"So, here's the program schedule," Linda said, flipping to a page in the folder. The name badge in mine said that I was Alex Hudson but Linda told me that would be fixed by morning. "The inspiration behind the program is Dr. Celeus Light."

"Ah—'Lightness in Living'—catchy."

She pressed on. "He studied in India under some of the great maharishis. Apparently, some of his healing techniques have worked miracles, although he's been poo-poo'd by the medical establishment." She glanced up at me. "That's one of the reasons I'm interested in finding out what he has to say. I'd never admit this to another of my patients but there's so much in Western medicine we don't know. And there are so many procedures we could be doing but are afraid to because we're crippled by the insurance companies. But that's a major rant that I won't get into." She took a deep drink from her water glass.

The brochure pictured a tall, slender man in his forties, with dark hair and bronzed skin. He wore some kind of modified sari with purple and gold trim, making him look like a cross between Gandhi and Caesar. In the photo he was shown in a Jesus-like pose with his hand stretched out to a small child. A real man for all cultures. Despite all the obvious image management his credentials looked impressive, including degrees from major universities in both America and England. The testimonials from doctors and patients alike were glowing.

"Tomorrow starts with an orientation class," Linda said. "I think there are only a few doctors attending the special sessions with Dr. Light. I'm hoping to get some individual attention and lots of information. At least half the attendees are people who are here to experience the treatments and work on their own problems, or so I'm told." Linda turned to the program schedule. "Each day starts with a yoga class, then meditation, then nutrition classes, followed by lunch. In the afternoon you get a massage or some other spa treatment, philosophy lectures, and group discussion."

I sent her the perkiest smile I could manage. My early

awakening, sketchy meals, and the hour-long drive were taking their toll and for a couple of seconds I wondered what I was doing here.

Our meals arrived, an artistically arranged pile of julienne vegetable strips in yellow, green, orange and red for me. Rice with black beans and glazed carrots for Linda. Pungent spices wafted upward from the plates and we picked up our forks without another word. Finishing the meal with ginger tea and an almond cookie, my energy rebounded. I suggested we check out the rest of the facility and learn our way around.

Linda glanced at her watch. "Good idea. There's a get-acquainted gathering at eight tonight, too."

She signed the dinner check, waving away my offer to split it. I glanced at the other diners as we left, curious as to which might be in our group for the coming week. Out in the lobby, Linda steered me toward a hallway to our left.

"According to my little map," she said, "the classrooms and a library are this way."

Through a short corridor, a doorway led to a good-sized vestibule where a reception desk sat with a lamp set to a dim night-light mode. Across the room, shelves held candles, incense and decorative bottles of various oils and potions. A display table contained an impressive array of Dr. Light's books. I'd just picked up one entitled *Shedding Stress From Your Life* when a voice startled me.

"Are you ladies here for our program?"

I jumped and set the book back in place.

"Yes, we are," Linda quickly chimed in. "I'm Dr. Linda Casper." She extended her hand. "And this is my associate, Charlie Parker."

The woman greeted each of us with a smile and warm handshake. "I'm Shirley Broussand." Cinnamon brown hair framed her face in soft chin-length waves and was scattered with gray strands. Tiny creases radiated from the corners of her vivid green eyes. Her skin had that particular gray-tan hue of a long-term vegetarian and her long, thin face reinforced the fact. She wore a gauzy skirt and top in a shade of sage that accented her eyes and brought out the luster in her hair.

"I'm afraid the offices are closed right now," she said. "I was just locking up."

"Oh." Linda sounded disappointed. "We thought we'd get a look at the place, so we'd know where we're going tomorrow."

"This is it," Shirley said. She gestured to indicate the vestibule. "Nicki will be here in the morning and she'll give a quick tour of the facilities. I'd offer now, but I'm off to get things ready. Are you coming to the gathering tonight?" When we nodded she smiled. "That's great—I'll see you there."

Subtly, we'd been ushered to an outer door and found ourselves standing in a beautifully landscaped courtyard. The evening temperature had dropped about twenty degrees already and I buttoned my denim jacket.

"So that was Shirley," Linda mused. "She's the one I corresponded with in getting this set up. Funny how phone impressions never come out right. I'd pictured her as a heels and business suit type with hair in a French roll."

We chuckled over that and strolled the courtyard, discovering that it was flanked by a number of offices on one side and a low adobe wall on the other. Beyond the adobe wall the night was pitch black. Knowing that the resort sat at the top of a hill, I assumed the terrain dropped off and there were probably fabulous views by daylight. Openings in the courtyard led back to the dining room and, eventually via a softly lit winding path, to the parking lot where I'd left my Jeep. We strolled as far as the parking lot then turned back toward the lobby.

Near the front desk a discreet sign pointed the way to the Lightness in Living group.

All this vegetarian, spiritual, lightness of the soul stuff was completely foreign to me but I'm game for new experiences. Signs directed us through another exit to a secondary building where the spa and massage rooms were located. The reception was to be held in the lobby of the spa building. We entered a world of luxury and quiet good taste. The walls were faux-finished in shades of umber and gold. Massive wooden columns framed the doorway, with smaller versions of them leading to other corridors and the hidden wonders beyond.

Cushy leather chairs had been pushed to the corners of the room to accommodate the dozen or so people who had already arrived. I noticed that the reception desk had been converted to a bar, serving something that looked fruity and slushy. A dark-haired girl poured the mixture from a blender jar into small crystal goblets. I supposed that booze was out on this healthy regime.

A quick glance around the room told me that no one seemed to know anyone else yet. They stood around awkwardly with their glasses of whatever-flavor smoothie, openly ogling the surroundings but not making eye contact. Linda seemed more at ease than most of them. She'd snagged drinks from the bar for both of us and quickly made her way to Shirley Broussand. I had to admire my friend for her easy ability to fit in nearly anywhere. It's a characteristic that I've not seen in many doctors, that quick rapport with all types of people.

I left Linda and Shirley to their conversation and began to snoop. If Linda's innate ability is rapport, mine is observation. I admit it, I'm nosy.

I slipped past a couple of women who appeared to have just met each other and slid through the archway leading to a series of treatment rooms. Doors stood half open and tiny lamps illuminated each room with cozy warmth. I ascertained that there were three treatment rooms with massage tables, followed by locker rooms for men and women. A locked door—I checked—stood at the end of the hall. Across the hall from the locker rooms a door led to a bubbling circular spa at least fifteen feet in diameter. A door beyond that sported a small sign saying "Mud Baths."

The voices from the lobby had dropped to a hush. Something was happening. I made my way back and cozied up to one of the pillars, as if I'd been there all along. All faces turned toward Shirley as she took a position near the entrance.

"First, I'd like to thank you all for coming to our little gathering tonight. You'll be getting to know each other much better in the coming days, but this gives you the chance to begin to put names and faces together. Doctor Light will be here in a minute to share a few words with you." A murmur of approval went through the room. "But first, I'd like to quickly go around and have each of you introduce yourself and let us know where you're from."

I hate this kind of thing. I shrank beside the pillar and let a few others step in front of me. However, my own reticence didn't mean I wasn't curious about the others.

Mouth shut, ears open, my mother used to say. I find I learn a lot this way.

After Shirley introduced herself, she gestured to the woman on her left.

"I'm Nicole Mayhew, from New York. My husband Gerald is here, too, but he didn't make tonight's party." Sleek aqua suit—probably Versace—gold Rolex, huge diamond on the left hand. Long hair, light brown with golden highlights, perfect teeth. She couldn't have been more than twenty-five.

"Dina Carlotti." An accent that made the name roll off her tongue. "I am from Venice, Italy." Slender, pretty, dark hair down to her waist, casually dressed in black slacks and sweater.

Linda introduced herself next, mentioning only that she was a physician from Albuquerque.

"I'm Tahlene Wexton-Smith, from Sidney." She didn't offer more. The Aussie accent piqued everyone's interest— we Americans are suckers for that. College-aged, wearing harem pants, a tight fitting wool jacket and two knitted scarves—one blue and one green—wrapped around her slender neck. A half-inch of tanned skin showed between the edges of the pants and the jacket. A froth of untamed blond hair bushed out from some sort of cloth band around her head.

The woman next to me spoke next. I noted graying shoulder-length hair with a bad case of static electricity to it. "Uh, I'm Trudie Blanchard. I live in California and I'm a nurse, uh, I used to be a nurse. I've had some health problems recently and lost my job. I want to learn more healthy ways to take care of myself because I've been depressed a lot lately and—"

"Thanks, Trudie, good to meet you," Shirley interrupted. I admired her ability to take control. "Let's go on to Charlie, over there by the pillar. Now don't be shy."

Ugh. I pasted on a smile and gave my name.

Luckily, the next woman took over quickly. "Dr. Patricia Girard, Harvard, Oxford. I live here in Santa Fe now and come to Dr. Light's seminars every couple of years just for a break. With my incredibly huge practice, I simply have to get away now and then."

"Um, yes, Pat. It's great to see you again," Shirley said.

I registered a fifty-something woman who'd probably already had a couple of face lifts. She wore skin-tight white jeans with a black T-top and short, fitted Indian-blanket jacket. Strands of turquoise nuggets hung around her neck and a wide silver bracelet clamped her right wrist. East Coast background latching onto Southwest chic, unfortunately, without the fashion model body to quite pull off the outfit.

"We'll have a few others joining us tomorrow and, as I mentioned, you'll be getting to know each other much better over the coming days," Shirley said. "Now I know you are all impatient to meet the spiritual leader of our conference so it's my great pleasure to present Dr. Celeus Light." She turned toward the door behind her. Precisely on cue, the tall carved doors swung open. Celeus Light, dressed in white baggy trousers and a white peasant shirt, pressed his palms together in a prayer posture, bowed slightly to the group, and bestowed us with a benevolent gaze. Was that actually harp music coming from behind him? I felt my bullshit sensors go up a couple of points.

"Welcome, and peace to everyone," he began. "You are about to experience one of the most enlightening weeks of your life. You'll find new methods of health care, new ways of preparing and eating the nutritious food that fuels your body, and a whole new attitude toward the stresses that everyday life sends your way." He relaxed his pose and shook his dark head. "Seriously, folks, I think you're going to have a great time here. Please, feel free to come to me with your concerns and share your experiences. I'm here for you, truly."

Around the room, shoulders relaxed and breaths were expelled. I noticed for the first time that aside from Dr. Light the group were all women. The magnetic charisma worked, and they gravitated to him like metal shavings.

I settled back into my pillar and finally took a sip of the drink Linda had handed me. It was a curious combination of fruit and vegetable, with an under taste of something else, vitamins probably. I rolled it around in my mouth and decided to go look for water. I'd seen a drinking fountain near the locker rooms and headed that way. The remainder of the drink went down the drain as I swished the glass with water. A good long sip took the rest of the taste out of my mouth.

"Not quite to your liking?"

I flinched.

Chapter 4

Drake brought the Jet Ranger in and worked to avoid the young guy who was attempting to guide him as he set his ship down in the landing zone set up by the job's helicopter manager. They'd put in a long day and now the sun was nearly behind the mountain, casting an orange-gold glow over the forestry compound, making the Ponderosa pines appear nearly black in contrast.

Ridiculous, he thought, making eye contact with the guy holding the two useless batons. Government jobs. They always found someone who'd had a couple weeks training and assigned him to direct a pilot with twenty years experience. Charlie always teased him about his frustration. What was the point, she said, of getting angry at a bureaucracy. Just do the work and collect the money. She was right, of course.

He pulled the rotor brake and brought the slowly turning blades to a full stop, letting out a contented sigh as the engine noise subsided. No matter what a pain the government jerks could be, this was what it was truly all about. That feeling of control over the aircraft, that adrenalin buzz as you soared through the air. And not all the government guys were jerks. Three of the men in the local Pecos office were great guys, including the two who'd spent the day airborne with him counting elk in the high meadows. He felt sorry for Milo, who always got queasy after a few minutes of staring down through the trees from the circling helicopter. He would be better once his feet hit the ground. Drake would suggest they all go out for a beer after he finished shutting down and securing the aircraft.

A sharp tap on his side window grabbed his attention.

"Drake!" Ernie Pacheco called his name through the Plexiglas. "Call for you." Ernie held up a pink message slip.

Drake felt his eyebrows pull together. It was unusual to get a call out in the field. Anyone wanting to schedule a new job would leave a message on his office machine, knowing that he would get back to them at night. Family would call his cell. He opened the door and took the note from Ernie. "Thanks."

"Beer later?" Ernie asked.

Drake looked up from the note. "Huh? Sure. I was going to suggest that. Wait a sec." He knew the number on the note. Charlie's office in Albuquerque. Since she wasn't there, it had to be Ron calling about that damn court case. He pulled his cell phone from his jacket pocket, flipped it open and noted that there were two voice mails but no signal. "Ernie? Let's plan on the Doble Seis for that beer. I'm buying."

"Johnny has a cooler," Ernie began, "but I guess it has to do with the message?"

"Yeah, I really ought to return this call." Drake unfastened his harness and climbed out of the aircraft. Pulling the tie-down gear from the cargo hatch he looped the strap over the rotor and pulled it taut.

"I'll see who wants to go," Ernie said.

"Thanks, I really appreciate the ride." It was always a hassle, being out of town without a vehicle, but that was the nature of the work. On longer jobs he had a buddy who drove along, bringing fuel and extra parts. But this one wasn't supposed to take more than a couple of days, and the Santa Fe airport was near enough for refueling. He ducked into the men's room at the forestry office—a relief after a full day at the stick, with only one quick break while he scarfed a sandwich at noon. Everyone else took an actual lunch hour, but for some reason they didn't seem to think pilots needed to eat or pee. His breaks usually only came while the aircraft was being fueled.

Ernie's pickup truck was parked beside the forestry building. Looked like Johnny and Milo had decided to come along. They were already sitting in the back seat.

They drove north on I-25 for about five miles to the nearest exit, easily spotted by the lighted sign depicting a pair of red dice showing sixes. The Doble Seis was the local bar, a tiny adobe building at a crossroads, run by a crusty old Spanish guy who'd probably been there since he was a kid and his father was the old guy serving up the beers. Drake opened his phone again, while the others headed inside. He had a good signal here—just that little difference between being along the Interstate or tucked back behind a ridge in the Sangre de Cristos. Both voice mails were from Ron.

"Order me a Tecate," he told Ernie. "I'll be right in." He dialed, wondering whether Ron would still be at the office or if he'd already gone home for the day. He stared out to the west, where the sun sat on the horizon like a fat orange ball, the bottom edge of it going flat. Two rings and he heard Ron's standard "Y'ello."

"Hey, what's up?" Drake asked his brother-in-law.

"Got a call from Rick Valdez," Ron said without preamble.

"And?"

"They're moving the date of your deposition up."

"Crap." It slipped out. "Sorry. I know I agreed to this." *Before I knew that the pilot in the crash was a friend.*

"Yeah, you did." Ron blew out a breath. "I mean, we all did. We took the case and managed to commit ourselves. None of us knew how long it would drag on."

Drake forced himself to relax and tried to keep the tension out of his voice. It wouldn't be a good idea to fracture family relationships. The current case had caused them all a lot of stress but he'd get through it.

"That's okay," he said. "Not your fault. Maybe moving things forward will get it all over with that much sooner."

"Exactly." Papers rustled as Ron undoubtedly searched through the usual mess on his desk. "I told Valdez that you were out on a job and they'd have to work around it."

"Good. I'm not messing up my contract with Fish and Game, even though I'm getting decent money for this other thing."

"They don't expect you to. I'm supposed to call them back and let them know your schedule."

"Two, maybe three more days here," Drake told him.

"Should be done by Wednesday, but maybe we better plan on Thursday."

Ron made a sucking sound, like he was pulling air in through clenched teeth.

"Problem?"

"Well, I kinda let them believe that Wednesday would work out."

Drake forced himself to count to three. "Okay. I'll do my best. No promises, though. Can't rush the government, you know. When all these elk are counted, they're counted. The cheesy lawyers can hold on." He wanted to make the point stronger than that, but held back.

"You want to tell Valdez, or shall I?"

"I'll do it. Give me the number."

"Thanks." They ended the call before Ron could say anything about catering to the customer, keeping the lawyers pleased to earn their future business. Drake, frankly, didn't give a damn. He'd quickly discovered that legal work was not his forte.

He dialed the number Ron gave him and got a voice mail system. After punching a few more numbers to get to Valdez's personal mailbox, he left a message telling the man, truthfully, that he'd be subject to financial penalties if he left the forestry job early. Wednesday was a possibility but Thursday was the earliest he could promise. Sorry to be so vague, but after all they were the ones who'd moved the date forward. He kept the message polite and as positive as he could manage, then clicked off. He blew a sharp breath out and walked into the dimly lit bar.

He wanted one beer, just a relaxer, then he was eager to get back to his bunk for the night. He ought to call Charlie before he got back to the cell phone dead zone, but wasn't sure whether he'd catch her. No doubt she and Linda were having a great time getting the spa treatment.

Chapter 5

I nearly dropped the glass into the drinking fountain. "Oh, Shirley. I . . ." I ran out of words.

"It's okay. I can have Danielle pour the other flavor for you. That one's pretty sweet."

"No, really, it's okay. I just haven't had enough water today. You know how important that is." I smiled stupidly.

"Oh, absolutely. And you'll be happy to know that our water throughout the building is filtered for purity."

I took another sip from the fountain. "Very good." A thought flashed through my mind, back to this morning's hastily chugged bowl of Coco Puffs and the fact that I had skipped lunch altogether. Maybe Linda had another motive in bringing me here, to convert me to a healthier lifestyle. I probably should take the program more seriously.

"Nice facilities," I commented, putting my nice-face back on. "I peeked into a couple of the treatment rooms."

Shirley flashed me a warm smile. "Linda told me you

were a private investigator. It makes perfect sense that you would check out your surroundings."

"I hope you don't mind."

"Oh, it's fine. While you're here, our home is your home. Do look around."

"And that part about being a private investigator. That's not exactly true."

She tilted her head to one side.

"I'm a partner in an investigation agency. But I just handle the financial end of it." Except that I often find myself going further than that, as evidenced by several close calls in recent years. "It's become more of a sideline anyway. My husband owns a helicopter service and I help out there pretty often."

A flash of interest. "You have quite an amazing life, don't you?" she said.

"Well, it's been fun, I have to admit." I found myself sharing the details of how Drake and I met in Hawaii. She listened with interest and I felt a rapport building.

The tone of the voices in the front room changed in intensity and she pulled herself back to the present moment. "Guess I better get back to the group. Nice to chat with you," she said. I followed her back to the spa lobby to find that Dr. Light had left and the crowd was dispersing. Linda stood near a big potted plant, looking around for me.

"I wasn't sure if you were still here," she said.

"Oh, yeah, just checking things out." I briefly described the rest of the facility. "Take a peek, if you want. I'm sure Shirley won't mind. I think I'll head back to the room."

She said she'd do the same. Once settled, I decided to give Ron a quick call since we hadn't ended our last conversation on the best of terms. The phone rang four times and I glanced at my watch. After nine.

"Y'ello," his voice finally said.

"Hey—just checking in. How'd the weekend go?" Keep it light, Charlie.

"Huh. Jason was feeling better by the time we met up with Bernadette, but of course all three boys blabbed about how much junk they ate at the fair and how sick he'd been. I got the usual devil-glare from her."

I made sympathetic noises—I've seen Bernadette's devil-glare—then filled him in on everything I'd done at the office this morning, letting him know that I wasn't shirking my duties.

"I talked to Drake awhile ago. His deposition is set for this week. He didn't sound happy about it."

"He's not looking forward to being grilled. Nobody would."

"It's more than that."

"When he started the investigation he didn't know Mike Walters was the pilot. And he's putting together some new evidence. Take a look at the notes in the folder."

"Charlie, I know how he feels about this case. But he can't back out on us now. He offered to help with the research and now we're getting down to where we need his expertise."

"I know that. He knows that. He'll be there." Not exactly with bells on, but I know my husband. He's nothing if not reliable.

A half-minute of silence from Ron. I could hear the wheels churning. He'd earned his living and built a career on poking into other people's dirty little secrets. He wasn't above snapping pictures of people in compromising situations, and he certainly wasn't above working with shady law firms in proving a case. Graham and Valdez weren't a bad firm, they just latched onto a lot of big-money cases that often put good people in a bad light. I knew this was really at the heart of Drake's attitude.

"Well, you know where I am." I said. "Anything you want me to check out in Santa Fe, give me a call." We hung up.

Linda came out of the bathroom. "Problem?"

I shrugged. "Brother versus husband. It'll resolve itself soon." There wasn't much else to say.

By the time I finished my bedtime routine in the bathroom she was deep into a book and I could barely keep my eyes open.

Chapter 6

When the alarm went off at six-thirty the next morning I found I'd spent the night mulling over Drake's upcoming deposition through a series of strange dreams that included my own heart-thumping experience in our simulated crash. I sat up in bed and gazed around the murky pre-dawn room. Nothing to be gained by fretting over it. I decided I would do my best to get into the spirit of the coming seminars and give Linda the help I'd promised.

My roommate was not an early riser. She groaned at the sound of the alarm and rolled over. I decided to grab first use of the bathroom, so I snagged a clean set of clothes and headed that way. By the time I'd showered, dressed, and dried my hair Linda was sitting on the edge of her bed. Her blond curls stuck out at odd angles and her face was puffy with sleep.

"Good morning, Mary Sunshine," I greeted in a sing-song voice.

She threw a pillow at me. "I hate that phrase. My mother used it on me every day of the week, including Saturday and Sunday," she growled.

"I know. I remember you throwing pillows at her too." I laughed and tossed the pillow back. "I'm finished in the bathroom."

She stood up and tugged her oversized T-shirt over her thighs as she shuffled toward the open doorway.

I located an in-room coffee service in a small alcove near the door and started the process for some wake-up brew. I wasn't sure how this whole nutrition program would go, but I couldn't live without my daily caffeine jolt. A few minutes later I poured two cups, slipping one of them onto the vanity in the steamy bathroom. Behind the shower curtain, Linda dropped a heavy plastic bottle and cursed. She wasn't always dimples and grins.

Thirty minutes later we joined some of our group for a breakfast buffet, which consisted of fruit, whole grain muffins, and herbal teas. Made me glad I'd already managed my one cup of coffee. I piled fresh strawberries and melon onto my plate and added a large muffin, wondering if it had come from Sweet's Sweets.

Across the dining room, I spotted Nicole Mayhew with an older man. Her husband, apparently. I guessed him to be about double Nicole's age, salt and pepper hair, clean shaven, and dressed the way you'd expect a businessman to be in a resort atmosphere. The tie was gone but otherwise he could walk right into a boardroom. She wore a white slacks suit today, with gold accent jewelry, her light brown hair twisted up into a not-quite-formal up-do. With those types, it always seemed to take a few days to go casual.

Dina Carlotti was sitting alone at a table, so Linda and I asked if we might join her.

"Certainly." She smiled widely, her voice friendly. "I'm very pleased to meet you again. Charlie, is it? Is that not a man's name in this country?"

"Yes. Actually, it's a nickname for Charlotte. My brothers stuck it on me as a kid. Guess I'm just not the Charlotte type." I forked a cube of melon. It was sweet and delicious.

A tiny crease of puzzlement crossed her brow and quickly left. "And, Linda."

"You're very good with names, Dina," Linda answered. "I always have a hard time with them."

"Well, you are wearing a badge," Dina said. Her lovely smile brought grins to all of us.

"You mentioned being from Venice," I said. "What brings you to New Mexico?"

"Oh, yes. The opera. I performed here last summer and loved this city very much. I wanted to come back at a time when I did not include work."

"You're an opera singer?" My preconceived picture of heavyset women with large mouths and huge bosoms went out the window. Dina probably weighed one-fifteen on a bad day and stood no more than five-four. It was hard to imagine lusty vocalizations coming from her petite little self.

"It is true," she said. "People say I do not look the part. But what can I say?" She shrugged and picked up her fork. "I am a singer since childhood. A professional for twenty years."

"What's your main interest in the program here?" Linda inquired.

"My health. You see, my mother died last year from breast cancer. It is in our family. I think if I can study healthy ways to eat and ways to relieve the stress of my travel, maybe I can have a better chance."

"That's a very smart idea," Linda said.

"And you?" Dina asked. "You told us last night you are a doctor. So you are here for Dr. Light's medical presentations?" When Linda nodded, Dina turned to me.

"Me? Oh, well . . ." I shouldn't admit that I got talked into the whole thing. I peeled the paper from my muffin and broke it in half. "I'd like to learn more about all of it. And I must say that the massages and spa treatments sound like they'll be wonderful."

"Oh, *sì, d'accordo.*" She popped the last of her strawberries into her mouth.

I'd managed to polish off the whole bran muffin and my bowl of fruit. "Guess it's about time to report to class, ladies."

We pushed back from the table and started toward the main lobby. As we crossed it, a man dressed all in black came through the front entrance, two deferential younger men at his side. Through the glass doors I could see a stretch limo with its doors standing open. Emerging from the limo stepped a woman with the distinct look of a secretary and another wearing jeans that barely concealed her pubic area and very high stiletto heels—obviously *not* a secretary. A chauffeur was pulling suitcases—a number of them—from the trunk of the large black car.

The man in black turned to one of his gofers and said, "Take care of things, will you, Pete? Get everyone settled."

Pete didn't look as if he had any choice in the matter. He headed toward the desk.

"Now where the hell's this meeting supposed to be?" The man at the center of things gazed around the lobby. His gelled black hair stood in spikes, carefully arranged to look like it had not been arranged. His thin face was somehow familiar, yet not.

"Who's—" I whispered to Linda.

"The rock star, Rex Storm," she mumbled back.

Whoa. His face clearly showed the ravages of the good life. I tried to remember the last time I'd caught a look at him on TV. Maybe five or six years ago. Deep lines now etched the corners of his mouth and gravity had begun its takeover. His scrawny frame clad in skin-tight black jeans and silky black shirt open nearly to the waist made him look like a fifty-year-old trying to be twenty. As I recalled, he was younger than my brother, putting him at about thirty-five. Drugs, booze and the high life, I guessed.

A cell-phone cheeped and he pulled the tiny instrument from a pocket in his black leather jacket. Although his voice carried clearly and he made a big point of revealing that it was his agent on the line, Linda, Dina and I ignored him and headed across the lobby toward the vestibule where we were to check in for our classes.

"Is he attending our seminar?" I asked once we were out of earshot.

"Afraid so," Linda said. "I saw his name on the list but didn't really believe he'd show up. Do *not* repeat this, but word has it that his body has become so toxified that major systems are shutting down. He's making a last-ditch effort to save his skinny little ass."

I had to laugh. It's rare to hear a judgmental word from Linda.

Entering the classroom wing was like walking into

another world. Soft lighting and subtle incense set a mood of relaxation and spirituality. Behind the counter, Shirley and her helper handed out packets. Mine contained a new name badge—I was no longer Alex—along with a couple of booklets that were clearly study materials.

"I'm going to head over to Room . . . I don't know . . . it's here somewhere . . . the first of the medical lectures," Linda said. "Catch you at lunch?"

"I'll get all the handouts and notes I can," I assured her.

She walked down the hall and I turned to peruse the books on sale at the table. Dr. Light appeared to be a prolific writer, with a variety of intriguing titles. Dina gravitated toward the candles and incense on the shelves, and I noticed a number of other people beginning to arrive. Patricia Girard, the doctor with the numerous degrees and big turquoise jewelry, grabbed her packet and headed off in the same direction Linda had taken. Nicole Mayhew and her husband arrived. He seemed a bit impatient and I noticed that she watched him almost constantly.

"I'm really looking forward to this, aren't you?" Trudie Blanchard, the former nurse, stood next to me at the book table. Her eyes looked a bit wilder than last night and I noticed that her shirt had some kind of day-old food stain on the front.

"Sure. Are you attending the medical sessions, or nutrition and fitness?"

"Oh, nutrition and fitness, definitely," she said. Her voice came out low and whispery, as if everything she said was confidential information. "I'm not in the medical field any more, I guess."

Before I could comment she reminded me. "I lost my nursing job, you know. And I don't even know why." Her voice went whiny on the last word. "It was just a conspiracy, I think. Hospital politics. You know how that is."

I nodded at all the right places.

"Well, I'm thinking about getting a lawyer. I mean, at my age, it's not easy. I've applied at lots of places. No one seems to be hiring right now. Well, it's taking its toll on my health, I'll tell you."

Before Trudie got the chance to elaborate, Shirley called for attention.

"I'd like to take everyone on a brief introductory tour of our facility," she announced. "If you'll all follow me." We trailed along.

"You visited the spa building last night. Today we'll be in this wing of the resort. The first room on the left is our library. It's open to all of you, for your research and reading enjoyment. Feel free to make yourselves comfortable there."

Double doors opened to a cozy place with big, overstuffed chairs, plump pillows and Oriental carpets. Shelves lined two sides with books and video tapes, and a small television monitor with VCR sat discreetly to one side. I felt the pull toward the bookshelves, but followed the tour anyway.

"The room on our right is the primary classroom where we'll be meeting. As soon as we've finished our orientation, we'll meet back here." As classrooms went, this one was extremely informal, with a mixture of chairs and floor cushions. Wide windows with gauzy curtains looked out to the beautifully landscaped courtyard. A white-board stood at the front, a tea service at the rear of the room. A few other interesting items, including a huge Chinese gong, merited further investigation later, maybe just one good whack with the special little gong-hammer . . ..

The next room on the right was the meditation room. "We'll be studying meditation methods this morning, then you'll be free to use this room any time," Shirley said. "There is group meditation at nine each morning and four each afternoon. We encourage all of you to attend and enjoy the benefits of the group energy." The room was square, with only one small window. A little statue of the Buddha stood in the center of the room, with a variety of puffy cushions around him. Chairs flanked the walls and an intricate incense burner stood in one corner. I immediately felt the calm as I stepped into the room.

"Beyond this room, the doors lead to Dr. Light's private office and to the classroom used by the medical practitioners. We'll stay back, since they've already begun their session." Shirley also pointed out a couple of small offices as we walked back toward the vestibule. When we were gathered there, she indicated a door I'd not noticed before. "The yoga room," she said. "We'll start here first. Everyone wore comfortable clothing?"

I glanced at Nicole Mayhew in her sleek pantsuit.

"If anyone wants to change, the restrooms are just across the hall. Your instructor will be here in ten minutes."

I ducked into the ladies room and switched my jeans for stretchy knits, then went back across the hall.

The yoga room was a large place with wooden floors and mirrored walls, like a dance studio. Against one wall were racks with mats and blankets. Shirley directed us to take a mat and pick any spot we'd like. I kicked off my shoes and dropped my purse and papers in one corner.

Dina Carlotti took up a spot on my right. Trudie Blanchard moved in on the left. I really didn't want her letting me in on her ongoing secret battle with hospital politics, so I chatted quietly with Dina. Tahlene, our Aussie flower child, showed up late, having missed the tour. She staked out her mat in the front of the room and began doing some stretches after a quick hello to each of us.

Nicole Mayhew came in, looking like an ad for fitness wear, in a sports bra-type halter top and a matching royal blue pair of stretch capris. Her hair was up in a twist, held in place with a blue headband. Her husband trailed along, looking like he'd rather be anywhere else in the world, but was decked out in the latest in men's fitness gear.

"Hi," said Nicole, setting her mat in front of Dina's. "I don't think I met all of you last night. I'm Nicole Mayhew and this is my husband Gerald."

He grunted a greeting and allowed Nicole to set his mat into position on the floor. Gerald was probably a decade older than Drake, but I could easily see my own husband just as uncomfortable in a yoga class. My guess was that Gerald was here at Nicole's request, when his usual milieu was probably the executive office of a major corporation. For relaxation I could see him in the smoking room of a gentlemen's club with a Cuban cigar in one hand and a glass of Glenlivet French Oak Finish in the other. I felt for the guy and had to give him points for being a good sport.

A few other people wandered in, one of whom was Shirley's assistant at the registration desk. Soon the room was filled with colored mats. A large man in a maintenance uniform with some kind of embroidered logo on the chest stuck his head into the room, called out, "Rita?" and backed away when he saw the rest of us. Fifteen minutes had probably passed since we'd come in. Everyone looked around expectantly.

At last the door opened again and in came a woman carrying a portable boom box cassette player, a yoga mat, and a canvas bag that clattered when she walked. She wore a pink and green striped leotard with fuchsia bike shorts. Her curly brown hair was gathered on top of her head where ringlets sprouted from a cloth band like a springy whale-spout. White plastic glasses with square lenses slid down her pert nose. She nudged them upward with one wrist.

"Give me a second, everyone," she said. "I'll just . . ." She dropped the canvas bag and cassette tapes spilled onto the wood floor. She grabbed one and stuffed it into the player, remembering only after she'd pushed the Play button that she needed to plug it into the wall. That done, she adjusted the volume so the sitar music would serve as quiet background.

"There," she said. "Hi, everyone. I'm Rita, your yoga instructor. I'm here to help you. If you're new to yoga, please let me know if you have problem areas in your body. We'll tailor your program to those things that will benefit you most." She made us each introduce ourselves, a little ritual that felt like one of those 12-Step things where you say 'Hi, I'm Charlie' and they all greet you in return. Once we got that over with, she sat with her legs folded under her, butt on her heels, and we all followed suit. "Let's start with some deep breaths." She closed her eyes and breathed loudly. I did the same but wondered how I was going to know when she changed position.

"Now we'll move into Tadasana," she said in a lyrical voice. I sneaked a peek and found that she was standing up straight now but not really doing anything. I figured I could get this one right. We stood there for about two minutes and I swore I saw Gerald Mayhew rolling his eyes.

"Uttbita Trikonasana is also known as the triangle pose," Rita said a minute later, jumping her legs apart and then slipping into a strange spread out shape so smoothly that I couldn't begin to figure out how she got there. A glance at the others showed that few of them got it either.

Copying her position, I aimed my left arm straight up.

"Hold there, hold . . . " Rita said as she began to move around the room, pointing out subtle changes to each student's position.

"Focus eyes on the ceiling, everyone," Rita called out.

My neck felt as if it would snap but I managed to find the ceiling. Everything was beginning to feel a little topsy.

"Charlie, this wrist needs to be turned inward," Rita said, tapping my right arm with her toe. I nearly lost my balance and didn't quite accomplish the maneuver.

"Over there, blue outfit, what was your name?"

"Nicole." Her voice came out as a grunt.

"Nicole. Nicole, do you have any clue what we're doing here? That position isn't even close."

I sneaked a look to my left. I couldn't tell that Nicole wasn't doing the very same thing I was. She shifted her body forward and grabbed a deep breath before forcing herself back into the stretched-out posture.

"Much better," Rita said. She turned toward Gerald, whose position truly didn't look very close. I got ready for a critique. But just then Rita's attention wavered to the other side of the room. "What on earth are *you* doing!" She practically shouted the words.

Chapter 7

All heads turned, cartilage crackling. In the front row, Tahlene was standing, arms above her head, fingers linked. She swayed in time with the sitar music, stretching to the left and then the right. Her eyes were nearly closed and a dreamy little smile played at the corners of her mouth. Rita was practically on top of her by now but she stretched to the left, front, and right again before acknowledging her.

"I can't seem to begin yoga that way," she said. "So I'm just doing my own thing."

"This is a class!" Rita's face looked like something might burst. "You can't just 'do your own thing'." Her head bobbed furiously as she spoke and her square, white glasses slipped down her nose again.

Tahlene continued to sway to her own rhythm and it

became apparent that the only way Rita would bring her into line would be to get physical with her. She looked like she was considering it for a minute. She sputtered a couple of times and finally shoved her glasses back in place and stomped away.

"Class, we'll now move into a Downward Facing Dog." She resumed her place at the front of the room, reestablishing the idea that she was in charge.

I had no clue what a Downward Facing Dog was and couldn't even comprehend the official name Rita used for it, but I watched Dina who seemed to know her way around a few yoga moves. I did my best to copy her. On my left Trudie fumbled her way into a rough approximation of the posture.

"Heads down," reminded Rita. "Take slow, steady breaths." She seemed to be making a concerted effort to do the same as she stayed on her own mat and performed the move with us. "Hold that arm position, hold it, hold it . . ."

About the time I thought my eyeballs would pop she moved us into an easier position. Trudie let out an audible groan and a few of the others snickered.

"Rise slowly now," Rita said. "Deep breath, Sun Salute."

This seemed to be a popular set of maneuvers that everyone knew. Everyone but Gerald Mayhew and me. Trudie clomped along, about three beats behind everyone else, while Gerald and I each focused on someone who knew what they were doing and tried our best to keep up.

"Nice, nice," Rita coached. As we finished the set with hands in a prayer position, she glared at Tahlene, who had gone along with the maneuvers but at double speed.

Gerald glanced at his watch and nudged Nicole. They

began gathering their possessions.

"What?" Rita strode toward them while the rest of us held our prayer positions.

"Thanks, Rita, really," Nicole said. "Uh, good class."

"It's just that I've got this . . . call . . ." Gerald said. "Need to catch . . ."

Rita watched helplessly as they rolled up their mats and laid them aside then gathered their tote bags and folders. "Tomorrow, then. Same time," she said. The door closed a little too loudly as they left. Dina and I both had wistful looks on our faces.

"Okay, back to work," Rita announced. "Balancing. Feet directly under you. Deep breath. Lift your left leg, grab toes with the left hand. Balance on the right foot."

No one exactly felt balanced by this point but everyone except Tahlene made a valiant effort. Trudie swayed dangerously and had to let go a couple of times. When we made the switch to balance on our left feet, I took a giant step back to put myself out of Trudie's way. Sure enough, first try, she toppled onto my mat, landing at my feet. I dropped position to help her up. Once I had her back on her feet again, I caught sight of one of the other girls tiptoeing out the door. Rita had clearly lost her fragile control.

By the time we got to the final few moves, the class was down to about half its original size. We were in a posture that required us to lie on our backs, hips raised, toes pointed skyward. Dina fumbled the move and muttered something about a bad back. She relaxed, leaving her feet on the floor and her knees bent.

"Hips higher," Rita said, nudging me on the rump. "What are we doing here with hips on the floor?" The *we* she referred to was poor Dina. The Italian singer tried to tell Rita about her back problems, but had hardly gotten the words out before Rita had grabbed her by the ankles and yanked upward. With one foot she shoved a foam block under Dina's hips, forcing them off the floor.

"Ow!" Dina rolled to one side and lay, panting, in a fetal position.

Rita didn't notice; she'd already moved on. I dropped my feet to the floor and asked Dina if she was all right.

"*Sì, grazie*," she said. She rolled to her hands and knees and did a couple of back arches to stretch out the cramped vertebrae.

The music had come to an end, reminding Rita that we'd had about enough misery for the day.

"Thank you, everyone, for coming to class," she said.

We all gathered our belongings and returned the mats to their storage shelves. I noticed that Rita had approached Tahlene and was conversing animatedly with a smile. She seemed to be explaining away her outburst, without actually apologizing for the prickly attitude she'd exhibited all through class. Tahlene wasn't buying it for a second. She gave Rita a look that sent the instructor into another round of pacifying non-talk.

From the front of the room, a cell phone chirped inside Rita's tote bag. She dashed for it, glanced at the number on the readout and answered with, "What now?"

I looked at Tahlene, who shrugged and picked up her mat.

"Forget it!" Rita barked into the phone. "I am not having this conversation."

Tahlene and I walked out, back to the calm ambiance of the incense-scented vestibule.

The medical seminar attendees were apparently on a break. I spotted Patricia Girard with a couple of men near the door. Linda was browsing the books on the table.

"How's it going?" I asked.

"Hey—great so far. I'm learning how to read your tongue." She stuck hers out, wide and flat, as if that would tell me something.

Ew! Did I need to know that?

"It's interesting stuff. I'll tell you about it later. How was yoga?"

"Interesting." My right eyebrow involuntarily twitched upward.

"Oh?" She glanced over my shoulder, where Rita and Tahlene were emerging from the yoga room. I turned in time to catch Tahlene heading for the restroom and Rita leaving by the outside door. Dina Carlotti stood near the reception desk, talking quietly with Shirley.

"Tell you about it later. I'm heading back to the room real quick to change back into regular clothes." The stretchy leggings were beginning to feel way too clingy. I was definitely ready for the comfort of my jeans and a soft sweater.

I took the courtyard pathway that led to another entrance to the guest wing, rather than crossing through the main lobby. Outside our door, I fumbled a minute for the key card that I'd dropped somewhere into the depths of my purse. I'd just stepped through the doorway when voices caught my attention.

"Sweetheart, we can't. This is too important. Please stick with it." Nicole Mayhew's voice sounded urgent. A door farther down the hall clicked shut.

I stepped into my room but didn't close the door.

Gerald's gruff baritone responded from the hallway with an unintelligible grumble.

"When it's about your health, no effort is too much," she said.

"I absolutely can't believe *she's* here, especially . . ." Their voices faded as they walked down the hall toward the lobby.

Interesting. Which 'she' I wondered. I shut the door, dumped purse and paperwork on my bed and quickly changed clothes. Ten minutes later I'd taken a seat in the classroom, watching the rest of the group assemble.

Dina walked toward me and I indicated the chair beside mine. "Is your back okay?" I asked. She smiled and nodded.

Gerald and Nicole sat across the room, she with notebook and pen at the ready, he staring at his watch and tapping one foot. Tahlene drifted in—drifting was a good way to describe her floaty way of moving. She gathered a couple of big floor pillows, kicked off her shoes, and made herself a little nest on the floor. She wore her fluffy blond hair in the same fabric-banded ponytail she'd sported in yoga class.

Trudie, who seemed to have latched onto me in yoga, took a seat in the row behind me, off to my right. I avoided eye contact; a new best friend wasn't something I needed right now.

"Good morning, everyone." Shirley greeted us with a smile. Her layered hair looked bouncy and she exuded an herbal freshness. Today's gauzy outfit was azure, the shade of a hazy day. "We're going to get right into the program this morning. Let's talk about the benefits of meditation on our overall health."

Her eyes went to the back of the room as a stir ensued. Everyone turned to look.

"Mr. Storm. Welcome."

The black-clad man we'd seen in the lobby this morning stood uncertainly near the back counter where the tea service was set up. He gave a little wave to the gathering at large.

"Come on in," Shirley invited. "Sit anywhere."

As he moved into the room, three other people followed. Since there were only chairs set up for the participants, the three spares didn't quite know what to do.

"I'm sorry, is everyone registered for the course?" Shirley asked in as diplomatic a tone as I'd ever heard.

"They're with me," said Storm.

The British-accented voice was one that had been heard by nearly everyone on the planet, outside the darkest reaches of the Amazon rainforest. Rex Storm, lead singer of the rock group Scriptor. They'd been so hot in the '80s that the National Guard had been called in to provide security at two of their U.S. concerts. They were one of those unusual phenomena who somehow appealed equally to male and female, ages fifteen to fifty, the Goths and Godly alike. I'd never followed rock music that closely, but even I had to admit that the heavy beat of their sound captured something primeval.

The last time I remembered seeing Rex Storm had been a news story about his breakup with his fourth wife, about five years ago. The publicity photo that flashed across news screens showed a vibrant man dressed in his traditional black with a sexy grin spread across his over-large mouth.

Looking at him now, I could see that the years had not been kind. His slender frame could now best be described as scrawny. His face was extremely thin, with the large mouth way out of proportion to his other features, probably the result of multiple face lifts. The blue eyes, always described by media as 'sexy bedroom eyes,' were now sunken dots framed by dark circles. I remembered what Linda had said about his being here to detoxify. I could certainly believe it.

Shirley drew our attention back to the front of the room. "Okay, let's get started." She rubbed her hands together. "Take a seat or a pillow, whichever suits you." She waited a moment for things to settle. Once Rex Storm took a chair, his little entourage placed pillows on the floor around him. Shirley let it go.

"The benefits of meditation in our everyday lives are many," she began. Using the white board and referring us to the workbooks we'd been given, she demonstrated the patterns of brainwaves during the meditative state.

I copied everything she wrote on the board, trying to follow quickly and keep my handwriting legible for Linda's later use. Shirley was a good instructor and I felt that my notes would accomplish the goals. I was also surprised to find that the substance of what she was saying appealed to me. When Shirley spoke of releasing thoughts and relieving stress, my mind flashed back to a few times during my helicopter flights when I could have used some technique to loosen a tight stomach and clenched jaw.

"Now that you know the theory, we'll put it into practice," Shirley announced.

Over the next few minutes she called each of us aside privately to receive a personal mantra. Armed with my little card with the three magic words written on it, I followed the others into the meditation room. Rex Storm came along, too, but I noticed that his followers stayed behind. Shirley must have drawn the line with him and his little groupies.

The lightly perfumed air in the meditation room exuded a feeling of peace and tranquility. I chose a chair with thick cushions and a high back. Others took cushions on the floor or chairs at various points around the room. By unspoken agreement, it seemed that each person left an empty space or two beside the next person. Gerald Mayhew took the seat closest to the door and Nicole settled on one of the cushions on the floor near her husband. Rex Storm sat near the incense burner and inhaled the stuff. I almost giggled but ignored the urge. If I could get into deep meditation I wanted to try.

Shirley cast her voice into a soft, relaxing tone and talked us through the opening steps. The room went quiet. As each person mentally repeated his or her mantra, the only sound remaining in the room was the soft susurration of shallow breathing. I remembered Shirley's instructions and willed my random thoughts away. A feeling of calm settled over me. Then a cell phone rang.

Chapter 8

A whispered expletive came from Shirley's chair. Five sets of eyes peeked through nearly-closed lashes. I watched openly as she rose from her chair and marched over to Rex Storm's seat. The phone emitted another ring. She took a handful of the wide collar of his silky black shirt and hauled him upward and out the door. As the door whooshed softly closed, I caught her words: "Mr. Storm—"

I checked out the room. Nearly everyone had given up the pretense of meditating. Nicole Mayhew surprised us all by taking charge.

"Come on, everyone, this is important. Let's get back to it," she said.

With a collective deep breath, we all closed our eyes and tried to get back to our peaceful state.

Forty-five minutes later, refreshed and feeling amazingly

light inside, I joined Linda in the dining room for lunch.

"So, how are you liking it so far?" she asked.

"Interesting. I've got notes for you on meditation techniques."

"So . . ." She cocked her head. "Did you like it?"

"Meditation was great," I said truthfully. "Really. I never imagined that thirty minutes of quiet time would make me feel so good. I'm going to start using it on those especially crazy days at the office."

"Good! I'm glad I didn't drag you up here for nothing. And yoga?"

"Well . . . that was also interesting."

"What."

I took a deep breath. "Okay. I've never been to a yoga class before, so I don't know what it's supposed to be."

"Yeah . . ." Those blue eyes fixed on me.

"Does the instructor usually yell at people?"

"Yell? You're kidding."

"Well, she got pretty testy with a few people. Half the class walked out before it was over."

A waiter approached our table. "You ladies are with the Lightness in Living conference?" At our nods he placed a small aperitif glass in front of each of us.

I took a whiff. Ginger?

"Our lunches are part of the program," Linda explained. "We'll be eating the food recommended in the nutrition classes. This is an elixir designed to help stimulate the digestion."

A tentative sip zapped me with a sweet-sour-hot flavor. Once past the initial surprise of the unusual combination, the taste really grew on me. I finished off the small glassful in a couple more swallows.

"So," Linda said, "you were saying about the yoga class?"

"Odd. I'd pictured it as a very soothing, centering experience. Rita, our instructor, was anything but centered, I'll tell you."

"Hmm, that *is* odd. Well, maybe she was just having a bad day." She shrugged. "You have a massage this afternoon, right?"

Our waiter reappeared just then, with colorful plates beautifully presented. Lunch consisted of a thick bean soup, a small salad, and a vegetable mixture of squash and tomatoes. Everything was delicious and we concentrated on nothing but food for the next few minutes. A minor stir began on the far side of the room. Pat Girard and two other doctors breezed through, on their way to a table.

"Well, I heard that she actually yelled at one of her students," Pat said as they took seats at the table next to ours. Her attire today consisted of a brilliant turquoise broomstick skirt and boots of the same shade, a burnt orange top and heavy squash blossom necklace.

I raised an eyebrow at Linda.

"Word has it that she won't be working here long," Pat continued. "In fact, her last job ended . . ." Her voice dropped as she fiddled with her napkin.

One of the other doctors, a tall, thin woman in her late forties, piped up. "When I was with Blue Cross we had this patient—" She seemed to realize how well their voices were carrying and dropped hers to a whisper.

"I certainly hope my doctor doesn't gossip about me in restaurants," I murmured to Linda.

"She certainly doesn't." She winked. "But you better be

nice to me or I might start." She took a spoonful of the rich, flavorful soup. "Besides, you're never sick. What would I say?"

"Good point. Plus, I've still got some dirt on you from eighth grade history class." We chuckled over the absurdity of it all, and at the three gossipers with their heads together over the other table.

Linda glanced at her watch. "Oh, gosh, I better make some calls before our afternoon sessions start. I've got someone else handling the emergencies, but I told Raylene I'd call in a couple times a day and see if anyone needs me." She laid her folded napkin on the table. "Take your time over dessert. There won't be a check so don't worry about any of that."

"Okay, see you later." I wasn't about to pass up dessert.

The waiter brought it a minute later, a stemmed glass of chocolate mousse with a fresh fruit garnish. He set a glass at Linda's place and rushed away before I could correct the error. Well . . . surely it wouldn't hurt . . .. Okay, I'll admit it right now, I finished them both.

When the waiter came back to make sure everything was all right, I commented on the fabulous chocolate concoction.

"Yes, very good, isn't it? It's also very high protein, you know. Made with tofu."

I did a hard swallow. He chuckled and cleared the glasses. "It fools everyone," he said.

I wandered leisurely through the main lobby on my way to the spa, refusing to feel guilty about the two desserts. If they were made of tofu, even chocolatized, they had to be healthy. Besides, I'd eaten all my veggies—I was entitled. In the reception area of the spa building a dark-haired young man greeted me. After checking my reservation he handed me a folded cotton robe and pointed me toward the ladies dressing rooms.

Ten minutes later I met my masseuse, Joanne, and was shown to a room where the light shone softly from indirect fixtures. Scented oil perfumed the air with a tantalizing aroma of spices and flowers.

"I see that you've signed up for our signature massage, the Total Body and Soul Experience," she said. "It's designed to both invigorate and relax, to improve the flow of energy through your body, and to infuse you with a profound sense of peace."

A tall order. "Sounds fabulous," I said.

"I'll leave you alone for a couple of minutes. Leave your robe here and lie down on the table, face up. Just close your eyes and relax."

After that big lunch I'd probably be doing well if I weren't snoring before she came back.

As it turned out, Joanne was absolutely right. I did feel both invigorated and relaxed by the end of my hour and a half. I floated out of the room wondering what it would take to hire her away from here and have her just stand in the corner of my office. I could go for one of those treatments every afternoon. I showered and changed, using the herbal shampoo and conditioner provided in the locker room.

By the time I drifted back to the room for nutrition class, I felt ready to meditate some more then report for happy hour. The tension of the morning in Rita's class was nearly forgotten. I did my best to focus on the information on food preparation, but they didn't cover one single thing you could defrost and reheat in under five minutes. I'm not exactly a crack chef, you've noticed, and I found my attention wandering. Luckily, the handouts covered the important stuff for Linda's benefit.

When the class took a short tea break I surreptitiously peeked at the readout on my cell phone. I'd missed a call from Ron an hour ago. I ducked out to the courtyard and called him back.

"Where are you?" he said querulously.

"Geez, grumpy, you need to relax. You know where I am. Santa Fe. I told you about the whole thing with Linda." I felt my mellow mood slip. Took a deep breath "What's up?"

"Drake's deposition has been moved up to this week. I need copies of all of your simulator data."

Although I'd left notes about all this on his desk, I told him where to find it, working to keep my voice level. Clearly I was picking up on Drake's attitude about the case; getting it over with might be the best thing to put everyone's tempers back on an even keel. I spoke with Ron for another minute then made the excuse that I needed to get back to class.

I trailed back inside, my former state of elation now almost completely gone. At least I wasn't sleepy anymore, so I diligently began taking notes on the six food tastes and the importance of eating the right combinations of food for your body type.

The entire group had made it for the afternoon session, including Rex Storm, who'd apparently taken the chastisement seriously after his cell phone incident this morning. He'd taken a seat as front-and-center as one could get, grabbing the limelight even here. Nicole was studiously taking notes while Gerald lounged in a half-sprawl in his chair. Dina sat straight up in her chair, obviously taking it easy on her tender back muscles.

Trudie, I noticed, had stationed herself as near to Rex as she could and spent more of her time staring at him than watching the instructor. From my vantage point, it became clear that Trudie's fascination with the aging rock star could easily border on obsession. I wondered if Rex had picked up on it.

Chapter 9

I left the afternoon meditation session, again feeling refreshed and relaxed all at once. I headed for the room, thinking it might be a good time to catch Drake.

He answered his cell on the third ring and I could hear jukebox music and voices in the background. To keep from shouting above the din, he excused himself to someone there and told me he would step outside.

"Sorry, hon," he said. "Those guys can't seem to just quietly drink a beer after work."

"I talked to Ron earlier. He told me about your deposition being moved forward."

He made a snarling noise. No surprise.

"Maybe we could meet in Santa Fe for dinner before you go back to Albuquerque?" I suggested.

He jostled the phone a little and I heard him flipping pages in that little notebook he keeps in his shirt pocket. "Yeah . . . day after tomorrow should work. I think we're finishing up the job here by early afternoon. Could we make it a late lunch? Early dinner?"

"Either. You set the time and I'll be there. Meet at the airport?"

We'd just finalized the plan when I heard a key card in the lock. "Linda's back—gotta go, love you."

"So, did you pick up any more gossip from good old Pat?" I teased as Linda came into our room.

"Sheesh—that woman!" She kicked off her shoes and flung herself onto her bed. "I'm amazed she made it through medical school. Truly, she spends more time poking into everyone else's business than studying the material."

"Speaking of which, here are the notes I took in class today." I handed her several sheets, along with the handouts Shirley had given us. "And you were right about the massages. The one I had today was fabulous."

"I told you. Boy, I could've used one myself." She rolled over and rested her head on her crossed forearms. "I think I'll schedule one for tomorrow."

As it turned out, we ended up at the spa at the same time on Tuesday. After another of Rita's contentious yoga classes, I was more than ready for it.

"I hate to agree with Pat, but I can't believe Rita still has a job. Especially at a place like this," I told Linda as we made our way to adjoining changing rooms. "She's alienated everyone in the class already, and it's only the second day. Dina didn't even come. She's nursing a sore back from the first class. And Gerald Mayhew skipped too. He strikes me as a guy who doesn't put up with a lot."

I gathered my clothes and stuffed them into a locker. Here I was, being as bad a gossip as Pat. I better watch my mouth.

This time I got an entirely different massage treatment, one that involved dribbling warm oil over my forehead. As awful as the description sounded, the reality was quite pleasant and I found myself once more leaving with a sense of peace and contentment.

"I'm not calling Ron at all today," I told Linda as we sat in a bubbling hot spa an hour later. "He and Drake are just going to have to work out their own stuff on that helicopter case. I'm not getting into it. I'm here to enjoy myself."

"Live in the moment, Charlie," she said. Her voice sounded drowsily happy.

"It sounds sensible, doesn't it?"

"It *is* sensible. All this worrying takes its toll on your body, you know."

"Yes, doctor." I grinned as she squinted at me.

She was right about that and I knew it.

Dinner consisted of a big salad with a wonderful variety of greens, dotted with spicy chunks of tofu. More of that stuff. I'd never found anything appealing about it, but had to admit that the chefs here knew what they were doing. Everything was delicious. Dessert this time was a warm fruit cobbler with a crispy topping. I couldn't spot any tofu in it, but you never knew.

After dinner, Celeus Light gave an inspirational talk in the courtyard. Everyone bundled up in sweaters and sat on cushions around the glow of an open fire pit. Beyond the plantings of bright chrysanthemums and the low adobe wall, everything was velvet black. Light's talk was about letting go of anger and stress in our lives. His charismatic voice flowed in soothing tones, softly coaxing us to shed negative feelings, switching them for an attitude of joy. He glided among the participants, his flowing long jacket brushing at shoulders as he passed through the group.

I sat cross-legged on my cushion, as did everyone, with my hands lying in my lap. With my head slightly bowed and eyes nearly closed I checked out the rest of the group. Once again, Gerald Mayhew didn't seem to be taking the class very seriously. He clearly was here at Nicole's insistence, although I couldn't help but remember her comment in the hallway, about his health being their reason for attending. Rex Storm, surprisingly, was very much getting into the mood, eyes tightly closed, body swaying slightly as Light talked. Trudie, his forty-something groupie, sat close and timed the swaying of her own body so that she could occasionally bump shoulders with Rex.

Pat and her two doctor friends formed a tight little group on the opposite side of the fire pit. They were all clearly enthralled with Dr. Light. Dina listened closely, but kept her eyes open and hadn't yet fallen under the power of the swaying bodies around her.

Light was in his element. Clearly, as I listened to his cadence I could tell that he picked up the mood of the audience and fed back from it. The longer the talk went on, the more they swayed. The more they swayed, the richer his voice became. I felt myself being pulled in, yet I held back. There was just something too cult-like about it.

I glanced over at Linda. Her eyes were closed but she

must have sensed my gaze. She peeked at me and puckered the dimple at the side of her mouth. Well, at least she wasn't lost completely in the trance.

Wednesday morning dawned clear and chilly, with that special brightness that New Mexico autumn mornings have. I groaned and looked at the bedside clock. Six. The sun had not cleared the mountains yet, but I needed to move.

"I think I'd like a walk before starting the day's festivities," I said to Linda, who yawned widely and groaned. "Want to come?"

"Yeah, I'll make myself get moving."

We dressed in jeans and sweaters and put on our walking shoes. The chill morning called for jackets, so we grabbed them and headed out.

"I've wanted to explore the grounds ever since we got here," she said, once she'd stretched her muscles a little. "Gotta balance classroom time with some physical activity."

We headed down the long driveway, planning to turn around once we got to the main road, then walk along the hillside past the parking area and back up to the dining room in time to catch some breakfast. The morning air felt crisp, the air tinged with the scent of wood smoke and chrysanthemums, reminding me that my birthday was coming up in a little over a month. Those autumn smells always bring back the reminder that the final family cookout each year was usually my birthday lunch, a picnic with a bunch of friends. This year, Drake and I had the added bonus of our planned trip to Kauai in November. Despite his misgivings about the deposition, it was probably a good thing that they'd moved the date up. He could be done with it and enjoy the vacation.

Linda and I conversed little at first, using the brisk pace and high altitude to wake ourselves up and get the blood flowing. When she asked about Drake I admitted that the camaraderie between my husband and brother had seen better times.

"I'm meeting Drake in Santa Fe this afternoon, maybe grab a late lunch, talk things out."

"Well, watch out that you don't get caught up in their whole conflict, yourself."

"Hey, I'm not feeling at all angry toward either of them. I've let go of my negative emotions, just as Dr. Light suggested." I negotiated around a pothole in the road. "Just don't ask me about it next week. My positive outlook may be a bit strained by then."

We passed by the portico and circled to the left, beside the spa building, then cut through the parking lot. At the edge of the hill we picked up a walkway that would lead us through the rear courtyard and back to the guestroom wing. About the time the tip of my nose felt like it would freeze, we got there.

"Do you know that guy?" Linda asked.

I looked up to see a dark-haired man staring into one of the rooms, hands cupped around his face at the window. He turned and gave us a quick stare. I didn't recognize the slender form, dressed in khaki slacks and dark blue bomber jacket, or the stern facial features under black brows. When he noticed that we'd stopped walking, he jammed his hands into his pockets and quickly followed the sidewalk toward the lobby entrance.

"Odd, don't you think?" I said

"He's not one of our group. Could be another guest, though."

"Staring into someone's window?"

"Not very logical, that's for sure," Linda said.

We watched as he entered the lobby and disappeared from sight. I noted the window he'd been peeking into, wondering who he'd been spying on. Entering our hall through a side door, I counted rooms. We'd caught him at the window of Room 14, right next to ours.

As soon as Linda had unlocked our door, I strode to the telephone and called the front desk.

"There's a man who just entered the lobby a minute ago," I said. "Has dark hair and he's wearing khakis and a dark blue jacket."

"Um, I don't see him, ma'am. Shall I page him?"

"No. I just caught him peeping into the windows of Room 14. Is there security here at the hotel?"

"Oh, yes, ma'am. Of course they can't be everywhere at once, but I'll . . ."

"Yes, get the word out. He's probably leaving the grounds by now, but have them watch for him. Who's registered in Room 14?"

"Well, I can't divulge that information, ma'am, but I will let the guest know about this."

It was the most I could hope for. But it didn't mean I couldn't use my own resourcefulness. I went back out into the hall and knocked on the door of Room 14. Shuffling noises came from within the room and an unsteady hand fiddled with the door knob. When the door opened, I found myself facing Trudie Blanchard.

Chapter 10

Trudie was fully dressed, although her hair still held the tangles of sleep and her face seemed thinner, with puffy bags under her eyes. Her restless eyes darted back and forth, not staying on my face for more than a second or two.

"Did you just see a man peeking in your windows?" I asked.

"Uh, no," she murmured. "I just got up." She rubbed her hands together and tucked them against her ribs, under crossed arms.

I quickly explained what Linda and I had seen and gave her a description of the man. Her eye movements quickened.

"The front desk should be calling. I asked them to. But I thought I'd tell you myself." In answer, the phone rang at that moment. She jumped. "There you go," I said.

I turned and heard her close the door behind me. Trudie was a hard one to figure out, but I'd done my part to warn her. I went back to our room, where Linda was fluffing her hair in the mirror. I gathered my yoga clothes and other items for the morning classes. We headed for breakfast a few minutes later. I noticed that Trudie didn't show up.

The yoga room felt chilly. Most everyone was moving around to warm up. Gerald Mayhew finally decided that was ridiculous and he turned up the thermostat. Trudie wandered in, looked around—I guessed she was hoping Rex Storm would be there—then parked her mat next to mine. Following the others' example, I stood and stretched a bit. After twenty minutes of this we all began to wonder where Rita was. She'd been late the first morning, but this was pushing it. I looked around and sensed the indecision in the rest of the group.

"Well, we could all go out for a nice strong cup of coffee," I said.

"No," said Dina, "we should be to sticking with our program."

Heads nodded, some reluctantly.

"If everyone does not mind . . . I have taken many yoga classes. I can perhaps show?"

"Great idea," Nicole chimed in. "Dina, you know the postures really well. Why don't you lead the class?"

"Yeah. You're a whole lot nicer than the grump," Gerald said. Nicole shot him a look.

"I can lead until she comes," Dina offered, looking around the group.

Everyone agreed enthusiastically and took their positions on the mats. Within minutes, Dina moved us into the first pose and explained the purpose of the mind/body connection in yoga. This was something Rita hadn't talked about and I found myself really feeling that I was getting something from the exercise. I began to agree with Gerald. The class was much more productive without Rita at the helm. I wondered if we could convince the directors to dump Rita and keep Dina for the rest of the week.

As we ended the class with savasana, I felt the rejuvenating energy flow through me. Finally, everyone began to quietly gather their things. I noticed that not one person had left during the class. Even Trudie seemed more centered, less jumpy than at any other time since I'd met her. I caught the eye of one of Shirley's assistants and gave her a thumbs up. She let me know with a nod and a smile that the word would get to the right people.

I wandered through the lobby on my way back to the room to change clothes again. At the front desk, complete with entourage, stood Rex Storm. Surrounded by about two dozen pieces of luggage, undoubtedly all filled with black clothes, he was in the process of gushing to Shirley about how sorry he was to cut the visit short. Prior commitments, and all that. So much for detoxifying. In three days? I aimed a little wave in his direction and headed down the hall.

When I entered the classroom for the morning's nutrition discussion, I noticed a smaller than usual crowd. I helped myself to a cup of tea at the back of the room. Shirley came in and set a plate of cookies near the tea setup.

"It's one of our chef's specialties," she said. "And, yes, they're made of all-natural ingredients. Very healthy."

I reached for one, of course, turning it over and eying it for tofu bits. "Did you hear about this morning's yoga class?" I asked.

She laughed. "Oh, yes." She dropped her voice. "We've known for a long time that Rita wasn't working out. We just weren't sure how to get rid of her. Poor girl has had a lot of personal problems recently. It just didn't seem fair to cut her job at the same time. Maybe she'll save me the trouble by quitting."

"Well, it was pretty obvious that her heart wasn't in that classroom the past few days. I'm sorry to hear about the other problems."

"I know. Despite our efforts at bringing peace and love into people's lives, sometimes shit happens." She allowed a worldly grin to sneak out. "Rita's divorce hit her hard, but then those things aren't easy for anyone, are they?"

She walked across the room, leaving me to wonder about Rita's personal life. We rarely see the whole person. I'd certainly learned that in my involvement with Ron's investigation business.

Shirley called for attention and everyone began taking seats.

"Today, we want to look at food preparation techniques," she said. "I'm going to come down against your microwave ovens and packaged foods, I'm afraid."

That drew a little twitter from the group and a surge of fear from me. No microwave?

She grabbed a stack of papers and began passing the handouts around the room. Yesterday we'd covered body types and the ways in which different people metabolize their food and the amazing ways that our bodies fight off various diseases. I flipped through the pages Shirley gave me, making sure I had copies of everything for Linda.

"Now—" Her voice was interrupted by the sound of a distant scream. By the time it repeated for the third time, pounding footsteps followed. Our group were now on their feet. I sniffed for smoke, looked outside for flashing lights, saw nothing. Leaving our workbooks behind, we moved en masse to the door.

"What's going on?" Shirley asked a passing secretary.

"Don't know," the girl said. "Something out back."

We headed for the exit to the courtyard. Out in the bright sun, the drift of people were all heading toward the low adobe wall at the edge of the compound. I worked my way forward, and found that they were crowded around Tahlene.

"Give her some space," the resort manager said as I walked up.

The crowd moved back about an inch.

"Tahlene? What's wrong?" I asked, over the heads of a couple of bellmen.

"Charlie!" She looked relieved to see someone familiar. Her hand reached out and I slipped from behind the bellman to take it. "Oh, Charlie, it's awful!"

"Calm down," I said. Her fingers gripped my hand with painful force and her whole body was shaking.

The resort manager stood before her. "Miss, can you tell me what's the matter? Can I call for help?"

Tahlene's blond curls bobbed. With her free hand she grabbed the green knitted scarf at her neck. She bunched and twisted the yarn repeatedly.

"Tahlene? Talk to us," I coaxed.

"Th-the wall . . . over the wall."

"Here, let me . . ." I pried her fingers off me and stroked her arm. "Let me see."

I walked to the wall and looked over. The ground dropped away all along this back side of the resort. In some places the drop began a few feet away from the adobe wall, but in this spot it fell away immediately. Erosion had created a steep gully with sharp exposed rocks. A cactus lay in shreds near the top. My eyes followed the direction of its broken arms and I leaned outward to see below. About thirty feet down, smashed against rugged boulders lay a twisted body. It was Rita.

Black specks floated in front of my eyes as vertigo threatened. I reeled slightly before catching myself. I turned and bumped into the manager, who now stood at the wall.

"Call the police," I said quietly.

He glanced downward and turned quickly. "I will. Keep everyone back."

Well, yeah. That was a real no-brainer. I turned to Tahlene and patted her back. "Let's get you inside," I said. Shirley stood at the edge of the group and I put the shaking Australian girl in her capable hands.

Commandeering two bellmen, I asked them to gather the little crowd and take them inside. "Offer them free drinks or something," I suggested. "We need to calm them down but keep them on the premises."

The older one picked up on the importance of the request and began moving. The younger guy was itching to peek over the wall, but followed the example of his senior man. Together they rounded up the twenty or thirty people standing around and headed them toward the lobby. I noticed Linda in the crowd but she didn't try to push through. She followed along with the bellman's request.

What had happened? The questions immediately descended upon me. Accident? I looked over the wall again, willing myself to be dispassionate. Clearly, the fall had killed Rita. Her neck lay twisted at a horrible angle. Blood covered her face and matted her brown curls. One arm was flung out behind her, the other pinned under the body. I swallowed hard.

Had she sat or stood on the wall and lost her balance? Had she gotten the hint that her job was in jeopardy and jumped? Rita, a suicide? I had to admit that I didn't know her well enough to judge. Or had something more sinister happened? Granted, Rita didn't have many admirers here. Her rigid rules and drill-sergeant attitude hadn't won any friends.

I scanned the ground on both sides of the wall. Remarkably, there were all kinds of footprints. As dangerous as the area obviously was, a well-beaten path led along the wall outside the safe zone. Had Rita been walking along and not noticed the section where the path was cut away by the gully? Possibly, if it was dark out.

I didn't remember seeing her at the firelight gathering last night. In fact, I was pretty certain she hadn't been there. Maybe she'd come to work very early this morning. Maybe she was staying at the hotel as a guest. I realized I didn't even know whether she lived here in Santa Fe or not. I needed more information.

Sirens began to sound in the distance. I could hear their progress up the road, then the long drive into the resort, and eventually at the front door. They finally died with a long groan.

Two men with EMT kits strode through the courtyard followed by a uniformed police officer. I pointed to the spot.

"Oh, geez," the first technician said. "I know the answer to this, but we're gonna need climbing ropes to find out for sure."

The other guy turned toward the lobby. "Is there another way, without going back through that crowd?" he asked.

I indicated the walkway to the parking lot. "Go past the spa building and this will take you to the front door."

"Nasty fall," the police officer said. She was built stoutly, a Hispanic woman of about forty, wearing a dark uniform and a belt full of weapons and cuffs. Her name badge said C. Montoya. She pulled a report form from a metal clipboard she carried.

She stared over the wall again and turned to me. After asking my name and getting my answer she said, "How is it you know the victim?"

"She's a yoga instructor here at the resort," I said.

"And how well did you know her?"

Wait a minute. Where was this going? "Barely." I responded. "You'll need to talk to either the resort manager or to Shirley Broussand, her supervisor. They, and the young woman who discovered the body, are inside."

Montoya folded down the cover of the clipboard. Wedging her pen into the clip she motioned me to lead the way. As we walked I heard her speak into her radio, requesting detectives.

Chapter 11

Two detectives arrived a few minutes later and officer Montoya was sent outside to help the recovery effort. In a divide-and-conquer maneuver, the detectives split the seminar group into manageable units and put us into separate rooms. Somehow, probably with input from Shirley, they made sure the groups consisted of people who didn't already know each other. Linda had been shuffled off to the library; at least she'd have something to read. I found myself in the meditation room with one of the doctors from Linda's medical group and a young woman who worked for the resort. Despite the incense-laden air in here, I couldn't imagine clearing my mind of its whirl of thoughts.

One at a time, the detectives called people into a small office across the hall. Waiting my turn, I positioned myself in one of the chairs that faced the open door so I could see others come and go. Most didn't spend more than ten or fifteen minutes, probably furnishing everything they knew about Rita and leaving the detectives with their own names and addresses for possible future contact. I caught glimpses of the faces as they left and nothing appeared out of the ordinary.

At one point Montoya tapped on the door and went in, carrying her report forms and a few zipped plastic baggies. She stayed about five minutes and left empty handed. By this time my two roomies had done their bit and been dismissed. I began to wonder if the detectives had forgotten me, despite the fact that I sat in plain view of their doorway. Finally I got the signal and walked across the hall.

"Ms. Parker, come in and sit." I did, surprised that they knew my name.

"I'm Detective Gallegos, my partner is Detective Greene." The man speaking to me was probably in his late thirties, slim, with black brush-cut hair and big dark eyes that would have looked great on a soap opera star. Greene was ten years younger, reddish blonde hair, green eyes, with signs of a few pimples lingering around his jawline. Both wore jeans, chambray shirts, and jackets. Greene's was a tweed blazer and Gallegos wore black leather. I nodded to them both.

"We understand that you're a private investigator?"

"Uh, that's not exactly true," I said, wondering where he'd gotten this information and guessing it was common gossip around here by now. "I work for one. My brother."

"But you're familiar with investigative protocol," Gallegos insisted.

"Somewhat."

"Okay." He seemed happy with that. "You're observant. Anything about this situation with Rita Ratwill that looks hinky to you?"

"I hardly knew Rita. Didn't even know her last name until this minute. I've been in her yoga classes the past two days. Today she didn't show up but we went on without her."

"Word is she was about to lose her job. Lots of complaints about her teaching style."

"That wouldn't surprise me." I glanced over at the baggies Montoya had left with them. They appeared to contain a few fabric fibers stuck to cactus needles, some hairs, a little bit of dirt. "Did Rita live here in town or was she staying at the hotel?" I asked.

"Local. She'd worked at another yoga center off and on for a couple of years, just became an instructor here the last six months or so, according to Shirley Broussand."

He seemed pretty open with the information so I decided to push it and ask for more. "So, what do you think? Could someone have pushed her?"

"It's looking accidental. Nobody here seems to have a motive. Her car's in the parking lot, engine barely warm. Looks like she arrived for work early this morning, for some reason sat on that little wall out there and fell over. There were some clothing fibers on the adobe. Lab will take a look at everything, naturally."

I shrugged, unable to come up with anything more plausible.

"Ms. Parker, one more thing," Gallegos said. Hmm… shades of Columbo. "Linda Casper, who's rooming with you I believe. She said the two of you saw a strange man hanging around outside one of the rooms this morning?"

"Yeah, I'd forgotten about that. We saw him peeking into the window of Trudie Blanchard's room. He walked away quickly once he saw us. I called the desk and asked them to watch for him, but they hadn't seen him. I also told Trudie about it, so she could be alert for him."

He wrote all that down, although I felt sure he'd gotten the same story from Linda.

"Did Ms. Blanchard seem concerned?" he asked.

"Trudie—how can I say this? Trudie seems concerned about everything. She's an odd woman. I'm no psychologist but she's talked about herself a lot in our classes, has a number of insecurities and there are mood swings. I don't know. She's got some kind of psychological issues."

"And how did she act when you told her there was a man outside her window?"

"Didn't say a lot. She tends to operate in a haze about half the time. I guess that's how she acted then."

"Thanks for the information, Charlie," he said. Greene still hadn't said more than a couple of words. Gallegos reached into his jacket pocket and pulled out a business card. "If you think of anything else…well, you know the routine."

"Another question, if I might," I said. "Did Rita have anything else with her? I didn't notice her little boom box tape player or her canvas tote bag that she always brought to class. She might have notes or personal papers . . ."

"I think Montoya found some things," he said. "We still have to review all the evidence. We'll keep an eye out for them."

He thanked me again and stood to indicate that the

interview was over. I picked up my purse and headed toward the classroom where I could hear the buzz of voices. Shirley's stood out above the crowd.

"Could everyone be seated for just a moment?" she called out.

I stepped into the room and grabbed a seat near the back.

"Thanks," she said. "We've had an upsetting morning so far. I'm truly sorry for the disruption to a week that's supposed to bring peace and harmony to your lives." A mild rustle went through the room. "I think the best way to do that is to get back with the program right away. So, check your schedules. I'll be starting the nutrition class in this room in ten minutes. Medical people, I believe Dr. Light will be arriving any moment now for your sessions. If anyone was scheduled for a massage this hour, by all means, I'm sure you're ready for it. Lunch will be delayed until one o'clock, and we'll do our best to work in everything else for the day. If we can't fit it all in, well this course is all about finding peace, so we're not going to stress over it, right?"

As the group began to disperse, I worked my way to the front of the room to sit where I usually did. Linda spotted me and reached for my arm. "We gotta meet up at lunch," she whispered. "There's more to this story."

I gave her a puzzled look, but the flow of bodies carried her out the door. What was that all about? I did my best to take notes on organic growing methods and the benefits of various spices, but probably missed a lot of it. My eyes kept scanning the room. I didn't believe for one minute that Rita had simply sat down on that adobe wall and toppled over backward. She had her ditzy moments but that scenario didn't seem likely. So, she either killed herself—over losing a job she'd held for only a few months?—or someone helped her fall.

Among the other attendees, I could sense a restlessness. They were itching to get together, as were Linda and I, to compare notes and to pass on information about the morning's events. When Shirley finally wrapped up and declared it lunch time, there was almost a crush to get to the door.

In the lobby I spotted Gallegos and Greene coming in from the courtyard. I veered my path to intersect theirs.

"Anything new?" I asked.

"Not really," Gallegos answered. "We found the tape player and tote bag you described. In her car. Looks like she'd arrived early this morning. There'll be an autopsy and we can get time of death. We'll also know whether drugs or alcohol played a part." He seemed impatient to get going.

"So you're thinking it's . . ."

"Probably an accident. Honestly, we haven't found any reason to doubt that."

"Detective? I've been wondering—who's Rita's next of kin?" One of my many random thoughts during class had been about whether Rita and her ex might have had children.

"Husband," he said. He thumbed through the little notebook in his hand. "David Ratwill." He caught the expression on my face.

"I was under the impression she was divorced."

"ID card in her wallet listed him as her emergency contact. I dialed the number on it and a recorded voice says 'You've reached Rita and Dave' . . ." Greene nudged him and Gallegos remembered that they were on the way out. I watched the two of them walk toward the main entry before

I headed to the dining room. Nearly everyone else was seated. I found myself torn between positioning myself in the middle, hoping to catch bits of the other conversations, or finding an isolated place where Linda could tell me what she'd so urgently wanted to say. Curiosity won out and I took a table between the one the Mayhews occupied and where Dina Carlotti and Pat Girard had just been joined by Trudie. This could get interesting.

Linda bustled across the room and sat down.

"Wasn't Rita divorced?" I asked her.

"I thought so."

"Me too." I cocked my eyes toward the other tables, indicating that we better keep our voices down.

"He wasn't an ex, according to the police," I said. "David Ratwill. The police believe the two were still living together."

"So, what else did Rita say that wasn't quite true?" She raised her golden eyebrows in a knowing way.

I wondered.

Voices from the next table drifted toward us. ". . . heard that she didn't drive up here this morning. She came last night and spent the night with one of the men." The comment came from Pat. The woman really seemed to thrive on innuendo. So far, very little that I'd heard through her little grapevine had turned out to be true.

From the Mayhew table, Gerald's muffled voice spoke urgently to his wife. She shushed him, glancing around the room. I recalled the fragment of conversation I'd heard in the hallway on Monday and wondered what their story was. In nutrition class, they'd indicated that Gerald had received some type of dire medical diagnosis and was here to work on improving his health. Nicole, however, seemed to be the one taking the classes seriously. She took notes and really got into the yoga and meditation. That might not be remarkable, but the urgent tone of the few words that drifted my way told me that something serious was going on with those two. I wondered if it related to Rita in some way.

The waiter appeared with our customary bean soup and spiced vegetables. I resisted the urge to beg him for a Big Mac in place of the standard healthy fare. Later, I promised myself. When I drove into the city to meet Drake for dinner I would figure out a way to sneak French fries into my diet.

As I sipped the hot soup I found my thoughts drifting back to each encounter with Rita. I couldn't get it out of my head that there were probably quite a number of people who didn't like the woman—the Mayhews, Dina and Tahlene among them. On Monday I'd been about ready to kill her myself. I remembered the bit of argument I'd overheard when her cell phone rang after class and wondered who Rita had been talking to. All in all, Rita seemed abrasive, argumentative and frustrating in her refusal to listen to anyone's wishes.

The Mayhews finished their lunch quickly and left. Conversation at the table with the three women began to dwindle. Dina was the first to excuse herself and Pat followed close behind. Trudie sat there, gazing almost hungrily at Linda and me. I wavered between repulsion at her neediness and a desire to find out if she knew anything more about Rita.

Linda finished the last sip of her ginger tea and began to gather her things. "Well, I'm really ready for a massage," she said with a grin. "Coming?"

I picked up my purse and stood up. From the corner of my eye, I saw Trudie also stand. She cleared her throat loudly and stepped toward us.

"Are you going to the spa?" she asked. "Mind if I tag along?"

Curiosity won out. "Sure," I said.

"That was pretty weird about Rita today, huh?" she said as we crossed the lobby. "I couldn't believe it. That policeman said she might have jumped. I don't think so, there was someone … Well, at first I couldn't believe it, but then you know in a lot of ways I could because I've suffered from depression a lot of times too. And sometimes it just hits you, you know, that you think you're doing fine, but then a bad spell hits and you just suddenly wish you were dead. And maybe that's what happened with Rita. I mean, maybe she just woke up this morning and came to work and had something happen that gave her bad thoughts and all of a sudden she was depressed and she just followed her impulse." She rattled all this off in the time it took us to cross the walkway between the main building and spa building.

"But then I guess it could have been purely an accident and she sat on the wall and leaned too far back, but wouldn't a person reach out and catch herself if she started to fall backward? Well, I mean, unless she was depressed and secretly wished it would happen. You know, lots of people don't have the courage to purposely kill themselves but if an accident is about to happen they won't do anything to stop it. I read this thing one time that said lots of accidents could be prevented but that lots of people subconsciously want to get hurt. Sometimes they really want to get killed. And when I feel depressed sometimes I feel that way too. But I'm lucky because I have this really good doctor and he makes sure I get these pills that keep my moods even and

I don't get the depression all that much anymore, just once in awhile, like, around the holidays and stuff but mostly I don't."

"Trudie," Linda said gently. "We're here. This would be a good time to take a deep breath and get ready for a nice, relaxing massage, don't you think?"

Without giving Trudie a chance to get going again, we collected our robes from the attendant and headed for the locker rooms. While Trudie chatted away with the desk person, we ducked into changing rooms.

"Whew!" I said. "Get me into that massage room!"

I heard Trudie come in and latch the door of a changing room. Linda and I both remained silent as we stripped out of our clothes and put on robes. I actually tiptoed over to the lockers and manipulated the door cautiously for maximum quiet as I put my clothes away. We sneaked back to the spa lobby and were lucky enough to be met by our respective masseuses before Trudie got back.

"How's it going today?" Joanne asked as I stretched out on the table. "Sad about this morning, isn't it?"

I nodded and murmured affirmatively.

"Well, we're going to put all that out of your mind," she assured me.

Good.

"Starting with our special oil of clove, geranium, and other essential oils suited to your body type, you'll find yourself losing those tight muscles and that pinched place between your eyebrows."

"Ahhh . . . yes. You're so observant, Joanne."

Ninety minutes later, she'd fulfilled her promise and I left the spa feeling like I could put all the Rita stuff behind me during my dinner with Drake.

I went back to the room, changed clothes and left a note for Linda, in case Drake and I ended up staying in town late.

I'd just tugged the door shut behind me when I recognized the voices of Gerald and Nicole. Before I'd turned to face them, Gerald bumped into me.

"Oh! Sorry," he said. "Didn't see you there." He snapped his tiny cell phone closed and dropped it into a pocket.

"It's okay," I said. "Look, I wanted to let you guys know that I was sorry about what happened to Rita this morning."

"How did you--?" Nicole didn't realize that I'd been bluffing.

"I'm used to being observant," I said, handing them my card from RJP Investigations. "You did know her before this seminar, didn't you?"

Nicole started to speak, but Gerald shushed her.

"We better not talk out here," he said. He nodded toward the door to their room, across the hall. He moved to unlock it. This was about to get interesting.

Chapter 12

Okay. You've guessed that this Lightness in Living conference isn't our first encounter with Rita Ratwill," Gerald said after securely closing the door and motioning me toward a chair near the window. "When we got to the first yoga class Monday morning, I didn't recognize her at first. She used to work in a law office and she wore suits and had her hair in a much more businesslike style."

"It was those square white plastic glasses that I noticed," Nicole piped up. "She always wore those. But she didn't seem to remember us. Not surprising, really. We only went to their office once or twice. It wasn't until she, uh . . . died, that I learned her last name."

Gerald shot her a look and continued. "The law office was her husband's. David Ratwill was head of a firm that sued my company. Of course, he was young and eager and snapped up the case immediately."

"What was the case about?" I asked. "Just generally."

"Oh, I can tell you exactly. You probably heard about it on the news, roughly two years ago. The guy who thought he'd become an instant millionaire suing AceChem because his son was born with severe birth defects. Claimed our pesticide was used on the apples that his wife loved so much and her eating them caused the defects."

"And you own AceChem? I do remember that one," I said. "They won some enormous amount but AceChem is appealing."

"On the grounds that the wife's repeated use of illegal drugs during her pregnancy was never brought out in front of the jury. On the grounds that every one of our products is FDA approved and EPA tested—don't even get me started on the joys of dealing with those agencies—and any burden of proof should rest with them. Common sense is dead, I tell you." His face grew red as he paced the floor.

"Gerald, your heart—" Nicole said.

He took a deep breath. "I know. Okay, so Ratwill's fledgling firm gets this big case. The dollar signs are glowing in his eyes. He's promised the client untold riches, obviously. Truthfully, the case was so flimsy that our attorney was every bit as surprised as we were when he won it. Lifelong judge who should have been disbarred twenty years ago for his antics and a bleeding-heart jury who saw absolutely *nothing* they were shown except that poor little kid with breathing tubes and missing limbs."

"Yeah, as I recall, that image made the news on a regular basis too," I said.

"Why is it that no one, not the judge, the jury or the

media gave a shit about how the kid got that way, they just wanted a big corporation to pin it on."

Nicole signaled him again to slow down.

"I know. I've now got a heart condition and a stress-related cancer over this thing. Does anybody care how *my* health conditions came about?"

"But the appeal—is that going well?"

"Extremely. A new judge has already ruled that the mother's drug use has to be admitted. He's also allowed documents proving the government approval of every one of our chemicals. So, yes, I think we'll win ultimately. Problem is that our insurance company already paid out a big chunk, not all but a lot, of the judgment. With the verdict getting overturned, David Ratwill and his client will be required to repay that money. Will we ever get it? Not likely. Ratwill went right out and spent his greedy share— big house, yacht in the Bahamas, art. Cash accounts that seem to have mysteriously disappeared. None of it but the real estate has a chance of selling for its full value. The client paid medical bills for their poor kid. How can I ask for that money back? But not to do so admits guilt to a certain degree in our convoluted legal system. In short, it's a total mess."

"What did Rita have to do with any of this?" I asked.

"Nothing directly, not with our case, anyway. She'd quit the law office awhile back, apparently went the New Agey way and started teaching yoga. My guess is that she saw David getting into financial trouble and wanted out, asap."

Maybe that was the reason Rita referred to David as her ex, rather than admitting she was still married to him.

"Not that it makes any difference to your situation," I said, "but the police are leaning toward ruling Rita's death an accident. If anything comes to mind that might change that, you could tell the police or give me a call at that number on the card I gave you."

Gerald glanced at the wrinkled card, which he'd kept in his clenched fist. "Sure," he said.

I didn't get the feeling that any outcome to the Rita investigation would take priority over Gerald's other problems, but it was worth a try. I left a couple of minutes later and headed toward the parking lot. I saw a woman walking toward me with her head lowered. "Dina? You okay?" I asked.

"Charlie?" The voice was soft.

Dina Carlotti stepped out from between two cars. Her eyes looked moist and her smooth dark hair was rumpled. I repeated my question.

"Um, yes, I think so." She walked toward me, wadding the fabric of her tote bag in her fingers. "I have been thinking so much about poor Rita."

"Well, it's sad. But you hardly knew her." I thought of the way Rita had practically forced Dina into one of the yoga positions, despite her back injury. "Not to speak ill of the dead, but she wasn't exactly the nicest person any of us have met."

"That is true. She just . . . I saw what a struggle she had in life."

How well *did* Dina know the dead woman?

"Didn't you just meet her on Monday, like the rest of us? I mean, she hardly shared her life story with us in these three days."

"Oh, I did not mention? Rita and I attend some yoga seminars here in Santa Fe last summer. She was only recently separate from her husband. I think there were many problems with money. She talk about going back to California for a better job." Dina fiddled with the tote handles again. "I did not know her well, but her impression is of a lady who knew better times. She once had money to spend and to travel. She told me she once watch me perform in Venezia."

Interesting.

"What about this week? Did you talk to her much?"

"No. Sadly, she did not recognize me at first. I introduce myself, then she remember, but was very, how you say, distracted. I asked her to have dinner on Wednesday, that is tonight, and we would talk. Maybe then she would tell me how her life was going. But now . . ." Her eyes welled up again.

I moved forward and hugged her. "Oh, Dina, I'm so sorry. I didn't realize . . ."

She gripped me tightly for a few seconds then pulled away.

"I know. A sad person, Rita was." She took a deep breath and swiped at her eyes with the heel of her hand. "Nothing to be done, though. It is time for my massage."

"That will help," I assured her, patting her shoulder as she walked away. I tossed my bag on the front passenger seat and started my car, mulling over the past hour's revelations. How coincidental was it that three people in our group just happened to know Rita from elsewhere? And wasn't it a tad early to consider a suicide verdict when Rita had made dinner plans for tonight? Even if she'd been feeling down, it seemed that meeting an old friend, someone she'd confided in before, would be incentive enough to stick around for another day or so anyway.

I didn't like the accident theory and I didn't like the

suicide option. So what was left? Well, with any luck the police would begin to piece it together soon.

I really didn't relish the idea of becoming sucked into a murder investigation.

Chapter 13

Drake stared at the horizon. The Santa Fe Airport came in sight, sitting out in an open spot with nearly three-sixty views. Some light industrial businesses flanked it on the east side, toward the city, while acres of native piñon and juniper stretched off in every other direction. He radioed his approach, got the go-ahead and set up the pattern. The elk count had gone well, they'd spotted over five hundred head, and his Fish and Game guys were happy. They'd scheduled him for another count in the Jemez in two more weeks. He brought the aircraft around to a southerly heading and aimed her into the wind.

Charlie's Jeep sat in the small parking lot, he noticed, and he caught the familiar sight of her slender figure as she walked toward Zia Aviation's fueling station, hands jammed into the pockets of her leather jacket. She'd flown in and out of this airport herself many times and knew just where he'd be landing. He dragged his attention away from his wife and concentrated on the ground. Wouldn't do to make an awkward landing in plain sight of the tower.

"Hey there, handsome," Charlie greeted, as soon as he'd touched down and opened his door. They shared a long kiss as the engine wound down and the main rotor began to slow. "How'd the job go?"

"Good." He liked the way she always showed an interest in his work. Not surprising. She'd been on enough jobs with him now that she knew a lot of the people and how their routines went. And she was turning out to be a pretty damn good pilot herself.

"What kind of food do you want?" she asked. "I thought about the Blue Corn, but then I got to thinking about seafood."

"Seafood it is," he said. "I've had plenty of enchiladas this week."

He climbed out of the cockpit, retrieved his old Thermos and jacket. "If you can hold on to these . . ." He handed the items off to Charlie. "I'll get this finished up."

He walked around the aircraft, making sure everything looked clean, noticing a faint trace of oil near the rear cowling. Have to check that out before next flight, he noted. A young guy from Zia was walking toward him and Drake told him to go ahead and fill the tank. The day was cooling and his high altitude work was done, so no harm in having the extra fuel weight.

He watched the young guy for a moment since he didn't know this one, making sure he followed safety procedure and watching to be sure fuel didn't slosh onto the Jet

Ranger's side. While the kid finished fueling, Drake loosely tied the main rotor. He'd be leaving again, probably before dark, so there was no point in bedding her down for the night.

"Where can we get seafood in the middle of the afternoon?" he asked Charlie as they walked toward the parking lot.

Her mouth did that funny little squinch that happened when she was thinking. "I think The Horno doesn't open for dinner until about six. I'm guessing it's going to be Red Lobster."

Drake didn't mind. Personally, he thought the chain places did a good job for a decent price, and he knew Charlie couldn't resist those cheese biscuits they made. He draped an arm around her shoulders and nuzzled her hair as they walked. Too bad they weren't going home together, but she'd already told him that she really ought to get back to that spa place tonight.

Plus, he knew it wasn't going to be an early evening for him. He'd be lucky to get much sleep at all, with the work he still needed to do on the lawsuit before touching base with Rick Valdez tomorrow. He gave Charlie another squeeze before they separated and went to their opposite sides of her Jeep.

She sometimes drove like a bat. He kept his mouth shut. Upside was that they arrived at the restaurant within a few minutes and got a table immediately. The smell of those biscuits was already filling the air by the time the waiter took their order and brought the first basket.

Charlie filled him in on what she'd been doing at this conference or retreat or whatever it was that her friend Linda had talked her into. Apparently a yoga teacher that nobody liked very much had fallen off a wall and killed herself, and then there was this guru sort of guy that ran the show. Drake smiled and nodded at all the right places but knew that his mind was being pulled in about six directions. He didn't mind that they ate quickly and she drove him back to the airport right away. He did give himself over to the parting kiss and resulting surge. Twining his fingers through her long auburn hair and breathing her breath, he almost wanted to say to hell with Santa Fe and lawyers and elk and all that. But he didn't.

He watched her walk back toward the gate, looking very fine in those jeans, and he sighed. Back to his responsibilities.

He checked the aircraft one more time, belted himself in and spooled up the engine. It was nearly five and the sun would be going down by the time he reached Double Eagle airport on Albuquerque's west side.

It was almost six-thirty by the time he'd landed and watched the tug put his aircraft into the hangar. He retrieved his pickup truck and drove to the RJP Investigations office near downtown. Ron's Mustang sat in the parking area behind the gray Victorian building and lights were on all over the place. He shook out the tension that had settled in his neck.

Drake entered through the back door, into the old house's kitchen. Kid voices came from the hallway and one of the little creatures zoomed through the doorway and nearly crashed into him. The munchkin slid to a stop and stared up at him with wide dark eyes.

"Hey, slow it down a little," Drake told him.

An ear-piercing shriek came from the front of the building, followed by Ron's roar—"Jason! Cut it out!"

Whichever kid—Justin or Joey—had nearly collided with Drake now raced away, heavier-than-possible footfalls thundering down the hardwood floors in the hall.

"Boys! Right now!"

Drake shook his head and allowed himself a moment of secret gladness that he and Charlie had not let themselves in for this. He reached the bottom of the stairs and called out to Ron.

"Up here," came the response. "In my office."

Drake waded through a tangle of plastic soldiers and little-boy bodies at the foot of the stairs and headed up. Ron's office looked about the same as usual, a solid layer of papers covering the top of the desk and Ron sitting in his chair with the phone to his ear.

"I'm on hold," he said, waving Drake toward the visitor's chair.

Since it was stacked with books, Drake opted to stand.

"I've got the Valdez file here somewh— Yeah, Bill, I'm here." He shrugged at Drake and turned his attention to the phone.

Drake wandered into Charlie's office, where he knew he'd find a little oasis of calm. The exact opposite of her brother, Charlie kept everything filed away or ordered with precision. Her phone, stapler and calculator stood in straight ranks on the desktop. Her chair was pushed into its cubbyhole, and her computer monitor and keyboard hadn't moved from their standard placement. An Oriental rug in pastels added a feminine touch, along with some potted plants that hung in the bay window. Atop a bookcase stood a tin 'cookie jar' undoubtedly filled with dog biscuits for Rusty. The one concession to untidiness was a pile of mail, which Sally the receptionist must have left in the center of the desk—precisely in the center, he noted.

"Okay, all set with that," Ron said. His appearance in the doorway startled Drake.

He held out a thick manila file, and Drake sensed a slight hesitancy in his manner.

"Hey, man, things are fine. I know I came off a little testy yesterday."

Ron shrugged. "It's okay. Charlie said you were dreading the deposition."

"That's all it is. Really."

Ron gave him a little pat on the shoulder and handed over the file. "I've added some reports on the legwork I've done—addresses, phone numbers, interviews with a couple of the family members."

"Good. Good." Drake felt the previous awkward moment drift away. He fanned a few of the pages. "All my notes in here?"

"Yeah, everything so far. Charlie filed some data from your simulator tests in there somewhere . . . I don't understand all the technical lingo."

"I've got a few more things at home, photos and notes that I never did type up. But I'll get it all in order tonight. I'm supposed to call Valdez at ten in the morning to go over my testimony. Deposition's at one o'clock."

Ron reached over and flipped open the cover of the file. "I stuck a note inside here," he said, indicating a yellow Post-it, "with the address of the downtown office where you're going. One of the families has a Santa Fe firm representing them, and that guy's name is right . . . here. David Ratwill."

Something about the lawyer's name felt familiar but he wasn't sure why. "Okay." Drake took a breath and looked his brother-in-law in the eye. "Guess I'm ready."

He threaded his way back through the mass of kids and toys at the foot of the stairs and walked out to his truck. Tossing the file on the passenger seat, he started the engine and realized he was clenching his jaw. Why was the idea of giving a deposition bothering him so much? He knew perfectly well why, although he hadn't said anything to either Charlie or Ron.

Like a flash, the whole scene from Seattle came back in a rush. Five years ago. The crash which killed a search and rescue crew he worked with, the calls from media, then from lawyers, finally from the FAA. What was the cause of the crash, they all wanted to know. How had a high-time pilot lost it and planted the craft into the side of a hill? Upshaw had never wanted to preflight the aircraft. Thought that was for wimps and suck-ups. If the helicopter was checked over every couple of days he thought it was fine. He ragged Drake more than once for being so meticulous in his inspections, checking every hatch, wiggling each moving part. Huh! He never bothered with that stuff. Their job was to get off the ground fast—lives were at stake in search and rescue and you didn't mess around. He held to that position right up to the day he died.

He died, and left everyone else to answer the questions. Drake knew exactly what had happened. A mechanic, earlier in the day, had opened a hatch to check fluid levels and Upshaw had called him away on some other duty. The mechanic had told him about the open hatch and was told, according to his later sworn statement, that Upshaw would take care of it. But then the pilot became distracted with concerns of his own (probably a woman, although Drake never mentioned that part of it), and when the call came a few minutes later, Upshaw had hopped in and been airborne immediately. Mere minutes into the flight the hatch door ripped off and flew into the tail rotor. It was all over.

Lawyers flocked to the scene, crawling all over the company records and the maintenance facility like cockroaches. The media pounded everyone with questions and the operator had to issue orders to the crew not to talk. But people want to talk, to speculate, to offer their 'expert' opinions, so the frenzy continued for months. Then the subpoenas came. Drake had managed to keep his mouth shut up to that point but you can't ignore a court order.

At the deposition the lawyers came at him from all sides. He told what he knew, which, first hand, wasn't much. He'd been off duty that day. He only knew Upshaw's work habits and what the mechanic had told him. He passed that along, but the lawyers weren't really interested in getting at the truth. They'd dug out the maintenance records on the aircraft since the day it rolled out of the factory. They wanted to find a mechanical failure that could be blamed on either the helicopter manufacturer or the engine company. The deep pockets. You can't win a multi-million dollar suit against a dead pilot or a poor mechanic. They went after, and got, the maximum limit on the liability insurance but the cost of the lawsuit put the mid-sized operator out of business. Drake had ranted at the unfairness of it and at the win-at-all-cost attitude.

Even now, as he drove west on Central, he felt his blood pressure rise. Here he was in the middle of another one. This time, as a favor to his own brother-in-law, he'd agreed to do some basic research into the maintenance records and flight history of the European-made helicopter that had gone down. From day one, he'd regretted the agreement.

He wanted out, away from all the memories and emotions, away from the lawyers.

He turned off Central and wound through the quiet neighborhood that he now called home. The minute he pulled into the driveway he could hear Rusty barking from the house next door. Charlie'd left the dog with Elsa, the surrogate grandmother who'd adopted Drake as surely as she'd taken Charlie in as a teenager. He saw Elsa peek out through the front curtains and give a small wave when she recognized his truck. A moment later, Rusty came trotting out, crossed the two yards, and flung himself at Drake.

"Hey, boy." He rubbed the Lab's ears and tussled him for a minute. "You're sure glad to see me." A man could always count on a dog. He grinned as he watched the big canine head toward the front door, eager to get there first.

He gathered his jacket and papers from the truck and went inside. The house felt cold and empty. They'd only been gone four days, but it wasn't that. It was the fact that Charlie wasn't there. In the two years they'd been married, their lives had meshed so completely that he just didn't feel whole when she wasn't with him. He knew she felt the same because she'd said so. But for him, the feeling was tangible.

He flipped on lights and tossed the folder on the dining table. In the kitchen he opened the pantry and gazed inside. This would be a long night, he had the feeling, and he debated what he wanted that would keep him alert. He settled on a Coke and stuck a bag of popcorn in the microwave. Rusty kept watch as the kernels began to make noise and the buttery smell started to drift into the room.

When the snack was ready, Drake carried the bag and his drink to the table, the dog trotting along, never taking his eyes off the goodies.

Drake opened the folder he'd brought home with him, along with the others he'd kept here at the house. Among them were photos and notes he'd taken of the crash wreckage. The mangled helicopter now sat in a corner of one of the maintenance hangars at Albuquerque International, kept there by court order until the investigation was complete. Drake had been there twice in recent weeks.

The first time he felt as if he didn't have a clue what to look for. The twisted heap of metal held a story—he knew that. But it was hard to look past the blood stains and charred paint on the fuselage, the result of what happened when the aircraft went down into a flame-ringed field during a forest fire. Mike Walters and two fire fighters—gone.

He'd steeled his emotions that day. Taken pictures of the tangled metal from all angles. Avoided looking at the passenger compartment.

Now, after weeks of research and the data from the simulator, he knew a little better what to look for. He pulled every photo of the engine and studied them. Found a magnifying glass in a desk drawer and studied them closer. Answers. They were here—if he just looked hard enough.

It was nearly two a.m. when he stood up to stretch. He'd reread every page of the file, and now he knew what he was going to tell them at the deposition. He needed to call Valdez in just a few hours, and he knew the lawyer wouldn't like what he had to say.

Chapter 14

I watched Drake pull pitch on the Jet Ranger and shielded my eyes at the little cloud of grit that accompanied his takeoff. By the time the aircraft had become a tiny dot in the sky I'd walked back through the gate and started the Jeep. I'd almost gotten my grease fix at dinner, consuming fried shrimp and three cheese biscuits, but something was still nagging at my hunger module. Sweets. For only a buck I could get a hot fudge sundae at McDonald's and I'd bet money that it didn't have any tofu in it. I pulled out onto Airport Road, knowing the yellow-arched garden of earthly delights was just a couple miles away on Cerrillos Road.

It seemed that half of Santa Fe had the same idea. The line at the drive-up window snaked around the parking lot, nearly to the street. A small growl formed in my throat;

when I want my sugar, I want my sugar. I spotted an opening and whipped around the line of cars, into the one empty parking space near the door. Going inside was going to be quicker than sitting out here, and I could be back on the road in just a few minutes.

Surprisingly, for the number of vehicles outside, there wasn't much of a line waiting to order so I stepped forward and told the girl my wishes, adding a Coke to the order so I could be good and syrupy by the time I got back to tranquility base.

Turning from the counter, I nearly bumped into a man in a dark suit who was preoccupied talking into his cell phone.

I almost sputtered an invective but my newfound inner peace led me to simply turn away and take a deep breath instead. Although he was one of those who seems to believe that his conversation is important enough for the entire room to share, I shook my head and moved aside.

The guy continued to talk about some stock transaction, dropping his voice occasionally, as he ordered a meal. I busied myself at the soft drink machine, finding a lid and straw for my Coke, keeping one ear tuned to the counter so I could snatch up my hot fudge sundae the minute it was ready. I found myself watching phone guy's back, amazed at his agility as he managed both phone and tray. Finally, he ended the call and headed toward the seating area. As I walked to the counter for my ice cream, I saw his face clearly.

With his longish hair neatly combed back, wearing a dark suit with white shirt and tie, I wouldn't have picked him out in a crowd. In the persona of a high roller businessman,

Celeus Light looked like anything but the pious, spiritual man in flowing robes who presented himself to the Lightness In Living group.

Light never glanced my way as he walked toward a corner table. I decided on a quick change of plans and chose a table where I could observe him. I casually picked up a newspaper and sat with my shoulder toward his side of the room. He went on to a corner table where he joined another man, also dressed in suit and tie. I sneaked occasional glances over the top of my paper.

It was clearly a business meeting, with folders of legal-sized documents changing hands and signatures being applied. Curious. The man whose sole driving force in life seemed to be spiritual and above earthly concerns was certainly in full swing now on the other side of the worldly spectrum. Once it appeared that all the papers had been signed the two of them turned to their hamburgers. I finally got a clear look at the other man and was surprised to see that it was the dark-haired man I'd seen peeping into Trudie's window on Tuesday. This was truly becoming confusing. If he knew Dr. Light, why hadn't he gone directly to Light's office, rather than peeking into guestrooms? Why hadn't they met at the resort instead of here?

I folded my newspaper, capped my Coke, and walked out to my car. Keeping the restaurant's door in my rearview, I waited fifteen minutes for the two men to come out. Light walked over to a white Lexus, which I remembered seeing in the parking lot at Casa de Tranquilidad. My attention shifted to the other man, who had already climbed into a tan Suburban and was backing out of his parking slot. I quickly cranked my ignition and followed suit.

The Suburban pulled around to the back of the McDonald's building and signaled a right turn onto a side road leading away from the main drag. I noticed that Dr. Light had already gone out the main exit and joined the traffic on bustling Cerrillos Road. Staying behind the big SUV didn't prove difficult. He made a couple of turns, then pulled into the parking lot of a small office building. I drove past it in time to see the dark-haired man open his door and kick a foot out as he turned to gather items from the passenger seat of the vehicle. I pulled into the parking lot of the next building and watched.

He didn't notice me. With briefcase in hand and a newspaper tucked under his left arm, he clicked the remote switch on his keyring to lock his car before heading toward the front door of the one-story adobe. In keeping with Santa Fe's laws on signage, the office building had only one discreet, carved-wood sign on the front. Once the guy had entered, I pulled out and cruised slowly past. LAW OFFICES read the top line. In smaller lettering, turquoise against white, his name stood out among the three listed. David Ratwill.

Confusion reigned for a full ten seconds. David Ratwill. Rita's husband. What was his connection with Celeus Light? Why the business meeting away from either of their offices? Had the Ratwills known Light socially? Maybe Rita had gotten her job with the Lightness conference through that connection?

An impatient horn jolted me back to the present. I'd nearly come to a stop in the street. Now I'd managed to call attention to myself. I hit the accelerator. By the time I'd negotiated the traffic through Santa Fe and up the winding mountain road to Casa de Tranquilidad I still didn't have any real answers.

Meditation session was just letting out and people were milling in the lobby as I entered. I caught Linda's eye.

"Hey, how's Drake?" she asked.

"Fine. No problems."

She gave me a quizzical look.

"No, really. I just saw something really puzzling, though." I glanced at my watch. "Look, I have a massage in a couple minutes. Meet you later?"

"I'll be in the dining room at seven." I felt her eyes on my back as I walked through the lobby to the spa building.

By the time I'd shed my clothes in the locker room, donned my robe and showed up in the treatment room, Joanne was waiting for me.

"Boy, everyone's got tense muscles today," she said as she began rubbing my shoulders.

"That obvious, huh?"

"Don't worry about it. You're getting the energy enlivening massage today. First, we're going to relax you to the state of a puddle of mush then we'll rejuvenate you so you can face life with the energy of a tiger."

I visualized a bunch of tigers lying around and yawning those huge lazy yawns with lots of pointed teeth showing. It probably wasn't exactly the comparison she intended but maybe that wouldn't be so bad. I settled into the soft surface of the massage table and let my body meld with it. After thirty minutes or so of Joanne's gentle touch with some heavenly scented oil, I'd completely put aside the events of the morning and the strange encounter at McDonald's.

"Now just lie still for a few minutes while this herbal oil

does its magic," Joanne said in her most relaxing voice. "I'll be back in about ten minutes to start the enlivening part of the treatment." She pulled a light blanket over me.

"Okay," I mumbled. With my face buried in the table's oval slot, the word came out more like "umphm." I never heard the door close behind her.

I dozed lightly, only vaguely aware that the door had opened again. Quick ten minutes, I thought. A second later a hand clamped down on the back of my neck.

Chapter 15

"If you know what's good for you, you'll quit snooping around here." The voice sounded raspy, light, neither male nor female.

I struggled to get a glimpse of my attacker, but the hand held me firmly and the padded edges of the table blocked my vision on all sides.

"No one asked you to butt in here. Rita ended up as she deserved."

My voice struggled to scream but only muffled squeaks came out. I swung out with a fist, but contacted nothing. The attacker must be standing near my head.

"I mean it!" came the nasty whisper again. "Leave this alone or you die!"

The claw-like hand jammed my neck downward with

enough force to make sparks jump in front of my eyes, then it released me as suddenly as it had appeared. I fought against the sparks and raised my head until I could stretch the crackly feeling out of my neck. I whipped my attention to the door, but it was designed to open away from the treatment table and I couldn't see the person as the door softly swung shut. I clutched the light blanket in front of me and hit the floor on rubbery legs, nearly blacking out from the sharp stab in my neck. I staggered to the door and pulled it back.

"Help!" My voice croaked pitifully in the silent hallway. "Joanne!"

"Charlie? What is it?" she said, emerging from the reception area. "What's happened?"

"Did you see anyone come through here just now?"

"Several," she said, guiding me back into the massage room. "A lot of people are milling around."

I allowed her to steer me back to the table. I sat weakly on its edge.

"What's wrong with your neck?" she asked, standing in front of me and giving me the critical eye. "You're holding it crooked."

I gave her a quick recap. "I think that final shove did it," I said. "I saw sparkles."

She made me sit up straight and place my hands in my lap. "Hold still." With gentle hands on both sides of my head she straightened it, staring at me critically. "Does that hurt?"

"No, not really."

She walked around behind me and touched the sides of my neck and head, guiding, making minute adjustments to my position, touching the vertebrae carefully. "Nothing seems out of place, but you should probably have an X-ray."

I wanted to get off this table and start searching the building, not waste away the evening in some hospital ER. However, common sense told me that the person was long gone.

"I've got to find out who threatened me," I insisted.

"Well, I can see that you aren't going to lie quietly and let me finish the enlivening part of this treatment. You're about as enlivened right now as anyone I've seen." She moved around to face me again. "At least let me work those shoulder muscles for a minute. Bolting from the table like that wasn't good for you."

No kidding. Going from melted-butter relaxation to scared-to-death probably hadn't done my heart any good either. I allowed her to recline me once more and knead some of the tension from my shoulders and neck. After insisting once more that I didn't want to be taken to the hospital (I promised to drive myself there later), she gave me a hand in sitting up slowly.

"Now go take a hot shower and try to keep those muscles as relaxed as possible," she advised. "And get that neck X-rayed."

I made obedient noises as I slipped into my robe and headed for the locker room. After the prescribed hot shower I stopped at the spa reception desk. During my shower I'd mulled over the possibilities of my attacker's identity. While it *could* be anyone, guests were usually attended in the building and someone would surely know who had been in here at the time. We were given our white robes when we checked in for our appointments, we wore them from the locker room to the reception area, then we were escorted to a treatment room. Afterward, as I'd just done, we left the robes hanging in dressing rooms, where an attendant promptly tidied up after each guest. Anyone who came in could grab a robe and blend in perfectly.

"Can you tell me who had spa appointments this afternoon?" I asked the guy at the desk. He must have caught a hint of the trouble because he didn't question me. He ran a hand through his dark, spiked hair and consulted a sheet of paper on the lower desk, hidden from my view by the counter top.

"Mr. and Mrs. Mayhew, Ms. Carlotti, and Dr. Gaston are here now," he said.

"And thirty minutes ago?"

"The same. The late afternoon appointments have all finished and most left before you got here, Ms. Parker." Anticipating my next question, he added, "We don't book appointments during the dinner hour, and we have no evening appointments today."

I thanked him and wandered out. Neither of the Mayhews nor Dina seemed like likely candidates, and I didn't even know a Dr. Gaston. Presumably, he or she was one of the medical doctors here for the professional portion of the seminar. I could catch up with Linda in the dining room and ask her while she ate dinner.

Chapter 16

In the restaurant Linda had already gotten a table and our little glasses of digestive elixir waited at each of our place settings. Linda's concerned frown dissolved as I approached.

"Well, you *look* okay," she said. "Feel all right?"

"I guess you heard. How far has the gossip mill spread it so far?"

"Pretty much through the whole conference," she said.

"Oh, great." I'd been hoping to find out who'd threatened me without their necessarily knowing I was after them. Obviously a dumb thought.

"I want to examine your shoulder right after dinner," Linda said.

"It was my neck. That's the problem with gossip as a source of information."

She looked slightly chagrined. "You're right. So I'll want to look at your neck."

"Lucky me, being right in the midst of all these doctors." I told her what I'd learned, or rather not learned, in the spa. "I have a hard time believing either of the Mayhews or Dina was involved in this. And I don't even know Gaston."

"I do," she said. "Soft-spoken woman, about my age. I can't figure how she'd be involved in something like this, although she is a chiropractor. She'd know how to snap your neck without doing any visible damage."

Bright thought, that.

Our waiter came just then with salads, and I declined, not mentioning that I'd just filled myself with fat, sugar and caffeine.

"I think I'll go to the room," I told Linda. "I should check in with Drake and be sure he got home okay."

"Lie down and relax your neck."

Before I got out of the dining room I was interrupted four times by people wanting to know if I felt all right. Some were attendees I didn't even know, and one was Dr. Light himself. He seemed to study my face an extra few seconds, but didn't indicate that he remembered me. He was back in form now in his loose cottons. The earlier business suit image was completely gone. I felt myself itching with curiosity about his dealings with David Ratwill. But that was information best saved for later.

I went to the room and called Drake. He said he was eyeball-deep in the accident file and he sounded so preoccupied that he probably didn't hear a thing I said anyway. I purposely didn't mention the attack in the massage room. He would worry needlessly. We kept the call short and wished each other a good night's sleep.

I reached for the phone directory in the nightstand, a twinge grabbing my neck as I did so, and Linda chose that moment to walk into the room.

"Hey, what's this—there's no lifting heavy objects when you have a neck injury," she said.

"It's hardly a 'heavy object'." I held up the book, which was barely over an inch thick. "And I'm not really injured."

"That's for me, your doctor, to say." She snatched the book out of my hand and set it aside, making me sit straight and stare into her eyes while she did some mumbo jumbo, moving her finger back and forth in front of my face and making sure my eyes weren't tracking off in wacky directions or something. She ran her hands gently down the sides of my neck, and I have to admit that I flinched at one point when she pressed on a muscle.

"See, there's some tenderness here," she said.

"Well, yeah. When you jab me ruthlessly."

By this time her fingertips were doing a little dance up and down my vertebrae and I guess she didn't find any of them missing. "Looks like you'll live. I'll give you a mild muscle relaxant for tonight, and that spot should feel a whole lot better by morning."

"Thanks, doc." I gave a little eye-roll and she snicked my shoulder with her nail. "Just shut up and take your pills."

I did both, and within fifteen minutes I'd drifted into a happy slumber.

When Linda suggested that I skip yoga the next morning, just to give my neck an extra day to recover, I was secretly not unhappy. The classes were okay, especially now that Dina had taken over, but I knew I wasn't going to be able to really concentrate on the postures.

The minute my roomie left, I pulled the business card from my bag and made a call to Detective Gallegos at the Santa Fe PD. The short answer to my question was that they'd ruled Rita's death an accident.

"Suicide sometimes gets tricky for the family—emotions, religious beliefs and all," he explained. "So we avoid that unless we have a real reason to go that way. I'll admit this could have been either, so we went with accidental death."

I couldn't believe that David Ratwill didn't get closer scrutiny, especially given the facts that he was on the property that morning and that she was in the process of divorcing him, and I told Gallegos so.

"His alibi checked out." He wouldn't explain further.

My next call was to Ron, who had apparently just arrived at the office because I heard the kitcheny sounds of coffee being poured into a mug and the carafe going, clumsily, back onto its stand. Clumping footsteps up the stairs, along with Ron's labored breathing, took me visually into his office where he would rummage for a minute or so before finding a blank notepad to write on. I filled the empty space with a mini-lecture on losing some weight. He gave me some yeah-yeah-yeah about that.

"I need some information," I said. I filled him in on the threat I'd received in the massage room yesterday afternoon and the strange transformation of Celeus Light into Mr. Businessman, along with my following the other guy and finding out that it was Rita's husband or ex- or whatever, with whom Light had the meeting. "I'd like to know if any of this ties together. It just seems a bit much that I'm warned away from asking questions about Rita while the police are sure it was an accident. And how strange is it that Celeus and David Ratwill seem to be doing some kind of business together."

"David Ratwill, you said?"

"Ron, where have you been?" I wanted to pull my hair out sometimes.

"Taking notes," he said, somewhat defensively. I heard a loud slurp at the coffee mug. Okay, in all fairness, my brother isn't truly awake—usually—until cup number three.

"Write down these names: David Ratwill and Rita Ratwill. I'd like background on both of them."

"I can give you an interesting tidbit on David right now, if you'll just let me speak," he said. "He's a partner in the firm that we're up against in this helicopter case."

Now I needed coffee. This wasn't making sense.

"They're representing one of the victims' families, and they're wanting to find Starland Helicopters and S-Jet Engines at fault."

"I'm not really following."

He slurped again and went on. "It's a complicated story. Do you want all of it?"

"Just the highlights."

"Three families, several law firms. Ours—Graham and Valdez—represents the company that made the engine. Valdez thinks he's got a good case for pilot error rather than mechanical failure, really thinks that's how the case will come down. Drake's looking at the evidence, but doesn't think that's true. The Santa Fe firm is going for the bigger money—find fault with a manufacturer and go after their insurance. Widows and kids of those other two families get a pile of money, attorneys get a bigger pile."

I couldn't get a grasp on how any of this fit with Rita's

death or the person who sneaked into the massage room to deliver me a headache, so I suggested he concentrate on background that went further back. "Find out about David and Rita, when they met, how long they were married, and all that. Rumors here are flying thicker than bats on a starry night, and I've heard that they weren't officially divorced yet. See if you can find out whether that's true."

He mumbled some um-hm kinds of things, apparently scratching notes as fast as I could talk.

"Oh, another thought. If the names Mayhew, AceChem Corporation, or Trudie Blanchard come up anywhere along the way, pay attention to them. I have no idea where this might lead." By the time we hung up, my head was pounding. I found aspirin in my travel bag and swallowed three.

I managed to catch Linda between seminar sessions and we walked outside and followed the meandering path through the gardens. The fresh air and sunshine felt good after spending half the morning on the phone. After she asked how my neck felt she said, "There's the farewell dinner tonight and don't forget tomorrow's special meditation session led by Dr. Light himself."

I couldn't quite tell her how very little that excited me. I didn't mention the headache. I did not want to be sent to an ER and waste the rest of the day.

"Word is getting around that the police decided Rita's death was an accident," she said.

"I know, Gallegos told me. Can I be blunt? I think it's bullshit. Otherwise, why did someone feel it necessary to warn me away from the investigation by nearly breaking my neck yesterday?"

"Exactly."

"I want to keep attending the sessions for you, but I also feel like there was a reason I was threatened. I have to look into it." Once the conference was over the participants would scatter. I could let the police ruling stand, but that would leave a killer running free and I just couldn't bring myself to let go of it.

She gave me a light hug. "That's okay. I'm sure Dina can share her notes with me. And Shirley will give me copies of the handouts. You do what you gotta do."

"Thanks—you sure it's okay?"

"Absolutely." She glanced at her watch. "I need to make the next session. If I see you at lunch, we'll chat again then."

I felt like a rat for a minute as I watched her walk back to the conference center but my phone vibrated in my pocket before I could give myself over to too much guilt.

Ron. "Hey, got some new stuff for you."

I fished in my bag for a scrap of paper and pen and found a deserted bench where I could sit down.

"The background check you asked me to do on Rita Ratwill? Interesting stuff. Turns out she was once committed to a mental facility in California. Checked herself in, about two years ago. Stayed ninety days, felt all better and checked herself out again."

Two years ago. Somewhere around the time her husband was up to his neck in the AceChem trial. Had something about the case bothered Rita so much that she couldn't stand being around it? The Mayhews mentioned that she'd been working in her husband's office at the time. I realized Ron was still talking and pulled myself back.

"Sorry, Ron, what was that last part? My attention wandered."

"One of her nurses at the facility was a Trudie, spelled T-r-u-d-i-e, Blanchard. Didn't you mention that name to me?"

"Wow, how did you get that kind of info? I'm surprised they'd give that out."

"They wouldn't. Not to me. But Sally came to our rescue. Posed on the phone as Rita's sister, who was trying to track down her present whereabouts. Lucked out in finding a gabby nurse who'd also treated her."

"Really." I tried to imagine our sweet, open Sally managing a lie with a straight face but couldn't put the picture together.

"Yeah, apparently Rita confided to this night-shift nurse that the day gal was weird."

An understatement.

"Nurse says Rita felt tense and nervous every time Trudie entered her room. This nurse told Sally that she didn't know what it was, but it was like there was a big, deep secret between them."

"Something pertaining to Rita's care?"

"She didn't know for sure but doubted it. Medical information would have to be entered into her chart. Any treatment would be logged. When Rita told the nurse that she felt intimidated around Trudie, this other nurse checked the file but didn't find anything out of order. Her conclusion was that it was something personal, maybe just paranoid delusion."

"And yet Rita stayed there three months," I said.

"Yeah. According to the story, Trudie got hired on sometime during Rita's stay. She was put on Rita's case about a month before Rita left."

Puzzling. I tried to think back to those first yoga classes, remembering the way Rita and Trudie had interacted. I couldn't think of anything out of the ordinary. Rita's interaction with everyone had seemed strange at the time. They definitely hadn't acknowledged knowing each other.

Chapter 17

Drake rolled over and looked at the bedside clock. 4:37. The last time he'd checked it was 3:21. He groaned and turned back to his right side. On the floor beside the bed, Rusty stirred briefly in his sleep, but didn't even raise his head. Charlie's side of the bed was cold and empty. He missed her but it was probably just as well that she wasn't home. He'd be keeping her awake with this constant tossing and turning.

At five-thirty he gave up on sleep. Made his way into the kitchen and brewed a double strength, full pot of coffee. He rummaged in the breadbox and found two cinnamon rolls that had been there at least a week, but he didn't care. He crammed one down before the coffee finished dripping and the other as soon as he had a full mug in his hand. He let the dog out, brought in the newspaper from the front porch, and tried to read it. No use. The headlines were meaningless and the rest of the small type just became a blur. He went, instead, to his computer and started a search, almost hoping that the results would contradict some of the data he'd studied last night.

At five minutes to ten he placed the call to Valdez's office. After a brief wait, the secretary connected him and he steeled himself for the reaction.

"Rick? Drake Langston here."

"Hey Drake, all set for the meeting later?"

Meeting. Nice way of phrasing what was sure to feel more like the Inquisition. "Yeah, I think so. Look, there's something we probably need to discuss."

"Is it something quick, or do you want to come down to the office?"

Neither. "The office might be better."

An hour later, paperwork and reports gathered, and dressed in a coat and tie, Drake sat in the reception area of the offices of Graham and Valdez. He regretted the tie; the damn thing made his neck itch and it felt like a noose. He frankly didn't care what these guys thought about his appearance. He was there to present his findings, as the aviation expert. He mentally cursed Ron once again for suggesting this involvement, then himself for accepting the job.

"Drake?" Rick Valdez's chubbiness wasn't quite concealed by the jacket of his pricey suit. He was four or five inches shorter and probably forty pounds heavier than Drake, with black hair combed straight back, the teeth marks still showing. "Nice to finally meet you. Come on into the conference room."

Drake followed Valdez's waddly gait down a hallway and they entered a room on the right. A long table, with chairs for ten, filled the conference room almost uncomfortably full. The only other piece of furniture was a narrow sideboard where a sweating pitcher stood on a silver tray.

"Water?" Valdez offered.

"No, thanks. I'm fine." Drake's mouth felt stiff and he surreptitiously flexed his cheek muscles while Valdez filled a glass for himself.

"So, what've we got?" Valdez said as he took the chair at the head of the table.

Drake took the cue and sat in the spot immediately to the lawyer's left. He hadn't thought about exactly what order in which to present his findings, so he just started with the beginning. The crash itself. He reviewed the FAA and NTSB reports, but sensed that Valdez already knew all this, so he skimmed them quickly.

He hadn't told Valdez that he'd known Mike Walters from previous forest fire work, but he did so now. The whole process would have been triply difficult if he'd discovered pilot error and was forced to testify to that. Even in death, a friend's reputation should be respected. He told Rick about the simulator tests he and Charlie had performed last weekend. "We can safely say it was mechanical failure, as opposed to pilot error."

"You got a simulator to replicate an engine failure," Valdez said. "But can you tie that same failure to *this* crash?"

"Yes. I've found evidence."

Valdez scratched a short note on the yellow pad at his side. His tight expression told Drake that this was not the answer he'd wanted, not as attorney defending the engine manufacturer.

Drake continued, "The nature of the engine failure leads us to take a look at this nut . . ." He pulled out one of the photos and pointed to the piece of metal. "And this . . ." he dragged an engine diagram out but Valdez interrupted.

"I'm not very technical," he said. "You can just give me the highlights. Save the in-depth descriptions for the group this afternoon."

"Fair enough."

"Bottom line? Is this going to play right into their case that S-Jet Engines is at fault?"

"No. Bottom line is that it looks like a mechanic probably failed to safety wire this nut before signing it off and putting the aircraft back in service."

"Probably? The other side would jump all over that word."

"Okay, he did." Drake used his pen as a pointer. "See here? And here? These fittings are safety wired. The nut that came loose had no safety wire. This spot—" he indicated it "—is where the nut was. It came off in flight."

Valdez squinted. "The photos aren't real clear to me. Would a jury be able to understand all this?"

"I can revisit the wreckage," Drake told him. "We could bring the actual engine into the courtroom if we had to."

"Nah, that's even more confusing." Valdez rubbed at a spot between his eyebrows. "Our client isn't going to like this. S-Jet Engines believes they build the best equipment there is. We really wanted the pilot to be at fault."

Stop beating a damned dead horse, Drake thought. "Well, he wasn't. But don't you see? S-Jet is off the hook."

"So, you're saying that the accident happened by a mechanic's negligence."

"Mistakes happen. I've known a lot of good mechanics in my career. They aren't stupid. They go through a tremendous amount of schooling and there's a lot of pressure on them in their jobs. I don't want to wreck someone's career."

"But this one little nut would have caused the aircraft to go down?"

"I could give the full technical explanation of it."

"No, that's okay. As long as you know it. The people deposing you will ask. You'll be ready?"

"Yes." Whining about his distaste for the whole process wouldn't get him anywhere with any of these guys. Buck up and just do the job, he told himself. "I can present it where even you will understand it." He gave Rick a little smile.

"Good. That's the main thing. As an expert witness you have to get your points across clearly. If this thing makes it to trial, and especially if there's a jury, you better be sure everything you say can be understood by your average juror."

"I can do that."

"And our client doesn't want to pay out millions of dollars for something that wasn't their fault."

"I'm telling what I've found." Drake felt the muscle in his jaw twitch.

"That's what we're after, the truth."

Drake wondered how accurate that statement would be if he'd found the other way, that the engine manufacturer made a faulty part, or one of their assembly workers had made the mistake. But he kept it to himself. Clearly, Rick was on his side. It was the other side that was likely to get hostile. They wanted a big settlement from one of the manufacturers.

Valdez stood up and adjusted his jacket. "Lunch?" I think we'll have time for a burger at Lucky's if we go now. We're expecting the rest of the group by one, and it's always good to be here ahead of them."

Drake gathered his paperwork and tucked it under his arm.

"My secretary can hold that while we're gone," Valdez suggested.

"As long as it's secure. Those are my only copies."

They traversed the long hall again and Drake watched as the woman at the front desk placed his folder in a small safe beside her credenza.

They walked the four blocks to Lucky's, a dimly lit place where it seemed a lot of Albuquerque's businessmen gathered. One of those two-martini spots. Drake ordered an iced tea and noticed that Rick seemed to hesitate before doing the same. The lawyer dug into his burger plate with gusto, the moment it arrived, but Drake couldn't seem to get much beyond the first bite. His throat had a tight feel and his gut still churned. Maybe he should have had the martini after all. He picked at the fries that came with the plate, big thick-cut things that held a lot of ketchup.

By twelve forty-five they were on their way back to the fourth floor office and Rick had located another secretary with the combination to the safe, as the receptionist was now on her lunch break.

Ten minutes later, three suited-up lawyers entered, along with a guy in khakis and a stiff-looking button down shirt. Everything about him said mechanic. He looked as uncomfortable as Drake felt. They eyed each other, recognizing that they were part of the same industry but each not knowing what the other was likely to say. Drake was glad that they ended up at opposite ends of the table as everyone took their seats.

Drake thought he would begin by repeating most of what he'd told Valdez earlier, but it didn't turn out to be quite that simple. The head of the other team pinned him immediately on his qualifications to be giving testimony in the first place.

"You're a pilot, is that correct, Mr. Langston?"

"Yes." Valdez had cautioned him to give brief answers.

"Not a mechanic?"

"I've got several years experience in both, including mechanical work."

"But legally you can't sign off an inspection or a mechanic's report, can you?"

"No, sir." He glanced at Valdez and saw nonchalance. Come on, a little support here?

The other lawyer was ready with a barrage of questions, this time about Drake's years of piloting. Where had he worked, what types of jobs? Had he ever done any low-level work with a long line, as was the case at the time of the accident? Yes. Had he ever had an engine failure? Yes. Weren't such failures nearly always the fault of the engine or aircraft manufacturer? Not necessarily. Did he have any violations on his record for pilot error? No. Had he ever been involved in an incident or accident? No.

Drake felt his blood pressure rise. None of this had anything to do with the accident they were investigating, nor with the findings in this particular case. Under the jacket his shirt felt damp. He gave the requisite one-word answers. He looked toward Valdez from time to time. Wasn't the man supposed to object or something? Shouldn't there be some limits?

At the three o'clock break, he steered Valdez down the hall to a private office and asked.

"It's just a preliminary, Drake. Calm down. It's their job to establish your credentials. If they can discredit you, they can have all your findings tossed out, so that's all they're trying to accomplish."

"I don't like it and I don't like the games."

"Nobody does." Valdez handed him a candy mint from the dish on his desk. "Get a tough skin, buddy. It's nothing personal."

"What about those questions about my qualifications as a mechanic? I'm not one, you know. Shouldn't you have a mechanic in there with me, telling that part of it?"

"We do. Have a mechanic, that is. Bill Townley. He's being deposed tomorrow. The guy they brought today is here to look for inconsistencies, to help them spot anything they might want to ask later of you or Townley."

"So you're just using me, for what? As the appetizer in this little feast? The one they sharpen their teeth on before they gorge themselves in the courtroom."

"Drake, chill." Valdez put his hand on Drake's shoulder, giving little pats. "It's not personal."

"So, are they going to get to any questions about this actual crash? About the stuff I spent the last few weeks and nearly all of last night researching?" He worked to keep the anger out of his voice but it wasn't helping.

By 4:45 they'd asked exactly two questions about the crash and Drake felt like a dishrag that had been dunked in boiling water and wrung out four dozen times. He did manage to insert his findings about the loose nut and the photos which proved it, although one of the three opposing lawyers, a skinny guy with black hair and a lot of attitude, tried like hell to shut him up. They threw a few daggered looks at each other and Drake actually got a tap-tap on the leg from Valdez.

As if the fourth-quarter buzzer had gone off, precisely at five both teams gathered their papers and began to shrug into their jackets. They thanked Drake for being there and told him that they would probably want to talk with him again, after getting the mechanic's deposition the next day. 'Talk' they called it. Drake fumed at the disingenuous wording. He watched the mechanic at the other end of the room as he left, but the guy seemed just happy as Drake to be fleeing.

Chapter 18

I finished my calls and left the room. Crossing the lobby, I noticed Samantha Sweet's little vehicle parked out front again, the hatchback open. Sure enough, down the corridor that led to the ballroom she was wheeling a cart that almost seemed dwarfed by a four-tier wedding cake. She spotted me and nodded at the closed doors and I hurried toward her.

The maitre 'd arrived at about the same time I did and he quickly pushed open the double doors and secured them in place so Samantha could get through.

"Hey, Charlie," she said. "Thought you were coming to my rescue again for a second time there."

"Wow, beautiful cake." Tiny beads dotted the sides of the creamy layers, and she'd created delicate ribbons of frosting that made the whole thing look like a gift from one's fairy godmother.

"Thanks. Wedding reception here this afternoon."

Now that she mentioned it I noticed the trappings. Round tables set up for eight diners each, wait staff doling out place settings and folding napkins, bows being fluffed over draped linen, massive flower arrangements and a bandstand.

A woman in an electric blue suit, wearing a cell phone on the side of her head like some android appendage, and carrying a thick stack of papers on a clipboard emerged from another room just then. The wedding planner, no doubt. "Oh, *there* you are! It's about time!"

"Catch you later," Samantha said, straightening her shoulders and facing the jittery woman with a smile.

I left the ballroom disorder behind and walked to the conference center. On this side of the complex the halls were quiet. Shirley sat behind the reception desk, pecking at a computer keyboard, a pair of tiny reading glasses riding low on her nose.

"Everyone's in meditation right now," she said. "The session should be ending in about ten minutes. I'll be starting the nutrition class soon after."

Did I detect a note of reproof in her voice? Too bad. I didn't want to deal with criticism over my failure to take the program seriously. I had a few other things to deal with right now. I mumbled something polite and wandered toward the classroom. Maybe I could get a jump on the tea and cookies. Too bad they wouldn't be some of Samantha's decadent varieties.

Dr. Light stood by the windows that looked out to the courtyard. I nearly backed out but he'd heard the scuff of my shoes on the carpet and he turned.

"Lovely morning, isn't it?" he said. His smooth voice held no hint of recognition. Mine was just one in the endless stream of faces who came through this place and he didn't seem to remember that he'd seen me in town only yesterday and in the dining room after that. "Autumn is supposed to be a sad time," he continued, "signaling the impending death of the year, the final throes of glory before the winter freeze."

"Personally, I love the fall," I said. "The colors are glorious, the oppressive heat of summer is gone."

"Yes. True." His voice still contained that drifty, mystical quality. Nothing like the all-business tone he'd used when talking on his cell phone. I found myself wondering whether he rehearsed this whole enlightened persona thing.

"I'm Dr. Light," he said, extending a hand. It felt limp, as if his wrist had no muscles connecting the hand to the arm.

"Charlie Parker."

"Are you enjoying your experience and finding the lightness of the soul?" he asked.

"Well, I've found a little difficulty in concentrating on that. Rita's death has been disrupting to all of us. And I didn't realize you knew her husband David."

For an instant the mystic veneer vanished and a cold, hard light gleamed in his eyes. His smile froze in place. Then he caught himself and his face smoothed once again and his eyes became veiled and soft.

"No, I don't think so." He formed his eyebrows into a questioning little ripple. "My assistant handles employment issues with our various associates. I don't recall having much contact with the yoga instructor."

My bullshit meter pegged but I simply adopted a fuzzy smile like his and excused myself.

The ladies room was empty and I set my bag on the vanity and stared into the mirror. What the hell was going on here? Unless I'd lost every fragment of my instinct for human behavior, Light was a con artist of the finest kind. His ability to switch personalities was downright scary unless he had an evil twin out there somewhere, which I highly doubted. That cold, calculating look in his eye just now was no fluke.

I splashed some water on my face and considered the possibilities. Maybe the guy was certifiably crazy. Maybe he'd been institutionalized at one point and had come into contact with Rita in that context.

Voices in the hall alerted me that meditation was over and someone would likely be walking in here any second. I grabbed my phone and auto-dialed Ron's number.

"I can't talk but need another background. Celeus Light." I spelled it for him. "He's not who he says he is. Find out anything you can, especially if it involves his being in the same facility as Rita Ratwill."

The restroom door began to swing inward.

"Okay, gotta go," I added in a chipper tone.

Two women walked in, chatting quietly, their seminar tote bags slung over their shoulders. They entered the two stalls and I heard clothing swishing and zippers unzipping. I dropped the phone back into my purse and washed my hands.

Out in the corridor, people milled, waiting for the start of the day's nutrition class in fifteen minutes. I spotted Linda and waved to her. I didn't see Dr. Light anywhere.

"You made it," Linda said, giving me a hug.

"Yeah, got Ron handling some things in Albuquerque." We drifted toward the door leading to the courtyard and stepped out into the sun. Most of the others had either hit the restrooms or were heading into various classrooms so we had the courtyard to ourselves.

"So," Linda said, "I don't suppose you're going to leave the police verdict alone are you?" She aimed her dimpled grin at me.

"I'd like to. It would simplify my life a whole lot to just walk out of here, that's for sure."

"But . . ."

"But a killer would be walking around free. I just . . ."

"Have you shared your information with the police?"

"Tried to. I really did. Gallegos just wasn't interested. And what do I really *know* anyway? Rita's death wasn't an accident because someone came into my massage session yesterday and threatened me? I can't make the connection yet, and it's a sure thing they won't immediately see it either. Maybe if I can get something more, something concrete."

"Do you have any ideas?"

"A couple. Ron's doing some background checks for me." I caught myself before I told her of my feelings about Celeus Light. She always spoke so glowingly of him; I didn't want to shake her faith if it turned out my suspicions were groundless.

"Look, I gotta get to the ladies room, then make it to my class," she said. "Be careful, and I'll catch you at lunch."

We walked back inside. As Linda made for the restroom I ambled toward the library. A plan had begun to form and I knew she wouldn't like it. A plan that could get me into a lot of trouble.

I stepped into the quiet ambiance of the library. Soft

lamps glowed on two tables and the freshly plumped cushions on the sofa indicated that no one had yet used the room this morning. The lingering scent of sandalwood clung to the oriental carpet and to the upholstery. I strolled to the bookshelves and studied the titles.

An entire shelf contained books by Celeus Light. Idly, I picked up one and flipped to the back cover, noticing for the first time that he had co-authors for all his titles. A younger photo of him smiled back at me with his trademark image as teacher of all things mystical. A week ago I might have bought it.

The blurb describing him as a spiritual leader and world-renowned speaker didn't tell me anything I didn't already know. Except, maybe, how many of the words in the book were actually his own. One thing about it: if I ever wanted to become rich and famous I'd like to get the name of his publicist. He or she certainly wrote convincing ad copy.

From the hallway Shirley's voice rose above the general hubbub, calling everyone to class. I replaced the book and tucked myself into a corner so I'd be invisible from the doorway. Within two or three minutes the place got quiet. I gave it another five minutes and took two deep breaths.

A tentative peek around the corner assured me that both Shirley's and Light's classroom doors were closed. Nicki sat at the reception desk, writing in a ledger-style book, her back to me. Now or never, I figured.

I stepped out of the library, careful not to bump against the door jamb, willing my shoes not to squeak on the polished wood floor. I walked past each of the classes, trying not to look sneaky, in case Nicki moved from her spot at the desk. The big obstacle might be a locked door, but I got lucky. Light's office door opened without a sound and in one second flat, I was inside with the door closed behind me.

The overhead fluorescents were off but he'd conveniently left a lamp burning on the credenza. I crossed quickly to his carved cherry wood desk and scanned its top. Nothing. He was one of those executives whose environment shows no trace of actual work being done. A blotter, gold pen and pencil set, and telephone were the mainstays. The top drawer on the left contained a box of business cards—Celeus Light, Spiritual Leader and Meditation Guidance.

Two more drawers contained nothing more than stationery, pens, and various office supplies. The bottom drawer on the right was sized for files and was locked. Fat lot of good that did, since the key to the lock was in the drawer right above it. I was inside that baby in no time.

Unfortunately, the files weren't exactly of a top secret nature. Publicity materials for his various speaking engagements, dating back three years. Nothing before that. It looked like the kind of ego stuff a person would keep either to remind himself how wonderful he was or to convince the IRS that his business was legit. Other files contained employee information, belying his statement that Shirley handled all that. However, no file for Rita. Interesting.

I pulled the rack of files forward and found a few goodies behind them, against the back of the drawer. A small bottle of Scotch, Glenfiddich single malt. The good stuff, and probably technically a vegetarian item. I pulled out a small box beside the bottle—another box of business cards. These bore the name Robert Stanworthy, President, Stanworthy Financial. Financial what, I wondered. Advisor, accountant, stockbroker? There were numerous possibilities. I snagged a card from the box and tucked it into my purse, replacing the box and closing the drawer.

Umm, now what? A credenza behind the desk held a laptop computer, lid open but not turned on. Did I dare?

I'd considered the tantalizing possibility for about two seconds when something else caught my attention. The squeak of a shoe sounded right outside the door. Oh god. Nowhere to go and no time to make a decision.

The doorknob began to turn.

Chapter 19

My heart did a gigantic thud, then stopped. I'm dead meat, I thought. With no other choice, I grabbed my purse, ducked into the leg space under the desk, and pulled the chair in after me. There was no time to make sure I'd closed all the drawers, no time to be sure my feet weren't sticking out. It wouldn't matter anyway because if Light came in and sat down he would knee me right in the face. I held my breath.

As before, the door swung open without a sound. What had worked in my favor ten minutes ago now kept me in suspense. Another shoe squeak. Someone was standing in front of the desk, separated from my vulnerable backside by a thin sheet of wood.

A thunk sounded directly over my head, like a stack

of papers being dropped. I jumped, fortunately not hard enough to bang my head on the underside of the desktop. Another footstep and the door closed with a firm click.

Too close.

I cautiously pushed the chair away, crawling on hands and knees out of my confined space. I smoothed my jeans in an ill-concealed attempt to be sure I hadn't wet my pants. Finally, I remembered to breathe again.

After about four deep breaths I felt my courage returning. I really wanted to take a look at that computer. I weighed the possibilities. Staying here was clearly becoming dangerous. Taking the computer would be even more so. Not to mention that I'd be committing a felony and would need to sneak back into the office again to put it back. This is foolish, Charlie, totally, completely, insanely crazy.

Before I had a chance to talk myself out of it, I closed the lid on the computer and stuck it inside my jacket. With nerves stretched like over-taut wires and heart thudding audibly, I peeked into the hall. All clear.

Light's office was the last one at this end of the hall and I thought I remembered an exit to the courtyard just beyond it. I edged to my left and found it. As Elsa Higgins would say, I was as nervous as a long-tailed cat in a rockin chair factory all the way to our room. Luckily, Linda's absence gave me the whole place to myself.

I figured I had about fifteen minutes max. Light's lecture would let out and I could pretty well bet that he would go immediately to his office. The conference attendees would head for lunch, but he rarely joined them. I locked the deadbolt and perched on the edge of my bed. The computer booted up readily enough, lighting up with a blank screen with one word in the center: Password.

How was I going to figure that out? And how many tries would it give me?

I closed my eyes and took a deep, meditative breath. Try something, Charlie, anything. No time to waste here. I tried SOUL, LIGHT, PEACE. No luck with them. I pulled out the business card I'd just stolen. His real name was Robert Stanworthy. I began trying variations of that starting with STANWORTHY and finally hitting it with BOBSTAN. All right!

The moment the desktop icons revealed themselves, I opened the list of files. Luckily there weren't zillions of them. Partway down the list I came to one named Ratwill. I opened the document, which appeared to be a legal form of some kind. I scanned through enough whereases and therefores to learn that David's and Rita's names were both in there, but I wasn't going to be able to read and absorb the whole thing in the next three minutes. Now what? I needed a way to print it or copy it. I'd brought nothing in the way of office stuff with me.

Wait—Linda had brought her laptop computer. She'd been transcribing her notes onto it each evening. Maybe she had an extra memory card somewhere. I set Light's computer aside and dashed to the corner where she'd stashed her computer bag. Feeling like a real sneak, I unzipped the bag and rummaged through it. Two cards were stashed in a small pocket inside the case. One was labeled, the other looked new. I grabbed that one and plugged it into the drive on Light's computer.

The Ratwill file copied quickly, and I ran my eyes down the list of other documents. Several might have been interesting, given enough time to open each and read them, but I had no way of knowing. I debated the invasion-ofprivacy issues for a good ten seconds before copying two more files. I will delete them the minute I've read them if they don't have anything to do with Rita, I promised myself. I unplugged the card and dropped it into my purse, shut down the computer properly, and stuck it back into my jacket. This is so stupid, Charlie, you're gonna be cooked if anyone ever finds out about this.

Light's seminar was due to break for lunch in two minutes. I raced out of the room and down the empty hall. Out in the courtyard, I paused for a second and took two deep breaths. No one was around. In through the exit I'd used earlier. I scanned the corridor and didn't see anyone, although voices rose in a lively pattern from one of the classrooms. People would fill the hall in mere seconds, heading for the restaurant. In as smooth a move as possible, I opened Light's office door and stepped in. Without bothering to close the door, I whipped the computer out of my jacket and crossed the room.

Guessing at the placement, I set it back on the credenza and opened its lid. The voices in the hall were very close now. I did two giant steps across the room and paused in the doorway.

"Ms. Parker?" Celeus Light stood no more than five feet from me. My stomach lurched and I know my face must have drained of color.

"Oh, there you are!" How would I explain this? "I uh . . . I tapped on your door, but wasn't sure if you'd answered me. Little noisy here right now."

He fixed me with a long stare.

"Well, obviously you weren't in. I just discovered that." Stop babbling, Charlie. You're looking guilty as hell.

"No," he said in that smooth voice. "I've just come

from my lecture. What was it you needed?" Pat Girard stood behind him.

Damn good question. "I . . . well, I see that you're busy." I glanced past him at Pat. "I just wanted to get some advice on my meditation techniques, but it can certainly wait."

I skittered away before either of them could pin me down more specifically. By the time I got to the ladies room I seriously thought I would throw up. Bolting myself into a stall, I leaned against the wall and pressed my hands to my stomach. He's going to notice something out of place and he'll remember this encounter. Why on earth did I take the computer, and *why* did I cut the timing so close? And how much had Pat seen? Her mouth was probably the most dangerous weapon on the premises.

The butterflies began to subside and I reached into my purse and felt for the memory card. For a second I couldn't find it and the bile began to rise again, but eventually my fingers closed around the little piece of plastic. A slow grin began to form. Risky as it was, I knew I had something here about the Ratwills' financial situation. Light or Stanworthy or whoever he really was looked like he'd been working with David Ratwill to pull something against Rita. I just needed to put the pieces together. And to do that I needed to read these documents.

Tahlene stood at the sink when I exited the stall. "Oh, hey, Charlie," she greeted. "Missed you this morning in yoga."

"Yeah, my attendance has been a little spotty the past few days. I'm really sorry."

"No worries. We got some dishy gossip about Rita this morning."

"Really. I understand the police ruled her death an accident."

"Did you know she and Trudie knew each other a few years ago?" she said.

I feigned ignorance. "Really? In school or something?"

"More recent than that," she said, moving closer and lowering her voice. "Rita was a patient of Trudie's in California. At a mental facility."

"Interesting. I didn't realize that was the type of nursing Trudie did."

"I know. Seems a bit mental herself sometimes, doesn't she?" Tahlene parked her butt on the edge of the vanity and went on. "Well, she says Rita checked herself into this place, claiming depression. But she really, deep down, had lots of issues with her husband. Trudie says the husband was really a nice guy, called every few days, cared for her a lot. But Rita was . . . well, we've all seen how Rita was."

Sort of hyper, controlling, edgy. But she also worked for David at that time and they were in the middle of the big lawsuit against AceChem. Add the strain of an unhappy marriage and I could see how Rita might have been depressed. Then there was the other nurse's account of Rita's being afraid of Trudie. For the first time I kind of felt for her. I wished I could peel through the layers of all this and find out what really went on, not just what the latest gossip held. Maybe a lot of Rita's prickly attitude came from all the crap she was facing in her life.

"Did anyone else have anything to say about it?" I asked.

"Not really. The Mayhews sat there kind of quiet, interested, you know, but not saying anything. But they didn't really get the chance. You know how it is when Trudie gets started." She turned to the mirror and fluffed her hair.

The door opened just then and two women walked in, Pat Girard and another of the doctors. Did I just imagine that Pat gave me a peculiar look?

"Your friend Linda is looking for you," the other doctor said. "Said she'd meet you in the restaurant."

"Thanks." I walked out, leaving Tahlene at the mirror.

Linda seemed a little anxious as she scanned the dining room, before I finally caught her eye.

"Ah, there you are," she said, her dimples finally showing again. "I'd been wondering whether you'd make it."

The waiter arrived with the ubiquitous bowls of bean soup, salads, and steamed vegetables. With my stomach still halfway in knots, none of it looked appealing. I halfheartedly speared a carrot.

"I need to ask a big favor, Linda," I said after a couple of minutes during which I worked over the one carrot slice, while she eagerly tucked into her salad.

"Sure, what is it?"

"First I better apologize for missing so many of the sessions and not doing a better job for you, not doing what I'd agreed to."

She waved it off. "No problem. I'm getting copies of the handouts from Shirley. You know I really suggested this week to give you a break from your crazy pace and let you relax a little. Guess that little ploy didn't work."

"I never do seem to relax, do I?"

"No, and as your doctor, I should be giving you a lecture about that." She forked a tiny grape-tomato.

"So, this favor, am I going to get a big lecture if you find out it involves work? For me, that is."

She rolled her eyes, which I took as a signal to spill it.

"Can I use your laptop for a few minutes this afternoon?" I asked.

"That's it? Nothing involving a shootout, a chase, breaking and entering?"

Her wide, innocent smile told me she really didn't know, but my guilt reflexes kicked in and my hand clattered the fork against my plate. Luckily she'd chosen that moment to take a sip of water and she didn't notice.

"No, just something I need to read from a disk. I'm impatient and didn't want to wait till I get home."

"No explanation necessary. It's in the black carrying case in the room. Use it anytime."

The waiter came to clear our dishes, giving me a puzzled look when I told him I was finished. I'd probably consumed a total of three carrot slices. "Just not hungry," I told him.

At that, Linda narrowed her eyes. "You, not hungry?" she said after he'd left. "I've never seen you not hungry. Usually for something involving a big hunk of red meat or smothered in green chile."

Exactly. But I didn't want to seem ungrateful. "No, no. Lunch tasted good. I just had a little touch of something . . ." I fluttered my fingers in front of my stomach. "It'll be fine by the end of the day, I'm sure." Provided I don't get caught in any more crimes in the meantime. "Guess I'm thinking about what Drake's going through in his deposition."

To prove my robust health, I joined her in finishing off my entire dessert, something that tasted like genuine chocolate but probably wasn't. I didn't ask.

"Okay, I'm going to take a leisurely walk around the building, then I have a massage at one-thirty," she said, rising. "Help yourself to the computer, whenever."

What I really wanted was just to go home. I was tired of healthy food, healthy exercise, and lectures on good health, surrounded by gossipy, toxic people who wove their little webs of intrigue and somehow ended up dead. A margarita followed by a plate of green chile chicken enchiladas at Pedro's would do me fine. An evening at home with my dog and my husband and a great night of sex and sleep in my own bed would do me even better. I sighed and pulled myself out of my chair.

<h1 style="text-align:center">Chapter 20</h1>

My grumpy sense of malaise followed me to the room, where I stretched out on my bed for a minute, which stretched into thirty as I promptly dozed off. My ringing cell phone brought me back. I'd forgotten to switch it to vibration mode and thank goodness it hadn't gone off earlier in Light's office.

"Hey, glad I caught you." Drake's voice came through, his familiar tone always welcome. "I was afraid you'd be in classes and I'd end up leaving a message."

"Umm . . . I was goofing off. Taking a nap and having this wonderful fantasy about you and some green chile enchiladas."

He chuckled. "That sounds kinky. Or is it just that you're missing normal food?"

"I'm missing Pedro's, that's for sure. A week without

enchiladas is like . . ." I couldn't come with a good simile for it. "How about you? Deposition going okay?"

He made a growling noise. "So far they haven't asked many relevant questions about the crash. Mainly, they're just grilling me about my credentials."

We talked for a few more minutes before he clicked off, sounding discouraged.

With that mysterious cosmic oneness that makes everyone pick up the phone at the same time, mine rang again immediately. Ron.

"I forgot to tell you earlier, I got some interesting information on your Rita Ratwill and her time at Peaceful Haven."

"What's that?"

"Sally coaxed her buddy the nurse to fax us a copy of Rita's admission papers. Seems Rita didn't exactly check herself in."

"What?"

"Well, technically she did because it's her signature on the line, but the forms are filled out in David Ratwill's handwriting and he's listed as the attending relative who drove her there. According to this nurse, who found out from the administrative assistant, who overheard the conversation when they arrived, David practically carried Rita in the door. She was drugged out on barbiturates and barely coherent. David gave the answers to the questions but insisted that Rita wanted to check herself in. Something about being free to then check herself out once she got better. I don't know what the rules are on that, but it was the way they did it. This office girl said he actually held the pen in her hand and guided her to sign the form."

"That doesn't seem right," I said. "I mean, would

hospital personnel go along with it that way?"

"Don't know. This is a private facility and some further background shows that they aren't always on the good side of the licensing board. Maybe a sizable 'donation' came their way. Anyway, they went along with David on it."

"The police here have officially closed their case. Accidental death was the ruling and they seem happy with that," I told him.

"So? Thoughts?"

"It doesn't smell right to me. Too many unanswered questions, too many coincidences." I filled him in briefly on Trudie's timely appearance here and the fact that Rita hadn't seemed to remember her.

"I can't believe Rita wouldn't remember Trudie, even if a few years have gone by."

"Could Sally talk her contact person out of a photo from Trudie's old personnel file?"

He agreed to give it a try.

I told Ron about David's connection with Stanworthy a.k.a. Light, and the strange coincidence that they all managed to appear here in Santa Fe at the same time. I told him I'd gotten a document that linked Stanworthy and David, but hadn't had a chance to read it yet.

By the time we ended the call, I felt my old energy surge once again. I better look at the files I'd copied, before Linda decided to pop in. I pulled her computer out of its carrying case.

At a glance, the document filled with legalese and phrasing in triplicate didn't make much sense to me. Why don't lawyers just spit it out, why come up with three synonyms for everything they're trying to say? I scrolled through the pages, taking it a clause at a time.

I began to get the idea that David had contracted with Stanworthy's financial firm for management of some assets. On its own, it wouldn't have made a lot of sense to me, but taken in context with the Mayhews' assertions that David's firm was in trouble because of their appealing the judgment against AceChem, I began to see a picture.

David was in the process of moving assets offshore and getting things out of his name. Apparently, he'd put several million dollars and some real estate in Rita's name during the time she'd been tucked away at Peaceful Haven. Stanworthy had then moved those assets to hidden accounts in the islands, using the fact of Rita's incapacitation as his reason for doing it without her signature. According to a separate memo between David and Stanworthy, a power of attorney was among the papers David had gotten Rita to sign.

My big question was, why? If the marriage was already shaky, why would David want to take the chance that Rita would simply buy herself a ticket south, clear out the accounts, which were already in her name, and live the good life while she brushed up on her Spanish? Unless, of course, Rita were not getting any better and had to be permanently institutionalized. And could it simply be a lucky chance that Trudie happened to begin working at Peaceful Haven and become Rita's nurse? The implications were interesting but there were lots of missing pieces still. My brain began to feel fuzzy.

A walk would do me good. The bedside clock said it was well after three o'clock so Linda would be returning from her massage any minute. I popped the card out of her computer and stashed it again in my purse. By the time I'd put on my walking shoes, Linda's key sounded in the door.

"How was the massage?" I asked.

She moaned. "God, wonderful. I had that two-part one—energy enlivening, I think they call it."

The one which I'd received part one and missed part two. "I want you to learn how to do that massage," I said. "I'll be at your office twice a week for it."

"I'm seriously thinking about trying to hire Joanne away from here," she said. "That girl is good."

"I'm fuzzy-headed from too long a nap," I said. "I think I'll walk for a bit."

"Remember, there's a special two-hour meditation session before the farewell dinner. I hear the chef has planned something really good."

I acknowledged it but made no promises. I couldn't imagine trying to find that magical space between my thoughts when I had all this new information about David and Rita Ratwill buzzing through my head.

I took the corridor exit to the courtyard, deciding to pass through it to the parking lot, then down the driveway and circle back uphill, the reverse of the walk Linda and I had previously taken. As I passed the spot where Rita had gone over the wall, I glanced down. Aside from the broken cholla, nothing indicated that a woman had lost her life in this spot. It seemed that there should be some hint of a lingering spirit, some ghostly voice calling out for resolution. Nothing moved but a light breeze ruffling the brilliant yellow leaves on a cottonwood across the ravine. I picked up my pace and felt the quickening of blood flow, melting away my muzziness.

At the parking lot I decided to circle the parked cars to lengthen the walk by a bit. There were ten or twelve of them parked along the adobe wall, and half that many more in a second row. I skirted the wall and had nearly passed all the vehicles when my attention was drawn to my own Jeep. The front passenger door stood open.

Wait a minute.

I knew I'd locked it. I cut through the first row of cars and headed toward it.

What happened next, I don't remember. Something hit me from behind and everything went black.

"Charlie, Charlie!" Voices wafted in and out, going quiet and loud with an eerie effect. An underlying hum made it difficult to follow them. "She's coming around," someone said. I felt a gentle touch on my shoulder and fingertips on my wrist. "Pulse is strong."

Someone stuck a nasty chemical near my nose and I recoiled from it. My eyelids gradually opened and things came into focus. Linda's face hovered over me; her fingers pressed gently at the sides of my neck and face.

"Well, I think you're going to live," she said. "How do you feel?"

A stupid doctor question. I feel like people are hovering around and staring at me. But the only words my mouth managed to utter were, "Okay, I guess."

My brain sent signals to my various limbs, and very slowly they began to respond. I seemed to be lying flat on my back on gravel, with a bunched up piece of clothing under my head. Faces came into focus: Dina, Tahlene, Nicole. Samantha Sweet was there too. Somehow I knew it was a good thing, the fact that I recognized them.

"You have a pretty good knot on the back of your head," Linda said. "Any idea what happened?"

I rolled to one side and sat up, closing my eyes against the black sparkles in the air. "How long was I out?"

"Not long." Linda said.

I'd walked out of the room a little after four. Had probably walked five minutes to get to this spot. "How did you know–"

"The Mayhews just got back from a shopping trip in town. They must have driven up immediately after this happened. Nicole ran inside and called me from the lobby."

I rested my elbows on my bent knees, checking my various body parts for rips and scratches before attempting to stand up.

"Did anyone see anything?" I asked. "Someone was out here."

Samantha looked around the group. "I just finally finished setting up that cake and was driving out through the parking lot. Realized it was you in the middle of the crowd."

Dina spoke up. "Tahlene and I, we have just come from the spa. But it did not face to the parking. We run after Linda and Nicole when they come out here."

"I didn't notice anyone either," Tahlene confirmed.

I ran my hands over my face and through my hair. A large bump stood out on the back of my head and the area felt really tender. Samantha extended her hand and I pulled myself up. A surge of warmth passed up my arm, through my shoulder, along my neck, and the hairs stood on end. She met my gaze and said quietly, "There, it should feel a lot better now." Better than better, actually. A feeling of . . . how would I describe it? Peace?

Before I could dwell on it I realized Linda was talking again: "Nicole? Did you guys notice anyone in the parking lot when you drove in?"

She thought about it for a second. "No, well I didn't. We can ask Gerald. He went to put our packages in the room, once Linda came to take care of you. We drove in and parked over there." She pointed to a spot two vehicles away from mine. "Then we got some bags from the back of the car. We were walking toward the lobby when it caught my eye that your car door was open. You were lying on the ground right in front of your Jeep. I think I screamed. Gerald grabbed my arm and said we better get help. That's when we ran into the lobby and got Linda."

She piped up, "Yeah, in medical lingo we'd say you were out cold." She grinned at me, which let me know I would live. "After that kind of bump on the head I don't want you to go to sleep for the next few hours."

Like that would be possible. All I felt right now was outrage. Who broke into my car and who was waiting out here to ambush me?

"Where are the other members of our group right now?" I asked.

"There weren't any classes this afternoon," Linda said. "So I don't know."

"Some of us had massages and spa treatments," Tahlene said.

"A group of the doctors had planned to go downtown and visit the museums," Linda said.

I did a quick tally. Aside from the doctors, none of

whom I'd had much contact with, I knew the whereabouts of the Mayhews, Tahlene, Dina, and Linda. Presumably, Joanne and the masseuses were at their jobs. So that left Dr. Light, Shirley and Trudie unaccounted for. So far, Shirley'd done nothing to warrant suspicion but the other two were high on my list. I thanked the ladies for their assistance and assured everyone that I would be fine.

Dina, Tahlene and Nicole headed back toward the lobby looking relieved that their obligation was now over. I followed Samantha to her vehicle as she prepared to leave.

"How did you do that?" I asked, flexing the fingers on my right hand. "That little shock up the arm."

She sent an enigmatic smile my way and shrugged. "It's . . . I guess it's a talent. My friend calls it the healing touch." She got into the car.

I felt the back of my head. The bump was barely noticeable and there was no pain whatsoever. No ordinary talent, I'd say. What had just happened?

I shook off the weird feeling as she drove away. Back to practicalities. I checked my vehicle quickly. Didn't see anything out of place. I must have come along at just the right time to interrupt the potential thief before he could take anything. But why didn't he just run away, why hit me? Unless he knew I would recognize him.

Or unless he wasn't a thief; maybe he'd planned to rig the car in some way, damage it mechanically or plant an explosive?

Light/Stanworthy might be a fake, but would his repertoire include this kind of stuff? Trudie might be crazy but would she be this calculating? Would either of them actually know how to mechanically rig the car?

Chapter 21

With the afternoon's grilling still fresh, there was no way Drake could envision going home to an empty house and quiet evening of TV so he stopped in just long enough to change clothes and get Rusty. The two of them headed out to Double Eagle Airport, where Drake could finish his logbook entries from the Pecos job and check the aircraft over. It was due for an oil change and couple of minor inspections that he could do himself. The airport's A.I. and a couple of other mechanics were there, hovering around a private jet that had come in during the afternoon. Drake greeted them and walked over to the shiny white jet with its trim work done in burgundy. Rusty loped over to the hangar, sniffing the ground, establishing that this was a place he already knew well.

"What a beaut," Gordon, the A.I., said, looking up at the jet's cockpit.

"No kidding. Who's she belong to?"

"Some corporate type from Chicago. The pilots are sitting in the lounge. The guy and his wife got met by a limo about noon."

Drake nodded. He'd met lots of corporate pilots over the years, and sometimes looked at them with a little envy— easy hours and good pay. But mostly he saw that they did a lot of sitting around. Did a two or three hour flight, then sat around for a day or more waiting until the hotshot owner showed up and told them where they were going next. Not for him. He loved having his own ship, taking the jobs he wanted to take, and being in the middle of the action. He chatted with the guys for a few more minutes, and when Johnny Ramirez offered him a beer from his cooler, Drake took him up on it. With the first few sips he felt the day's tension receding.

He asked Johnny to pull the Jet Ranger out onto the tarmac and the two of them set out with the power washer to take off the small traces of grime. As Johnny dried the fuselage, Drake went over the windows with a soft cloth and let the mundane chore relax him.

The sun had set and they worked under the lights. The two jet pilots came out and watched from the sidelines for a while. Drake could tell that one of them had some helicopter time. The guy's face held that particular wistful look common to those who've had the chance to hover. Can't do that—and can't back up—in a Citation. He smiled their direction and they walked over to talk story for a few minutes, the one thing that every pilot of every type of aircraft has in common—stories. By the time Drake had finished polishing the windows, the chief pilot got a buzz from the cell phone in his pocket. The two men said goodbye and crossed the tarmac to begin their preflight for the return run to Chicago.

By this time, Johnny had finished his part of the cleanup so Drake had him pull the ship back into the hangar. The jet's engines started and a gleaming black limo was heading toward it, coming from the entry gates across the way. Drake quickly completed his logbook entries and left orders with Gordon and Johnny to start the hundred-hour inspection in the morning. He needed everything ready by next week for another job.

A sharp whistle brought Rusty to his side and the two of them headed through the lobby of the general aviation facility, toward the parking lot. Drake unlocked the pickup's door and the dog climbed inside. Before he could twist himself into the driver's seat an arm reached past him and slammed the door shut.

"What—" Drake started to whip around but a massive dark body slammed him face first against the truck.

Rusty was barking furiously, clawing at the driver's side window. A hairy forearm pressed against Drake's neck and beery breath warmed the side of his face.

"The mechanic didn't do it," the gravelly voice whispered.

"What?" His mind worked furiously, thinking of the instructions he'd just given to Gordon and Johnny.

"You're not going to testify that the mechanic was the one that brought that aircraft down."

Comprehension dawned. The court case.

The pressure on his neck increased, forcing his windpipe against the top of the truck's cab, cutting off his air.

"You hear me?" the voice rasped, like rocks against metal.

Drake couldn't form words. His throat closed tighter. He worked to produce a feeble nod.

"I said, did you hear me?" The lips were right against his ear, whiskery stubble scratching. The pressure on his neck eased a fraction and he nodded firmly.

"Good. When you go back there, you're going to tell them the engine failed."

"It did." Drake grunted out the words.

"It failed because the factory did something wrong." The arm jammed against him again, and sparks danced before his eyes.

His legs started to give way and he forced himself to stay in control. His arms felt like rubber as he swung ineffectively at the attacker. The window vibrated in its frame as the dog threw himself at it repeatedly. Just about the time Drake thought he was going down for the count, the guy gave one final shove. When the momentary blackness cleared he was gone.

Drake spun around, scanning the parking lot, but saw no one, only rows of parked vehicles. He leaned against the truck, lungs grabbing for air, digging his feet into the pavement to stay upright. He considered letting Rusty out of the truck and turning him loose to search out the attacker, but thought better of it. The dog was getting too old to stand up to someone that dangerous. A hundred yards away, at the far end of the lot, a vehicle started up and sped off in the opposite direction. The lot was so dark by now that he didn't even get a good enough look to know whether it was a car or a truck. It became no more than twin red lights, which quickly disappeared as it turned onto the frontage road and went behind a hill.

Anger replaced fear. By the time he'd opened the door and reassured the dog, buckled himself in and started the engine, he felt ready to kill. If only he had a clue who it was, he might have followed that urge. The only ones who knew what he'd said today at his deposition were the lawyers.

He headed for Interstate 40, his mind churning with possibilities. Flooring it, and not giving a damn about the consequences, he raced eastbound to the Rio Grande exit and roared down the off ramp. Less than ten minutes later he whipped into the parking lot at RJP.

A light was on in Ron's office and the rest of the place was dark. The back door stood locked and he pounded on it, impatient as he imagined Ron getting up slowly from his desk and looking out an upper window to see who it was.

"Ron! It's me. Open up!" The shout ripped Drake's raw throat, without producing much volume. Eventually the back door opened.

"What's up, man?" Ron looked liked he'd been dozing with his head propped on his hand. The hair on the left side of his head stuck out in tufts.

"How much do you know about this Santa Fe law firm representing those families?" Drake demanded.

Ron's eyes crinkled as he thought about it. "Not a whole lot. Never worked with them, ourselves."

"I was just threatened," Drake said. He'd fast-walked down the hall toward the reception area, where he remembered a large wall mirror. He flipped on a light and tilted his head back to stare at his neck. His Adam's apple looked like a plum and the entire front of his neck was as inflamed looking as it felt.

"God, Drake, what happened?" Ron finally looked as if

he were coming awake.

Drake briefly related the past half hour's events. "How did this guy know I was going back to testify again, if that information didn't come from the lawyers? There were six people in that room."

Ron scrubbed at his face with his hands, spiking his hair even worse. When he caught sight of himself in the mirror he smoothed the sides down and did a little pat-down to put the sparse top in order.

"Go over it again and tell me everything that happened," he said.

"I suppose the guy in the parking lot could have been the mechanic who worked on that aircraft," Drake said, after going over both the deposition and the assault at the airport. "He's the one with the most to lose, probably. But I hardly got into any specifics about that. I mean, those lawyers were so concerned with tearing me a new one that they hardly asked any questions about the accident itself."

They'd fetched cold beers from the fridge by this time and were in Ron's office. Drake had dumped the stack of books from the most comfortable chair in the room and put his feet up on the desk. Rusty lay within six inches of the chair, his ears perked and head cocked toward the open doorway.

"You went over the whole thing with Rick Valdez ahead of time, right?"

"Yeah, but geez, you don't think he'd sabotage me. That just doesn't make sense."

"No, it doesn't. I can't see him being behind it." Ron drained the brown bottle and asked whether Drake wanted another one. When Drake declined, he leaned back in his swivel chair. "This mechanic who attended the deposition.

What was his role?"

"What I was told, he was only there to hear our evidence. He's supposedly an expert witness for the other side. Their expert to counter our experts."

"So, aside from doing his research and presenting his side of things, he doesn't have any personal stake at all in the case?"

Drake shook his head. "Not as far as I know."

"You got your folder of notes with you?" Ron asked.

A shock went through Drake. "Shit! I don't know. They were in the truck." He jumped up and dashed down the stairs before Ron could speak.

He came back in under two minutes with the thick file folder. "Luckily I'm fanatic about locking my vehicle," he said to Ron. "Be sure to tell your sister that the next time she rags me about it."

"Offhand, you know the name of the mechanic who signed off on that work?" Ron asked. "Where does he live?"

"Manuel Salazar," Drake answered. He spread the file open on Ron's desk and paged toward the back of it. "Lives in Gallup."

"It's not that far, couple hours. He could have driven here this afternoon, if someone in that meeting tipped him that you were pointing fingers."

Drake thought about that. "I suppose. I've never met the guy, that I recall. Could have been him out at Double Eagle tonight."

"Tomorrow, I say we take a little drive over to Gallup," Ron said.

Chapter 22

Drake woke up well before dawn. He'd talked to Charlie after he got home last night and managed to skim past the attack at the airport with little explanation. She told him there had been an 'incident' at that resort place, but didn't go into detail, just that Linda wanted her to stay over and it was simpler not to argue with her friend.

When he spoke to her his voice was sounding like something off an old 78 record from the 1930s and she'd immediately asked him about it. He passed it off by saying he might be catching a cold. Following her advice of drinking a warm honey and lemon concoction helped for awhile, long enough to fall asleep. But by midnight he was tossing and turning. He renewed the honey drink a couple of times during the night, when he couldn't stand it anymore but nonetheless, he was awake for real by five. He put on a soft turtleneck, although a lot of the redness was already fading. The bruising on his Adam's apple would probably go through all sorts of color changes before it was really gone.

The injured throat was only part of the equation, he knew. His and Ron's plan to drive to Gallup today and confront Manuel Salazar seemed like a great idea at the time but during the night he began to question it. Now, after easing some warm oatmeal down his throat and wincing at his first tentative sip of fruit juice, he was torn between wanting to find the guy and dish out some of the same treatment and wishing he could just put his feet up and watch football until Charlie got home. Before he'd entirely decided which way to go, he heard Ron's car in the driveway.

He whistled out the back door for Rusty and the dog came inside. Drake filled his food and water dishes, figuring that would keep him happy for a few hours.

"Ready?" Ron asked when Drake opened the front door.

"Yeah." Meeting Salazar face to face would put a lot of questions to rest.

Ron hadn't eaten breakfast yet so they made a pass through the drive-up at the first McDonald's down the road. Drake declined. The drive to Gallup went smoothly enough. Most of the traffic on the interstate at this hour were eighteen-wheelers, bound for Arizona and California. Ron's style, Drake discovered, was to crank up the CD player and let Creedence Clearwater Revival drown out the sounds from the big trucks. "Proud Mary" precluded any attempts at conversation, which was just as well.

Manuel Salazar still worked at the Gallup airport, doing

mainly the types of routine maintenance that any fixed-base operator handles. Oil changes, hundred-hour inspections and that sort of thing. Once in awhile an airplane might come in with a problem and the local mechanics might have some real work to do, getting it airworthy before it could leave. Drake had spent a good part of his career around such facilities and pretty well knew the routines they followed.

He also knew, from the accident file, that Salazar had previously worked for Greenwood Aviation, one of the larger helicopter operators in the country. With a fleet of over a hundred craft, there was enough maintenance to keep a dozen or more mechanics busy. Between the routine stuff and the occasional hull damage from an accident, things were always hopping at those types of facilities. He sat back in the Mustang's comfy seat and formulated a few questions for Salazar.

The plan was to approach him cautiously. If it looked like Salazar might have been Drake's attacker they'd have to be careful what they said. If he wasn't, Drake could still use the time to ask a few pertinent questions about the case, a few little things to round out the information in his file.

They parked in the public area outside the main building on the airport property. Calling it a terminal was probably a bit hopeful, since there were only two daily commercial flights here, when an airline employee probably showed up to act as ticket agent, baggage handler and perhaps even flight attendant. But there was a lobby, a guy at the front desk who monitored weather reports and handled radio calls, and some public restrooms. Ron went there first, while Drake inquired about their mechanic.

"The full-time guy, Manny or part-time Leo?" asked the

desk guy, who wore a gray twill shirt with Marker Aviation logos on the sleeve and "Bob" embroidered over the chest pocket.

"Manuel Salazar," Drake told him.

"Yeah, he's back today."

"Back? Was he out?" Drake asked.

"Had the flu the last couple days."

Bob pointed toward a door that said Employees Only in bold red letters. Below the big lettering was another placard with all kinds of disclaimers about insurance regulations and such. Ron reappeared and the three of them walked past the few couches and chairs in the waiting area, pushing through into a large hangar.

"Manny!" Bob's voice echoed amazingly large in the open space. "Somebody here for you!" He turned and went back inside, leaving Drake and Ron standing there.

Three planes pretty well filled the space. A small one, something aerobatic by the look of it, was tucked into the nearest corner. It looked like it probably stayed there most of the time, in storage until some rich daredevil type of guy came out and put it through its paces. The other two were in the midst of maintenance. Cowlings were off the closer one, an older Cessna 210, and hatches were open all over the other, a nice Piper 301. The rat-a-tat of an air wrench bleeped through the air and Drake began to wonder whether Salazar had heard Bob's shout. He was about to call out again when a slender Hispanic man ducked beneath the wing of the Cessna and came toward them.

"Manual Salazar?" Ron asked.

The guy nodded hesitantly and paused about twenty feet away. Even at that distance, Drake knew this wasn't the man who'd pinned him against the side of his truck last night. This guy probably came up to Drake's shoulder and underweighed him by thirty pounds. Salazar gave Drake and Ron wary looks as he wiped grease off his hands with a red rag.

Drake stepped forward. "Manny, I'm Drake Langston. This is Ron Parker." He held out his hand and the other man took it. "We're with the investigation firm that's looking into the forest fire crash, last year. Do you have a minute?"

Salazar looked cautious. If he had a lawyer of his own, Drake knew this was when Salazar would have been advised not to talk. Even if he didn't, the guy might have watched enough cop shows on TV to know better than to volunteer information. Still, he decided to give it a try.

"I just want to get a little bit more about your side of it," he saying, keeping his voice gentle. "Can you take a break and chat for a couple minutes?" He nodded back toward the lobby.

"Can't really tell you anything," Salazar said. "I've been asked about it already."

"I know. I just wanted to see if there was anything we might add to our own files."

"I don't think so," Salazar said.

"Do you remember the day you performed that last inspection on Walters's helicopter?"

"Not really. I mean, I didn't until this came up and I had to go back through my logs. They showed me the aircraft log. Then I kinda did." He glanced over his shoulder at the two airplanes. "But nothing specific."

"You don't recall replacing the nut on the engine? Whether you used safety wire on it or not?"

Manny began twisting the red rag and shifting from

one foot to the other. "No. I don't. We do a couple dozen inspections a month. That was way over a year ago."

Drake nodded, giving him a moment longer. When Salazar didn't volunteer anything more, he knew it was time to let the guy off the hook. "Okay, thanks. I understand." No point in grilling the man; the lawyers would be doing plenty of that, if they hadn't already.

"Well, I better . . ." Salazar again glanced back toward his work area.

"Yeah, sure. Thanks, man." Drake watched him turn back, then looked at Ron.

"Guess that's it," Ron said. Under his breath he muttered, "Outside."

Drake followed, refraining from saying anything at all until they were back in the car.

"I take it that wasn't your assailant," Ron said the minute the doors closed.

"Nope. Couldn't have been. But he sure seemed nervous. Think it was just jitters over being questioned?"

"No way. He didn't give any real information either, did he?"

"Not a scrap," Drake agreed.

"Did you catch sight of the other guy?" Ron asked.

"Hunh-uh. Other than his legs. Bob said they had two mechanics. That must have been Leo."

"At one point, when you were paying attention to Manny, this other guy peeked out from behind one of the planes. I got a pretty good look at him. Great big guy, closer to the size you described last night."

"And . . ."

"And he sure was listening to our every word. You notice Manny didn't want to come outside with us, where he could really talk? I got the impression he wanted this guy to know that he wasn't giving us anything useful."

"Makes sense. He sure got antsy when I asked specifically about the nut." Drake put his hand on the door handle. "Maybe it's the other guy I really should be talking to."

"Let's wait on that," Ron said. "This is one of those times when we might learn more by watching than by asking a direct question. The guy's guilty, he's just gonna clam up. Probably worse than Manny did."

He started the car and backed out of the lot. "Let's just see what happens. We're not in any big hurry, are we?"

A short half-block away was a light-industrial park of small warehouses, the kind of area where shipping companies and home-grown manufacturers were often located. Ron pulled into a parking slot beside a place with "Navajo Candles" painted on a sign at the door. He made sure he had a good view of the side street.

"It's nearly lunch time. I'd be curious to see whether either Manny or Leo take a break."

Of the three slots marked Employee Parking Only at the airport, one had held a Marker Aviation vehicle, the other two had pickup trucks—one red Nissan and one white Dodge Ram. Drake was willing to guess which one belonged to Leo.

Within fifteen minutes the white Ram with its bulky driver drove past. Speed limit on the street was only thirty-five, so they had no trouble getting to the driveway before Leo made it to the stop sign at the next intersection. He made a left turn and Ron quickly got to the stop, where they could watch his next move. Leaving a couple of vehicles between them, they stayed behind until he took the entry ramp onto I-40, eastbound.

They stayed close, allowing no more than two cars between them, until it became apparent that Leo wasn't pulling off at any of the Gallup exits for lunch. Within ten minutes they'd bypassed the whole town. Ron let a couple of big rigs get between them and paced himself so Leo never got much farther ahead. Once they'd cruised past Grants, an hour later, it became obvious that Leo was probably going all the way to Albuquerque.

"Shit, it's going to be hard to track him without being spotted if we get into city traffic," Ron said.

"What do you want to do?"

"About all we can do is see how it plays out."

As they passed the casinos on the city's western edge, Ron closed the distance between them, back to the requisite two cars. Keeping the big Ram in sight had, so far, not been too difficult. Keeping Ron's Mustang out of Leo's sight could prove more chancy. After another fifteen minutes, Drake tapped Ron's arm.

"He's signaling." Sure enough, the Ram slowed for the ramp at 98th Street.

"This is where it's going to get tricky," Ron muttered.

He slowed and exited but now there were no other cars between them and their quarry. The Ram stayed to the right and pulled into a truck stop.

"Whew. Lucky for us," Ron said. He steered the Mustang to the car-sized gas pumps, watching as the Ram whipped to a quick stop in the parking slots in front of the convenience store.

"What now?"

"He's not getting out. Let's just watch."

The pumps weren't busy and no one was yet clamoring for their spot so they held tight. Within minutes a silver

BMW pulled in beside the Ram. A slim man got out and walked over to the driver's side of the Ram. He spoke with Leo through the open window, then went inside.

"I can't be sure from here," Drake said, "but that looks like David Ratwill, one of the opposing attorneys."

"David Ratwill? Charlie had me check that name—his ex was just killed in Santa Fe."

Chapter 23

The office had a hollow, unoccupied feel when Drake and Ron arrived. Something in the kitchen trash was going bad, Drake noted, along with a scum of old coffee in the bottom of the pot that always sat on the counter. Little touches that betrayed the fact that Charlie hadn't been here in several days.

Ron glanced at his watch. "Rick ought to be here any minute," he said. They'd phoned the lawyer from the truck stop and asked him to stop by. A lot of unanswered questions remained, about Salazar and Leo and how it all related.

Almost in answer to Ron's statement, a firm knock sounded at the front door. They traversed the long hall from kitchen to reception area and Ron opened the door to Rick Valdez.

"Let's go up to my office," Ron suggested.

"Maybe Charlie's would be better," Drake said after one peek into Ron's den of uncontrolled paperwork.

He ushered Valdez across the hall while Ron retrieved the files. The lawyer took a seat on the couch near the bay window and Drake grabbed a side chair by the desk, leaving Ron the desktop to spread out the papers.

"Do you know whether this mechanic Leo . . ." Ron searched for the last name, "well, Leo somebody, has some connection to our case?"

"I haven't heard of him before," Valdez said.

"Big guy, hairy arms, bad breath," Drake said. "I had close contact with him last night." He gave Valdez the quick version of the attack.

Valdez shook his head.

"He's up to something. We went out to talk with Salazar this morning and I got the distinct feeling that he wasn't talking because Leo was there in the hangar. Probably afraid of being overheard. Then Leo zoomed off to Albuquerque and had a little rendezvous with David Ratwill, a sly-feeling meeting at a truck stop on the west side." Ron was flipping through pages in the file as he talked.

"I don't know what," said Valdez. "But if he's talking to the opposing attorneys and passing information along, I want to know about it."

"Not to mention threatening your witness," Drake reminded him. "This wasn't just a friendly suggestion to quit the case."

Ron pulled a page from the folder. "Let me make some calls," he said. "This is Salazar's employment record."

"How about something from the kitchen?" Drake asked.

"Soda, beer? Whatever we have down there."

Both men asked for Cokes and Drake headed down the stairs. Through the back window, he spotted Charlie's Jeep in the small parking area. The driver's door stood open and one jean-clad leg stuck out.

He quickly put the encrusted coffee pot to soak in the sink and pulled the smelly trash bag from the kitchen waste can, yanking the ties together and heading for the back door with it.

"Hey, you're back!" he greeted as she approached the back steps.

She gave a quick glance toward the bulging trash bag and grinned. "You could have let Ron take the heat for that, you know."

He shrugged. "He's been pretty busy."

They shared a long kiss before he ushered her into the kitchen.

"Whose car, out front?" she asked.

He explained about the meeting with Rick Valdez and gathered the soft drinks for which he'd originally come downstairs. When he and Charlie entered her office, Ron was ending a call. He raised an eyebrow in greeting to Charlie, while Drake introduced her to Rick Valdez. She shook hands with the lawyer and answered politely, but he noticed she was eyeing the stack of mail on her desk.

"Okay, thanks. Appreciate the information," Ron said to the receiver. Hanging up, he turned to Valdez. "Damn employment regs. Can't get anything good out of people anymore."

As soon as it became apparent that Ron's phone call was winding down she shooed him out of the chair. The three men began to drift across the hall toward Ron's office as she switched on her computer and began sorting mail with a vengeance.

Valdez shrugged and Drake chuckled. "So, anything useful at all?"

"Actually, yeah. Interesting coincidence that both Leo Malone and Manuel Salazar worked for the operator in our case, at the same time. At the time of the accident."

"So, you're thinking maybe Leo had more to do with the nut not being tightened than Manny did?"

"Seems logical."

"But Manny has admitted that he's the one who did that particular part of the inspection," Valdez reminded them.

"Manny also says that he was called away partway through the work," Ron said, consulting the notes, "and he can't specifically remember attaching the safety wire."

"They use checklists," Drake said. "My question would be whether the safety wire step was checked off."

"My money says that it is now," Ron said. "Whether it was checked off that day or not."

"So, where does that leave us?" Valdez asked.

"With diddly squat unless we can get that original checklist," Drake said. "We might be able to have it analyzed for changes made after the fact. Do we have that?"

Ron pawed through the file again. "I don't. How about at your office?" he said looking at Valdez.

"Probably a copy, if anything. I'll have to check. This case has filled about five file boxes so far." He shifted on the couch. "But I have a secretary who's a marvel of organization. Let me ask her."

He pulled a cell phone from his inner jacket pocket and speed dialed, speaking to someone named Jen. He quickly explained what they needed and asked her to call back if she could locate it.

"What do we do if she doesn't come up with it?" Ron asked.

Drake piped up. "The operator has to have those records. You can subpoena them, can't you?"

"Time consuming." Valdez didn't look happy. "But yeah, we can." He stood up. "You ready for your next session in the deposition room tomorrow, Drake? Or do you want to spend a little more time going over things together?"

"Unless you know what they'll ask and can provide me easy answers, or unless you can give me a note from mom to get me out of this, I guess I'm ready."

Chapter 24

The quality of the faxed photograph wasn't great. Even knowing who I was looking at, I could barely tell it was a younger Trudie Blanchard. It was obvious why Rita didn't recognize her. This Trudie had very dark hair, pulled up into a tight knot on top of her head, contrasting the stark whiteness of her skin. Thick glasses with dark frames obscured her eyes—a disguise, or had she switched to contacts now? Her mouth was a hard line. I saw little of the uncertain, needy woman I'd met in Santa Fe.

Drake peeked into my office, looking like every other guy who ducks and runs when a woman goes on a cleaning binge.

"Don't worry, it's safe," I said. I'd downloaded forty-three email messages and trashed more than thirty of them.

Same with the regular mail. After sorting out the junk, there were really just a couple of bills to pay and one letter to answer. All of it could wait until tomorrow.

"Pedro's?" he asked, with that winning little-boy smile that always gets me.

"You bet." I grabbed my denim jacket and purse and switched out the light so quickly that he did a double-take.

Our favorite little haunt was empty this early in the afternoon. We'd caught them squarely between the lunch crowd and the happy hour margarita drinkers. We kept the chat light as we ate, because I didn't really want to share the drama of yesterday evening in front of Pedro and Concha, and because I was too busy stuffing my face.

"That was *so* much better than any chef-prepared gala dinner in Santa Fe," I said.

Thirty minutes later, we'd dragged ourselves away from the table and arrived at home. Rusty greeted me like I'd been gone for a month, but he does that even if I just run to the post office. But the sentiment was nice and I hugged him and sneaked him an extra doggie cookie.

Drake seemed distracted as he went to his home office and checked messages on the machine. He called the one client who had phoned, a rancher who wanted to patrol the perimeter of his eight thousand acres to be sure fences were intact for the upcoming winter. He offered to send me to do the job, but I was secretly glad when the rancher reassured Drake that there was no rush—the work could wait a few days. It was always a pleasure to work for a guy who ran his own show, rather than the government types who'd as soon fine you or dock you if things didn't go exactly their way. The guy had been pleasant and amenable to working on the weekend or even the beginning of the following week, if Drake were held over. For my part, there were things in Santa Fe that had not quite been answered.

I was in the kitchen, scooping nuggets for Rusty, when I felt Drake's presence behind me.

"Hey babe." He had that bedroom tone and in less than two minutes we'd abandoned our poor dog and closed the door to the sanctuary on him. I had to admit that I'd really missed having my sweetheart to snuggle every night.

Shoes and jeans began to pile up on the floor but when Drake took off his shirt I stopped cold.

"*What* are these horrible marks on your neck?" I demanded.

He wasn't to be deterred. "Hmm… tell you later," he murmured into the curve of my collarbone.

I took a deep breath. He clearly was feeling quite well, and it wasn't worth spoiling the moment.

An hour later, however, he wasn't going to get away without an explanation. We lay in the warm sheets, a tangle of arms and legs when I brought up the subject again. When I heard that he'd been attacked and warned away from his testimony, anger flooded me.

"Sweetheart, calm down," he said. "It's done. I know who it was and I don't have any reason to go near the guy again."

I sensed there was more to it and my skepticism must have showed.

"Okay, whole story? I have to continue my deposition again tomorrow. And what I have to say is going to nail this guy, Leo Malone."

He read my worried expression. "It'll be fine," he said. He pulled me into his embrace. "There's another witness, plus I think we can prove his guilt through aircraft records. My testimony is only part of it and Malone can't get rid of everything that implicates him."

That made sense and I relaxed a little. But not much. Any guy who would give such a drastic warning might very well go further.

He stirred again. "There's a weird thing, though. I forgot to mention it earlier . . . one of the attorneys on the opposing side is a guy named David Ratwill."

"What!"

"A Santa Fe firm. Ron said he's connected to that case you're working on?"

All at once my nerves felt wired. I lay there, puzzling over the connections, long after Drake fell asleep.

Chapter 25

Eight o'clock the next morning came way too soon for Drake's taste. He rolled over and put an arm around Charlie, wishing that the morning snuggle could last awhile longer. She mumbled something about his needing to get downtown and that brought back the apprehension that he was trying to hide from her.

"Hon, just chill," she said. "I can feel it in your muscles that this whole thing is really getting to you, but don't let it."

Easy to say.

"I mean it. You can't take this stuff personally. Those lawyers are jerks. Don't let it bother you."

"I know. And if it weren't for the fact that they're trying to make me look incompetent and stupid, I'd like to confront David Ratwill, in light of the things I know about him now."

"Actually, I'd like to ask him a few questions myself." She sat up in bed.

"Forget it. I know what you're thinking, and you can't go with me."

She almost muttered 'rats' under her breath. "But, hon, it would be so classic to see his reaction if he saw me there."

Actually, it probably would be pretty funny. But Drake didn't need the distraction.

"I'll bet David has no idea of our connection," she was saying. "With different last names, he probably has no clue . . ."

"Not this morning, Charlie."

She sensed the finality in his tone, he could tell by the slump in her shoulders.

"You're right," she said. "You have to keep your mind on your testimony. I need to go back to Santa Fe and get the rest of my stuff anyway."

By the time he made his way to Valdez's office he'd gotten himself all keyed up again and took a minute in the elevator to take a couple of deep breaths and force himself to repeat 'it's nothing personal' several times. The receptionist greeted him warmly this time and he put on a smile.

"Hey, Drake!" Valdez certainly looked cheery this morning. "Guess what Jen found?"

"The inspection checklist, I hope?" The two men walked down the hall to the lawyer's private office as they talked.

Valdez whipped out a sheet of paper, a photocopy of the familiar form. Beside each item on the inspection list was a checkmark on a short line. Next to the check, initials confirmed which man had performed each step. Drake scanned down the list; the tightening and wiring of the nuts would be near the end. Every line had a check and set of initials.

"What do you think?" Valdez asked. "I looked it over. Can't tell if the same guy made all those marks or not."

Drake shook his head. "I can't be absolutely sure, either, not on a copy."

"Let's hold off and not bring it up just yet." The lawyer lowered his voice. "See what the other side says first. If we have to, we can get the original."

Voices in the hall announced the arrival of the other team and Drake felt his stomach tighten. He was glad he'd opted for a light breakfast.

Valdez reminded him: "With everything you say today, just remember that this is the time for the other guys to show their hand. Don't bring up Leo or the fact that you went to Gallup yesterday, unless they ask about it. Don't speculate about Leo and Ratwill meeting—in fact, don't even let on that you know. I want the chance to find out what we can from them, so we have a little ammunition of our own."

Drake nodded.

"Next week it's going to be our turn to grill the hell out of their expert."

That made Drake feel somewhat better as he walked into the room and was forced to shake hands and smile at the men who would, for the next few hours, be his inquisitors. Again, there were three lawyers in expensive suits and their mechanic expert, who looked no more comfortable than he had two days ago.

"Mr. Langston, how are you today?" Malcolm Browne, the other partner in Browne and Ratwill, greeted him with pseudo-warmth. Drake smiled his own version of the social grimace and answered, "Just fine." He met Ratwill's gaze and, as if unconsciously, stretched his neck and passed a hand over this throat. He'd purposely worn a polo shirt with his jacket, open at the collar. The vivid purple had gone out of his throat now but the marks were clearly there. Ratwill didn't blink. Either he didn't know about Leo's little communication two nights ago, or he was able to stay extremely composed about it.

The third lawyer, whose name didn't stick with Drake, had crossed to the back of the conference table and staked out the same chair he'd had at the previous session. As the others took their seats, Drake sent a tight smile toward the mechanic, sending the message 'enjoy this, buddy, you're next.'

The session started much as the previous one, with questions from Ratwill about Drake's qualifications. He answered by rote, telling the truth but not letting the substance of the question or the manner of the questioner affect him. After an hour or so of covering the same ground the lawyers changed tactics, Ratwill appear to be getting impatient. While he took a break for a glass of water the guy in the gray suit started in with specific questions about the crash.

By the lunch break Drake was feeling a bit more relaxed. The things pilots did and the ways they would react to emergency situations were familiar to him. The lawyers had come up with nothing he couldn't answer with confidence.

At lunch with Valdez, over another burger at Lucky's, he found himself actually smiling.

"Don't get too calm just yet," the lawyer advised, swallowing a large bite of his green chile cheeseburger.

"Remember, these guys want to pin the accident on the engine manufacturer. Learning that the pilot wasn't at fault will go right to their goals."

"Okay, they're establishing that the pilot did all the right things," Drake said, "we're in agreement on that."

"Which is good. Finding some common ground with the other side isn't necessarily a bad thing."

Drake dipped a potato wedge in ketchup. "So are they going to ask me about the mechanic's role this afternoon?"

"My guess, probably so. But who knows with these guys."

In the afternoon session, Ratwill was absent. Browne took over and began with general maintenance questions, procedures that Drake knew well. He answered confidently when asked about the frequency of inspections and which procedures could be done by an Airframe and Powerplant mechanic and which would have to be signed off by someone holding an Aircraft Inspector license. He readily admitted that he had some experience with the work but was not licensed at either level. Browne clearly wanted Drake to be apologetic or become rattled, but Drake held his own.

"Now, Mr. Langston, in this particular accident case you've stated that the mechanic forgot to sufficiently tighten one of the nuts and did not safety wire it."

"I can't say whether he tightened it or not. I can say that in the wreckage of the engine, the nut had come off and there was no evidence that it had been safety wired, although the other nuts on that part of the engine were wired."

"So one small piece of wire brought down the whole aircraft. I find that very unlikely."

Drake opened his mouth but Browne continued.

"Isn't it far more likely that there was a defect in the engine's design or manufacture that caused the failure leading to the crash?"

"This particular engine has been in use for more than twenty years," Drake responded, "with few problems. I think that would rule out design flaws."

"*Few* problems?" Browne looked like an angler who'd just snagged the big one. "Then there have been engine failures."

Drake took a deep breath. "There have been engine failures, but—"

"Note the witness's admission that there have been engine failures." Browne turned toward the stenographer.

"This isn't the courtroom," Rick Valdez reminded.

Drake continued where he'd been interrupted. "But—in each of the documented cases—three in all, the failure was traced to either pilot error, an inspection not done correctly or other human error. I have documentation." He reached for his folder.

"Note this evidence for the record as well," Valdez said, giving Browne the same intent stare the lawyer had so recently aimed at the stenographer.

Drake pulled out the accident reports from the other three incidents, thankful that he'd anticipated this line of questioning. Browne quickly glanced at them and asked that copies be made for his files.

The lawyer continued questioning, throwing in a number of queries that didn't appear to Drake to have much at all to do with the case.

When Drake asked Valdez about it during the mid-afternoon coffee break, the chubby attorney shrugged. "Some guys like to think they're clouding the record with stuff like that. It might work in front a jury—throwing out a lot of irrelevant stuff to confuse them—but in this kind of proceeding it just wastes time. My guess is that he doesn't have much else. He was counting on being able to get you to admit that the engine design could have been at fault."

They were in Valdez's office with the door closed, having coffee and cookies that his secretary had left on the cherry credenza. "Why?" Drake insisted, "Why does everyone seem to think that corporations want to deliberately make their products fail? There's no logic in that."

"Logic, no. Money, yes." Valdez topped up his mug. "Get a case like this in front of a jury and nine times out of ten they want to sock it to the corporation with a big money award. Ratwill and Browne know that. They want enough evidence for the judge to let them take it to trial."

"No wonder every part on the damn aircraft costs so much," Drake fumed.

"Hey, the corporations know it too. It's easier for them to agree to pay ten million in a settlement than to risk having a jury hit them for a hundred mil. And the cost of appealing a judgment like that—it gets unbelievably expensive. They'll pay out of pocket—well, their insurance will."

"And everyone's insurance rates skyrocket because of it." Drake found himself pacing the carpet, remembering how his own insurance company had notified him last month that his rates would go up twenty percent come January first, despite the fact that he'd never filed a claim in his entire career. "It's not right, not when the fault lies with some mechanic's mistake. A mistake he might have made simply because the phone rang at the wrong moment or the boss pushed him to finish early so they could get the aircraft back in service by the next morning."

Valdez shrugged. "I know. There are no easy answers. People died and their families want somebody to pay."

"The word 'accident' has slipped from our vocabulary in recent times. Everything has to be someone's fault. And the more money it appears you have, the more likely it is that the 'fault' is going to be yours."

Valdez set his cup back on the silver tray and took Drake's. "I don't know what to tell you, other than we've got to go back in there and you need to unwind a little."

Drake sighed. "I know. I know I'm going to want to spout off to the creep, the same things I just said to you."

"Well, don't. If you think it's going to be a problem I'll ask that we continue this another day. Antagonizing these guys isn't going to change their ways. They'll either go after you with a vengeance, more determined than ever to win this case, or they'll just blow you off and go find another witness who'll say what they want."

Drake felt the tension go out of his jaw. "You're right. Pissing them off isn't going to help."

"So, shall we go back in there or shall I ask for a recess?"

"No, I'll go back in there. Let me visit the men's room first."

Drake knew his own nature. He'd simply go home and stew about it all night. Build an even greater anger and then come back the next day with a worse attitude. As he splashed water on his face and dried his hands he forced himself to calm down. Make your points, hold your ground, he told himself. Don't let the bastards get you down, as Charlie would advise.

Browne seemed subdued in the late afternoon session. He'd probably spent the coffee break with cell phone to his ear, down in the lobby of the building somewhere out of earshot, demanding that somebody come up with some evidence to contradict Drake's testimony. But Drake knew there wasn't any. He'd spent months digging through records, looking for anything that might weaken Valdez's case, and he hadn't found it. FAA and NTSB records on accidents were thorough. There hadn't been a case since the introduction of the S-Jet 1200 engine that would say differently. That knowledge kept his temper in check, and he found himself almost able to see the humor in the opposition's desperate moves earlier.

The gray-suited attorney resumed the questioning. But his queries were routine, re-covering ground that they'd already been over. As five o'clock approached it became apparent that the other team had no new information and Drake began to relax. As the others put on their jackets and gathered their files, they thanked him for his time.

"No problem, gentlemen," he responded. "It's really all about doing the right thing, isn't it?"

The lawyer gave him a funny look. Malcolm Browne almost hung his head but caught himself in time. No one from that side was going to admit that they weren't on the side of truth and justice—maybe just the American way.

"Let's go get a drink," Valdez suggested. "You've had a rough few days."

They stepped off the elevator and Rick's phone rang.

"Yeah?" Valdez said. A moment later. "What!"

Drake watched as the attorney's face registered shock. He stood still as Rick nodded a few times then ended the call. The stocky attorney turned to him.

"Manuel Salazar is dead."

<h1>Chapter 26</h1>

I rolled over and realized with a start that it was after ten o'clock. I'd slept like the dead after Drake got up and left. With a groan I pulled the covers up and rolled over again. The week of early mornings, combined with the assaults on my body, clearly left me needing extra rest. Finally, I dragged myself out of my comfy nest and into the shower, where I indulged in the full round of pampering that included both skin and hair conditioners.

As I'd told Drake, I needed to go back to Santa Fe today. If nothing else, I'd left most of my things there. It didn't seem right to ask Linda to clear out the room and deliver my stuff home to me. Plus, there were still too many unanswered questions. It's bull-headed, I know, but I wasn't going to just 'let it go' that I'd now been attacked twice. Someone thought I knew something incriminating. Somewhere amid the questions I'd asked or the files I'd copied from Light's computer, there was information that might help catch a killer.

I walked into the kitchen to look for something to eat. There on the kitchen table lay a gun. It was my Beretta 9 mm, freshly cleaned and loaded, along with a note from Drake. *Don't let anything happen to you*, it said. He was right, of course. Foolish of me to go back near the scene of the crimes without protection. I carried it to the living room and stuck it into my purse.

Back in the kitchen I stood at the open refrigerator door, debating among the various choices. Breakfast or lunch? The cool air was rushing out and Rusty now joined me to see what he might snag, as long as I was taking my time about it. I finally just picked up a package of deli turkey and made myself a sandwich, tossing small bits to the dog, noticing for the first time that he wasn't quite as spry in catching them. How old was he now? I really couldn't remember.

A tap at the back door interrupted, saving me from having to think too hard. My neighbor, Elsa, stood there, visible through the panes of glass.

"I know you're busy," she said.

I felt a guilty stab that I hadn't been over to check on her once this week.

"I brought you some tomatoes from the garden." She held out a bag and I savored the fresh, outdoorsy smell of them. "And I wanted to tell you that I'm going to be away for a few days."

Now that really *was* news. Since her sister in Denver passed away over ten years ago, I couldn't remember a single time Elsa had been away from home overnight.

"A lady from my church talked me into taking a trip with her," she said. "It's a bus trip to Vegas. We're going to clean out the slots!"

"Really? But there are casinos all over New Mexico. Why Vegas?" I had to admit that I've not seen that much sparkle in her eyes in a long time.

"Because we can, sweetie." She patted my hand. "At our age, there's no sense putting off anything."

"Well, I agree. You go and have a great time."

I watched her walk back through the break in the hedge, to her own back door. I could feel a smile coming on. Why not? I silently wished her luck. A glance at the kitchen clock told me that I better get myself in gear. I tried to explain to Rusty that he couldn't come along and that we would all be back in time for dinner. All he really got from the whole conversation was that he would get a rawhide chew in return for staying home.

All the way back to Santa Fe I contemplated the unsavory doings at the conference. For a bunch of people who were into peace and love and all that, there sure were a lot of unloving things going on. Like having my neck almost broken and then being knocked in the head. David Ratwill and Trudie were still my main suspects, although the more I thought about it, Stanworthy/Light was right up there too.

I negotiated the winding road to Casa de Tranquilidad and spotted Linda near the lobby entrance. I tooted my horn at her and went on to the parking lot. She was still standing by the door when I caught up with her.

"Have you seen Trudie today?" I asked. Stanworthy had too high a stake in this place and in his business to take a chance on being caught assaulting one of the attendees, even if he did have a lot to hide. Trudie, on the other hand . . . anything could be possible with her and she'd been here every day of the conference.

"How's your head?" she asked, ignoring my question as we walked to our room.

"Amazingly well." I remembered the nearly euphoric feeling when Samantha Sweet had helped me up. The lady had *some* kind of healing touch, for sure.

Nonetheless, Linda made me sit on the edge of my bed and submit to another head feel-up before she pronounced me fit for light duty.

"I need to track down Trudie. If she's the one who hit me I want her to know it didn't work."

"Charlie, don't get yourself into—"

"I just have a few questions for her." Such as, why hadn't she acknowledged that she knew Rita from California, and where had she been yesterday when I got whacked in the parking lot.

"I'll be either here or in the library if you need me," Linda said.

I walked next door to Trudie's room and knocked. Thirty seconds later I knocked again. I pressed my ear to the door but couldn't hear a thing. Maybe Shirley would know her schedule. As I recalled, most of the classes had wrapped up this morning but there were probably spa appointments and such this afternoon.

I cut through the hotel lobby and entered the reception area for the conference section of the building. No one attended the desk at the moment so I headed down the hall. Shirley's office was on the left, next to Light's. Her lights were on and I tapped at the partially open door.

"Hi, Charlie," she greeted. "Just getting a few things organized for tonight's farewell gathering. You'll be there, right?"

"I'll try." I tried to look regretful but couldn't imagine listening to Celius Light speak for hours. I noticed a canvas bag on the floor in the corner.

"That's Rita's," Shirley said, following my gaze. "The police couldn't decide who to give it to so it ended up here." She looked back up at me. "What can I do for you?"

"I'm trying to find Trudie and she's not in her room. Do you know if she had a spa treatment this afternoon?"

She sat down and hit a few keys on her computer. "Let's take a look at the schedule."

I took the chair opposite her desk and willed the computer to work a little faster.

"No, I don't see anything here," Shirley said. "In fact, I seem to remember her mentioning that she planned to take a nap, organize her papers, something like that. She's not leaving until tomorrow. I think we asked the hotel to arrange a shuttle pickup to the airport around noon." She looked away from the screen and turned her attention to me. "She's probably asleep in her room, just didn't hear your knock. You look like you could use a nap, too, Charlie. Take advantage of a couple of free hours."

"Yes, maybe I will." I stood up. "Is Dr. Light in his office?"

"I doubt it. He usually goes to the spa for a long massage before our final evening. Relaxes him."

I thanked her and left. Instead of exiting through the courtyard, I veered out to the main lobby. Two young clerks who'd been lounging against the front desk snapped to attention and became busy as I approached.

"Excuse me, my roommate went off this afternoon and must have taken my key with her. Can I get another one? Room 14."

The brunette picked up a blank card, hit a couple of keys and swiped it through a slot on her computer keyboard. "Here you go," she said.

That was way too easy. Her supervisor would have at least required a name and ID.

I headed down the hall and used the key on Trudie's door. It opened easily with nary a safety latch to stand in my way. As I'd suspected, she wasn't there. I poked my head into the bathroom and even whisked back the shower curtain to be sure. I made sure the door was closed tightly and decided to do a quick snoop-through.

As I'd noticed from my previous peek into the place, Trudie wasn't exactly a neatnik. Clothes were strewn over bed and chair. Her open suitcase lay on the floor in one corner, hair care gear and cosmetics lying haphazardly inside as if she tossed them there each time after using them.

Her conference tote bag and pages of handouts lay on the desk, again scattered about as if she tossed each day's new batch on top of the old. I riffled through them seeing notes in scrawling, lopsided script. Many of them were barely readable but those I could easily decipher seemed to pertain only to the class discussion.

My eyes landed on another note, this one on a small sheet of hotel notepad paper, stuck murder the edge of the desk lamp. Trudie hadn't written this one; the handwriting was too different--bold, slanting letters, decidedly masculine. *Meet me in the parking lot 4:00.* I glanced at my watch—it was after five. I didn't like the feel of this.

I took the note with me and rushed back to Linda's and

my room. I startled her at the desk.

"Trudie's missing. We've got to look for her," I said.

Linda stared at me as if I'd gone mad, but quickly recovered. My friends soon become accustomed to my dashes into the unknown. She pulled on a pair of sneakers while I recapped what I'd found.

"She was to meet someone in the parking lot," I said as we locked our room and headed across the courtyard. "I don't know whether Trudie is a victim or an accomplice but somehow this feels like it's tied to the attacks on me."

The parking area appeared unchanged since I'd arrived. There may have been a few different cars; I hadn't taken close notice of them the first time. We walked the perimeter of the lot, watching for anything out of place. I debated whether it would be worthwhile to note license plates and check them, but that would take a lot of time and something about this felt urgent. I just couldn't put my finger on it.

After fifteen minutes with no results, Linda began to get impatient. "Other than the note, is there any reason to think she actually came here?" she asked.

We stopped beside the last car on the last row. "No, I guess not."

"Does she have a car here?" Linda asked. "Maybe we should find out which one is hers and concentrate on that."

I thought about it. "No, Shirley said she was taking a shuttle to the airport."

"Then the other person's car? Have you figured out who she was meeting?"

I'd thought about that. Celeus Light's car, the pearl-white Lexus, sat parked in its usual spot and I'd surreptitiously laid a hand on the hood when we walked by it. It had not left recently.

"Charlie, she could be anywhere, couldn't she?"

"Technically, yes. But I have a feeling about this. She's somewhere here on the grounds."

"Then let's be logical about it. Maybe she's having a massage."

I didn't tell her that I'd already asked Shirley about that; after all, it was possible that Trudie had walked in and they accommodated her. "Okay, I'll try that. You don't have to come if you don't want to."

She glanced at her watch. "I'll give it another fifteen minutes. I have some patient calls to return and I really need to have a shower and wash my hair before the evening meditation starts."

We walked toward the lobby and circled through it, paying attention to its various alcoves and overstuffed leather couches and chairs. No sign of her. The doors to the dining room were closed, and a peek through the glass panes showed it to be empty of customers.

On to the spa, where a lone attendant stood behind the reception desk, flipping through the day's receipts, tallying something on a calculator.

"Sorry, all the appointments are finished," she said. "The last client left about ten minutes ago."

"Was Trudie Blanchard one of them?" I asked.

She looked a little put out, but pulled out her gilt-edged appointment book and opened it to the right page. "No, nothing for her, either scheduled or walk-in. I write those down, too."

"Could she be in the locker room? We'll be quick if you can let us look."

She barely concealed the expression that said 'it's Friday night and I have a date' and waved us through.

Linda and I took opposite sides of the corridor. She walked into the glassed-in hot tub room, scanning the water's surface and pushing aside the fronds of potted plants, while I took the locker rooms. At the Men's door, I tapped and called out loudly. The place echoed back hollowly. In the Ladies locker room an attendant stood by her station, folding towels.

"Is anyone still here?" I asked.

"No, Señora, all gone."

For extra measure, I called out Trudie's name but this room, too, echoed back at me.

Back in the corridor, Linda reported that the mud bath and hot tub areas were empty. "I better head to the room and get ready," she said.

"Okay, I'll be along in a minute. I'm going to take the back way and walk around the building once."

"Be careful. Walking around by yourself got you into trouble before," she warned. She turned back the way we'd come.

I remembered seeing an emergency exit at the far end of the corridor, beyond the ladies locker room, so I went that way. What was I going to do if I found Trudie, anyway? If she'd been the one who attacked me earlier, she'd no doubt try it again.

Foolishly, I'd left my purse, with the Beretta in it, in our room. I'm in pretty good shape, but against someone with the strength of insanity on her side . . .. I looked around for a weapon but found only a stack of clean towels. I grabbed one, nearly laughing at the absurdity of it. What was I going to do—snap her with it or blindfold her?

Nevertheless, I took opposite corners of the towel and spun the piece of cloth into a strong whip. The attendant from the locker room came out, her Casa de Tranquilidad smock gone now, her purse over her arm. She gave me a curious stare but didn't say anything as she walked out.

The place suddenly felt very quiet and I felt very alone. Just get this over with, Charlie. I headed toward the end of the hall where I'd seen the other exit. Then the lights went out.

The hairs on my neck bristled. I stopped, blind.

Chapter 27

Minutes ticked by in what must have actually been about ten seconds. I squeezed my eyes shut and opened them again. No emergency lighting but faintly, ahead, I could see the glowing green letters of a lighted Exit sign.

I faced it squarely and edged forward. I could only hope that no one had remembered to lock the door, or I'd have to traverse the whole corridor again to find my way back. I visualized the hall. Aside from the recessed countertop where I'd found my towel weapon, it was long and straight without obstacles. Light switches—I couldn't remember. But that's hardly the thing one notices right away. They had to exist. Dropping one end of the towel, I edged to my right and felt for the wall. It wasn't that far, probably twenty feet, and the tiny green letters actually sent a small glow to guide me. I could do this.

I hummed a little non-tune to keep myself company but quit when it echoed eerily off the tile walls. Brushing my fingertips lightly along the wall I moved forward, covering a foot at a time. I encountered a doorframe—something I didn't remember—and my fingers followed the recess across the door itself. I'd just touched the outcrop of the molding on the other side when a loud thump rattled the door.

I jumped back from it, a scream forming in my throat and coming out as a squeak.

Every logical thought told me to run, but I envisioned myself bouncing off the walls like the metal ball in a pinball machine, unable to get to my destination. I skittered frantically away from the door.

Another loud bump, then two, three, four.

"Who's in there?" I shouted. My voice careened off the tile.

I edged away and felt the opposite wall against my back. The echo of my words died away, leaving my raspy breath as the only sound. I forced myself to calm down, to breathe through my nose.

As my own noises died away I caught a faint voice. "Help me," it called.

Oh god, what was going on here?

Two more bumps and again, "Help!"

Not in the dark, I swore. If this is a trap, I want to at least see it before I walk into it. I extended both hands, feeling the wall behind me, edging always closer to the exit sign. At last, I encountered a double switch.

I rammed both switches upward. And blinded myself.

My eyes slammed shut against the cruel glare of fluorescent light on white tile. I cupped both hands over my face for additional protection.

Gradually, through slotted fingers I eased my eyes open and scanned the corridor. Empty, as before. Across from me, the door I'd touched was labeled with a small sign that said Employees Only. Another bump came from it, this one seemingly fainter than before.

Again, the voice, muffled. "Help me." It sounded feeble and not nearly so frightening anymore.

I lowered my hands and walked toward it. My towel-weapon lay nearby. I must have flung it away in my panic. I tiptoed to the door and listened.

"Who's in there?" By keeping my voice low, the horrible echo was minimal.

The answer came as a scraping noise on the floor. I tried the doorknob. Locked. Now what?

"Wait," I said. As if this person had any choice. "I'll be right back."

I rushed back to the reception area, flipping on more lights along the way. The desk consisted of a long granite top with two shallow drawers under it and banks of deeper drawers in columns on either side of the swivel chair. I yanked open the two shallow drawers first and was rewarded with the sight of a small compartmented tray that contained a ring of keys and a few loose ones. I grabbed them all.

As an extra measure, I also took a box cutter with a lethal looking razor blade concealed in a heavy metal handle.

Feeling considerably braver now, I approached the unknown door again.

"I'm back," I said. "I'm going to see if any of these keys work, so just be patient."

The answer came as a small scraping sound.

I glanced through the loose keys first, discarding them when they all appeared to be the small type used for filing cabinets. The keyring gave more choices, with several that could work on doors. I tried two before I came to the one that worked. I operated it with my left hand, pulling the box cutter out of my pocket with the right.

A prone figure lay face-down on the floor of the small supply closet, wrists and ankles bound with rope, hair matted over the face, clothing covered with dust. I retracted the blade on my weapon and stuck it back into my pocket.

"It's okay now," I murmured. "I'll get you out of here."

I knelt beside the dirt-covered form and rolled it toward me.

It was Trudie.

Chapter 28

Her eyes squinted tightly against the light and she groaned when I touched her.

"What happened, Trudie?" I asked. "Who put you here?"

Her mouth worked for a moment, then went slack. I felt her neck and found a fluttery pulse at her carotid artery. I tried to roll her onto her back but the closet was too tight. I'd have to get her out of here. I backed out of the tiny room and grabbed the rope at her ankles. She probably outweighed me by twenty pounds and the dead weight didn't make the job any easier.

Inch by inch, with a grip on her ankles, I dragged her out of the confinement of the closet. She wore an old, ratty running suit and sneakers so once I got the bulk of her body past the concrete floor in the closet and onto the smooth tile in the corridor she slid along much more easily. I rolled my former towel-weapon to form a pillow and cushioned her head with it, then I took the box cutter and cut away the ropes from her wrists and ankles.

Her breathing seemed shallow but steady. I grabbed another towel from the alcove and dampened it with cold water from the locker room. As I dabbed the cold towel on her forehead and temples, she stirred slightly and began to murmur. She didn't look like quite such a formidable enemy now.

"Trudie, it's Charlie. You're okay."

Mumbled words that didn't make any sense.

"Trudie, stay right here. I'm going to get help."

The nearest phone was at the reception desk. I'd left my cell in the room. I left Trudie on the floor with the cold towel on her forehead and rushed to the desk. What to do? I remembered the smelling salts Linda had used to bring me around. I'd try calling her first. With any luck maybe she hadn't already left for the meditation session.

She answered on the first ring. "Hey, where are you?" she asked.

"I never made it out of the spa. I found Trudie. She needs medical attention. Can you come or should I call an ambulance?" I gave her a quick description of Trudie's condition.

"I'll come. Give me three minutes. I just stepped out of the shower."

"You're a doll. I'll wait with her in the corridor outside the locker rooms."

I unlocked the main door and returned to the hallway. Trudie was lying where I'd left her, thrashing restlessly as if in a bad dream. I knelt beside her.

"Trudie, Trudie, calm down. Help is coming."

I stroked her arm and repositioned the wet towel, which had slipped.

She murmured something I couldn't understand.

"What, Trudie? What happened?"

More restless movement.

"Who did this?" I slapped lightly at the back of her hand. "Who were you meeting in the parking lot? Who left you that note?"

At the mention of the note and the parking lot, she mumbled louder. It was like she was still far away but had somehow come a little closer to me. I pressed the advantage.

"Trudie, come on, tell me who you went to see."

A mumbled word came out.

"Say it again, Trudie. I didn't hear you."

"Dav—David." More mumbled words came, something I took to mean "I went to meet David."

Puzzling. I thought he was at Drake's deposition. I repeated his name and she nodded ever so slightly.

"Don't worry about it," I said. "We've got help coming." I could hear sounds in the reception area now. "Back here, Linda," I called out.

A commotion sounded behind me and I looked over my shoulder to see Linda, wearing hastily donned sweats and a T-shirt and carrying her medical bag. Shirley bustled along behind her, dressed for the evening's social gathering in a gauzy purple skirt and beaded purple top. She'd fluffed her curly brown hair and even added a touch of lipstick.

Without a word, Linda knelt beside Trudie. She felt for a pulse and ran her hands along the sides of Trudie's face and neck, much as she'd done for me. Trudie's eyes began to flutter open. I stood up and backed out of the way.

"Can you hear me?" Linda asked. "Do you feel pain anywhere?" Her expert hands continued to examine, checking her patient's arms and legs as she spoke.

"No, I . . ." Trudie croaked. "Water—"

"In a minute," Linda said. She turned to me. "I don't think anything's broken."

"I'll get it," Shirley offered. She headed toward the reception area and returned a minute later with a small paper cup.

By this time Trudie had managed to sit up and she took the water gratefully. Her hands and face looked grimy with dirt from the closet floor and her hair stuck out in wild gray tangles. She appeared shaken and groggy—drugged?

Shirley found a wicker chair with a soft flowered cushion in the hot tub area and brought it into the hall. Linda and I took Trudie by the upper arms and helped her rise and get to it. She flopped onto the seat. I motioned Linda aside.

"What now?" I whispered. "Should we get an ambulance?"

"All they would do is take her to the hospital where she'd be admitted overnight for observation. I can do the same thing here, if she'll let me," she said. "Let's give her a few minutes to compose herself and I'll ask her."

I sneaked a look at my watch. Six-fifteen. No wonder Shirley seemed restless; Dr. Light would be well into his meditation session by now and here were three of their attendees, sidetracked. They'd made such a big deal of the special evening, I knew the size of the crowd would be important to them.

Linda knelt beside Trudie, talking quietly to her. The

patient looked better, a bit of color had come into her face now, although she still wasn't talking much. In Trudie's case that could be somewhat worrisome.

"Shirley, could you arrange for some soup to be sent to Trudie's room in about thirty minutes?" Linda asked. She looked to her patient for confirmation and got a small nod. "I'm going to sit with her for awhile and get her settled in for the night."

"I'm due back in Albuquerque tonight," I said, knowing this delay would set me back. "I'll help you get everything arranged before I head out."

Shirley didn't look terribly happy about the loss of three participants, but she didn't have much choice in the matter. She bustled away to handle her part of it.

"Come on, Trudie," Linda coaxed, "we're going to get you to your room."

She stood shakily and we slowly headed out.

A few minutes later, with Linda and Trudie settled into the room next door, I tossed clothes into my duffle. The experiences of this week had been interesting, to say the least, but I wouldn't be sad to see the last of Santa Fe for awhile. I planned to take a quick shower to wash off the closet grime, then pop in to say goodbye to Linda and to encourage Trudie to file charges against David for assault.

For my own part, I would phone the Santa Fe police on Monday and give them what I knew about David Ratwill and Robert Stanworthy. They could do with it as they wished.

Right on cue, I heard a sharp knock on the door to Trudie's room. "Room service," the voice called.

I stripped down and stepped into the shower. My spirits lifted as I soaped off the dust from the supply closet and fantasized about being at home again.

By the time I'd dried my hair, put on fresh jeans and sweater, and packed the last of my toiletries, I figured Linda and Trudie would be finished with their light supper. I phoned Drake and got voice mail. I left a message that I'd be on the road within fifteen minutes.

Leaving my bags in the room, I walked next door and rapped lightly at Room 14. C'mon, c'mon, I thought, tapping my foot. I knocked again, louder. "Linda, it's me." A frisson of unease shivered down my spine.

"Linda! Trudie! Open up!" Nothing.

I looked up and down the hall. Nothing seemed out of place. Where had they gone? Linda would not take off without telling me. At the very least she would have left a message on our phone.

I let myself back into Room 12 and found the card key I'd gotten earlier for the other one. Something told me to take along my gun and I tucked it into the waistband of my jeans. Every nerve ending went taut as I stuck the key into Trudie's lock.

My eyes scanned the room and I knew my fears were justified. Linda's medical bag had fallen off the desk; stethoscope and vials spilled over the carpet. The room service tray lay on its side against the table's legs. Thick bean soup ran down one wall, the bowl smashed in shards on the floor below. The lick of fear at my spine congealed into a hard place low in my gut.

I grabbed the phone, punched 9-1-1. "Two women have been abducted. Get the police here *now*!" I held on just long enough to confirm that they had the address before I slammed the instrument down and dashed out of the room.

Which way did they go? I debated for a second and

decided to try the rear exit, the one to the courtyard. I'd just reached the end of the hall when I heard a noise behind me.

Chapter 29

I whirled, reaching for my gun.

Gerald Mayhew's eyes grew large as he spotted me. I quickly concealed the weapon. "Gerald! Quick, come with me. I can use some help."

He glanced back once and walked toward me slowly.

"Linda and Trudie are gone," I said, my breath coming in quick bursts.

He raised his shoulders in a small shrug.

"It's David Ratwill. He's got them."

Puzzlement and anger crossed his face at the same time but he jogged the remaining length of the hall.

"It happened within the last ten minutes," I said, shoving open the door to the courtyard. "I'm hoping they haven't gone far."

Soft landscaping lights highlighted rocks and trees within the short adobe wall. Beyond that, dusk faded to black.

Suspecting that they'd head for a vehicle, I told Gerald I'd take the parking lot and I sent him to check the lobby. "Don't get physical with him," I cautioned. "I don't know what he'll do. If you can, just keep him there until the police arrive." I trotted toward the parking area, leaving Gerald looking like he wasn't quite sure what he'd gotten into.

As I passed the low adobe wall I couldn't help but look over it, at the place where Rita had gone down. It had to be David. I'd known from the beginning that there was something off when he'd showed up here. Poor Rita had known he was a threat to her, yet she'd been unable to do anything about it. Now he had Linda and Trudie and there was no telling what desperate measures he might take. I scanned the dark slope, looking for any sign of movement. In the deepening gloom I could make out only the dark blobs of trees and occasional tufts of yellow-blooming chamisa.

On toward the parking area I kept up a quick jog, trying to look every direction, watching for motion in the shadows and possible hiding places. The path narrowed, lit only by small sidewalk lights every twenty feet or so.

The overhead lighting in the parking lot was adequate for a person to locate a car, but hardly enough for me to tell whether someone was hiding out here. I skirted the edge, wary of another trap, watching for movement. At the far end of the second row I spotted a woman getting into a car.

"Joanne!" I ran up to her. "Can you help me?" I quickly gave her the same version I'd given Gerald. "We've got lots of ground to cover. Can you help me check out this side and the front of the building?"

Bless her, she didn't question me. She tossed her purse into her car, locked it, pocketed the keys and followed my lead. We edged the rest of the parking area, then headed down the long driveway that led from Casa de Tranquilidad to the main road. Small landscape lights shone up into some of the trees; otherwise it had become pitch dark out here. I wished that I'd thought to find a flashlight to bring. Joanne and I took opposite sides of the wide drive, alert for any sign of movement out in the blackness. How far could they have gone?

I knew a moment later. Ahead, in a wide spot in the road, a tiny light caught my attention.

"Joanne!" I stage-whispered. "Hold back. Get out of sight and be quiet." I pointed to the light. "If things start to get ugly, head back to the lobby as fast as you can. I've called the police already. Wait for them."

It was good advice and I should have taken it myself, but I couldn't let David take Linda away. That small dome light told me he was about to force the two women into a vehicle and then they'd be gone. I stepped to the soft grass at the dark edge of the drive and approached carefully, reaching for the Beretta's grip.

I got to within twenty yards when I heard their voices. I tiptoed closer, trying to make out the words. David held a gun on Linda; he jerked his head toward the Suburban, indicating for her to get inside. She stood her ground, her stocky body and legs-apart stance telling him she wouldn't go willingly. I felt proud of her.

Trudie stood by David's side, an eager look on her face. What the hell was she thinking? Trying to curry favor with the man who'd earlier left her for dead in a storage closet? Or going along with her partner? A confusion of possibilities rushed into my mind but I put them aside. Right now I had to get Linda out of this.

I watched David's body language. He held the gun casually, like a man who wasn't used to handling a weapon. Although he waved it at Linda, his grip didn't look firm. Could I disarm him without his getting a shot off first?

Trudie presented an unknown. She might turn on David, but I doubted it. At best, she might cave. At worst, she could easily turn on me. I edged closer, fifteen yards away now. I held the Beretta in front of me and flicked off the safety.

David's back presented an easy target to me. Despite the meager light, I had the advantage of close proximity and surprise. I could take him out.

Ron had asked me, when he began teaching me to shoot, whether I'd be able to kill a person if the situation arose. I didn't know then and I still didn't know. But I knew I'd be making that decision within the next few seconds. My hand wavered then steadied. He'd killed once. If he became more aggressive with Linda or if he turned on me, I could do it.

I went over the steps in my mind, back at the target range. My hands went automatically to my two-handed grip, the gun was hot, safety off. I lined up the sights, gauging distance and angle.

Linda's gaze flickered toward me.

Oh, god, this might be the moment.

David didn't catch it. Linda returned her attention to his face, refusing to let her focus come back to me. Good girl.

"I said, get in the car!" he shouted. That time it came through loud and clear. "Both of you!" He shook Trudie off like a mosquito.

This time Linda didn't resist. She climbed in and slid across to the far side of the big vehicle.

Trudie turned to David, a pleading look on her face. "I want to ride up front with you," she whined.

"Get in the b—" David looked at her but she was looking at me.

Oh shit. This is it.

He shoved her aside and turned his gun toward me. His frantic gaze darted about, trying to figure out whether I was alone. I couldn't afford to wait until he got off the first shot. I aimed high, hoping I hadn't misread him. My shot went right where I placed it, over his head, to the right of him, far into the forest.

Trudie screamed and hit the ground.

David's face crumpled in an almost comical way. His arms fell to his sides.

"Drop the gun! Way out there, in front of the car!" My voice came out much firmer than I'd anticipated and he obeyed. "Trudie! Face down on the ground, spread those arms!" She, too, followed instructions. I liked this.

"Linda, get out of the car and grab his gun. Come over here by me." Her white faced peered out of the dimly lit vehicle and she looked pretty shaky. "It's okay," I assured her. She did as I asked.

"David, down on the ground too. Over there." I waved the Beretta toward the front quarter of the Suburban. "Flat on your face, arms out."

"You can't—"

"Watch me." I re-aimed my gun and squinted to align the sights.

"You'll be in trouble . . . I'm a lawyer," he blustered.

"Good point." I fired another shot over his head,

pleased to see a wet spot form on the front of his pants. He dropped to the ground with a whimper.

<h1 style="text-align:center">Chapter 30</h1>

I'd just about let loose a few choice words for the Santa Fe Police Department when a cruiser rolled up the drive. I slipped my two spent casings into one pocket and the Beretta back under my jacket.

"Lay the gun on the ground and just tell your story as it was," I advised Linda.

By the time David whined about being fired upon, for which he had no proof, and Trudie babbled on with loads of incriminating testimony about how they'd planned to be together and how she would stick by David and visit him in the pen, the two officers were beginning to look harried. Linda pointed out David's gun on the ground and explained how he'd used it to abduct her from Trudie's room. I gave them minimal information and suggested that they check with Detective Gallegos in the morning. Meanwhile, they agreed that both David and Trudie should be held on suspicion until then.

The questions about my gun were starting to get a little tricky when my cell phone rang. I raised an eyebrow to the officer who'd been questioning me and he nodded assent to answer it.

"Where are you?" Drake asked. "You were supposed to be here an hour ago." He sounded worried.

"Little delay," I said. "I'm with the police now."

The officer beside me had heard Drake's voice clearly. Luckily, my husband knew better than to get into details over the phone.

"So, when will that be?" he asked, lowering his voice. I got the distinct feeling there was something important he wasn't telling me.

"I'm not sure. Soon?" I looked at the officer who was closing his notepad. "I hope?" He shook his head. "Maybe not."

"Call me before you leave Santa Fe." With that, he hung up.

I managed to stay composed until I'd given the officer my card, all my phone numbers, and my planned itinerary for the next two days. I confess that I fudged a little on the importance of my reasons for getting to Albuquerque, but it did gain me a smidgen of leeway.

It occurred to me that I might report some inside information to Ron and Drake. I turned back to the officer. "So, will David be in jail for a few days?"

He wagged his head in a somewhat hopeless gesture. "Don't bet on it. This guy has connections. I wouldn't be surprised if he's posted bond before I finish the paperwork tonight."

That was discouraging.

Linda was still in the middle of giving her statement when I left the driveway and made my way back to the resort. Gerald and Joanne, plus a small gathering of others from the conference, wanted all the juicy details but I put them off.

I managed to stay composed through all of that but as I gathered my bags and started to leave the room, I lost it. I set everything down and gave in to the shakes and the tears. I could have killed a man tonight.

More frightening was the fact that I knew I would have if he'd harmed Linda or turned on me. I'd been damn lucky he'd shown that flicker of hesitation, that moment which told me he was more afraid of me than I was of him. He'd killed his own wife—I still wasn't sure of all the reasons why—but against an armed opponent he'd backed down. Some people are like that.

I allowed myself a full ten minutes of self-indulgent blubbering. Then I washed my face and brushed my hair and composed my face.

I was rummaging in my purse for keys when Linda came in. We gave each other a tired stare and I felt the rims of my eyes prickle again. "I need to get going," I said.

"Nope. I don't want you out on the road," she said in her firmest doctorly voice.

"Linda, I already told Drake—"

"I don't care. It's an hour-long drive and you're too upset."

"I'm not—" But the anger in my voice made her point. I was too upset.

"Stay here tonight. Calm down. Let me give you a sedative."

Was the answer to everything found in a pill bottle? "No drugs," I insisted. "I'll be better off if I just . . ." I didn't know exactly what it would take.

"Okay then. Let's go to the meditation session. It's still going, and we could tiptoe in quietly."

I just couldn't envision sitting in a big crowd and managing not to scream in frustration, especially with Celeus Light in the room. My teeth gritted at the very idea.

"Linda, I just can't . . ." I started to say that I couldn't stand the phony leader, but managed to couch it in softer wording. She looked disappointed, but didn't argue. "You go. I'll be fine here in the room," I promised.

She didn't buy it. I would bolt the minute she left, and she knew it.

"Let's go have a bowl of soup or something light," she said. "I'm serious about you staying here tonight."

I wanted to pop out with a reminder that she's not my mother, a you're-not-the-boss-of-me comment, but I held it. "Let me call Drake first. He thinks I'm going to be on the road any minute."

She went into the bathroom while I placed the call. I speed dialed and asked him to give me a little more time. Despite the lateness of the hour I was still determined to break out of this place yet tonight.

Using the room phone I ordered two bowls of soup. Linda was right about that. I couldn't remember the last time I'd eaten and the lack of energy was dragging me down. I let her do the talking while we ate but something about the conversation with Drake kept nagging at me. I got the idea that there was still something he wasn't telling me, but didn't press it. Eventually, and when I wasn't quite so drained, I would figure out all of it.

Chapter 31

I awoke to the sensuous feeling of my body against my own sheets, the smell of Drake's aftershave lingering on the pillowcase next to mine. Unfortunately, he was not beside me.

Noises from the kitchen pointed me in that direction and I belted my cozy terry robe around me as I went.

"Hey there," he said, backing me against the fridge and kissing me. He tasted like blueberry muffins. Sensing my momentary distraction he pointed toward the kitchen table. My favorite mug, steaming with coffee, and a plate with two bakery muffins sat at my usual place. "Better have that so you can wake up. You were up way past your bedtime last night."

No kidding. It had been close to two a.m. when I drove

in and I'd barely kissed him and fallen into bed before going unconscious.

He topped off his own mug and rearranged the napkins in the holder. Set the salt and pepper shakers straight for the third time.

"What's the matter?" I asked once I'd downed one of the muffins and realized that he was working his way up to telling me something.

"Manuel Salazar, one of the mechanics who worked on Mike Walters' ship? He died yesterday. Pretty sure it was suicide."

"What? How—?"

"I don't know details. Rick Valdez got the call just as we were leaving the deposition yesterday."

"Why didn't you tell me last night?"

He shrugged. "It was late and you had a lot on your mind."

True, but he certainly could have interrupted me for this. I watched his fingers trace circles on the table for a minute.

"Hon, you're not somehow blaming yourself for this, are you?"

Another shrug.

"You can't have caused the guy to be *that* depressed. I mean, surely . . ."

"Maybe not depressed. Maybe he panicked. Maybe he thought we were about to haul him into court and accuse him of causing the accident. He was real nervous when Ron and I talked to him."

"But—" I couldn't think of anything else to say.

He exhaled loudly and stood up. "I know. I can't really

believe that I caused it but still—it's bothering me."

I walked over to where he stood staring out the window into the back yard. I put my arms around him and laid my cheek against the back of his shirt. Stroked his chest with my hands.

"Okay, your turn." He turned around to face me.

"My turn?"

"To spill the beans. There was a message on the home phone from a Detective Gallegos in Santa Fe," he said.

"What! Why didn't you tell me?"

"What happened last night with David Ratwill?" he asked. "And why did Gallegos want you to know he's out on bond. Out, why?"

"Let's make some breakfast and I'll fill you in." I had a feeling bacon and eggs would be a necessity.

I scrambled eggs and made them into sandwiches and carried two plates to the living room. Curled into one corner of the sofa I gave Drake time to reappear, freshly showered and wearing a soft pair of flannels and a T-shirt, before I launched into the full recount of the week's events. From the threat on the massage table to my bump on the head in the parking lot, I went over it all. He stopped me once in awhile to clarify some minor point, but mainly he let me talk. He actually let out a little snicker when I told him about David wetting his pants as the shot went over his head.

"And David Ratwill, the same attorney who's been ragging me over the helicopter crash, probably killed his own wife and is now out on bond?" He was pacing the living room by now, unable to relax and just enjoy my little tale.

I nodded and drained the last of my coffee while Rusty cleaned up the scraps of toast and egg from my plate.

"I'm going to have a hard time not punching him out when I see him, you know," he told me when he finally finished pacing.

"And what good is that going to do?" I set the mug on the coffee table. "I don't know for a fact that it was David who knocked me out or who locked up Trudie. In fact, I don't see how it could be, now that I look back at it. Even if he'd raced out of your deposition, he couldn't have made it back to Santa Fe and up to Casa de Tranquilidad in under an hour. Someone else must have done that little bit of dirty work."

He stopped with a jolt. "But David left the deposition early. I wasn't told why, but the other attorney from his firm handled the questioning all afternoon. David could have easily been back in Santa Fe."

Now I felt myself go still inside. All along, I'd felt that David was the one who pushed Rita, but until he held Linda at gunpoint I never quite fully believed that he'd also come after me and after Trudie. I'd been sure that her fantasies about David were just that. Now I had to rethink that whole idea.

"Did Gallegos want me to call him back?" I asked.

"Didn't really say. The message is still on the machine if you want to go listen."

I checked it and wrote down the number he gave, which matched that of the police station from his business card.

"I've got to go out to the airport and re-examine that helicopter wreckage," Drake said. "Do you want to come along?"

"Unless you think I know something about the engine that you don't, I better stay here and return Gallegos's call."

As it turned out, I decided to get my thoughts together before talking to the Santa Fe cop. Last night's events were still eating at me. First thing I did was to retrieve the memory card with the documents I'd stolen off Stanworthy's computer. I couldn't think of him as Celeus Light once I was away from the insulated atmosphere at Casa de Tranquilidad. The guy was a businessman, no matter what his followers might want to think, and I had to believe the meeting with David Ratwill that I'd accidentally witnessed days ago at McDonald's was going to be key to some kind of connection with Rita.

How could it not be?

Rita works in David's office for several years before their split-up. She's institutionalized for awhile—manipulated by David—then shows up a couple of years later working at Light's place as a yoga instructor. At the same time, Trudie the now-out-of-work nurse just happens to enroll in the Lightness conference? And Trudie has a huge infatuation with David. It was all too much.

I ruminated over all this as the pages of the document printed. The money transfers offshore were huge—I added up the various amounts shown on Stanworthy's spreadsheets. Setting that aside for the moment, I took out my little pocket spiral notebook and a large yellow pad. I transferred the few notes from the spiral and filled in the gaps, detailing everything in sequence, from the warning I'd received in the massage room to my own knocked-unconscious episode in the parking lot, to the showdown in the woods. David's peeping episode into Trudie's window was curious, to say the least, and I had to wonder at her insistence that it had been David she was meeting when she was lured to the locker room and stuffed into the closet. Later, when I caught up with them in the woods, she hadn't been afraid of David; she'd actually been hanging all over him as though the two of them planned to run away together.

And Rita. What truly was the story there?

If David had pushed his wife over the wall to her death, why on earth had he come back to Casa de Tranquilidad several more times? Logic would seem to tell me that a killer would stay away. But then, they always say that the murderer returns to the scene of the crime. My head felt fuzzy, trying to sort it all out.

The phone rang just then and I realized it was noon when the caller turned out to be Drake. He asked if I had planned on his coming back for lunch and seemed relieved to have the extra time without having to come home. Said he was finding the evidence he needed and would probably be there a couple more hours.

Drake's call reminded me that I hadn't reached Gallegos in Santa Fe yet. But I wasn't quite ready to talk to him. The fact that he hadn't been able to hold David Ratwill, even a day, bothered me as surely as all the strange links in the case.

My notes were piling up and I felt as though the answer had to be here somewhere. I just couldn't figure out where.

Rusty began to nudge at my leg and I realized he hadn't been out in hours.

"Let's go for a walk," I said. The magic word was 'walk' and he headed for the front door. I grabbed my jacket and his leash and we walked toward the park two blocks away. The autumn sky was brilliant with its typical deep blue and I wondered why on earth I'd spent the whole morning indoors. We might have another month or so of this fabulous weather before winter set in. I needed to make the most of it.

I willed all thoughts of the case out of my head, clearing space for answers, I hoped. We circled the park and found it deserted. The neighborhood is still mainly older people and they tend to stick pretty close to their own territory. The real outdoor girl of the whole lot is Elsa, with her huge garden every year. I let Rusty off the leash and he sniffed at the ground for awhile.

"Hey old man," I teased as I clipped the leash back on, "let's head home."

He trotted beside me, sprightly enough, and drank about three quarts of water when we got back to the house. I debated making myself a little lunch but the two muffins and egg sandwich had taken their toll on my appetite. I went back into Drake's office, where I'd left all my papers piled on the desk. The dog eventually came in and flopped down beside me, with all the energy of an old rag.

Lethargy was trying to set in and I dropped into Drake's desk chair and began to gather my pages. Two unmarked folders lay there and I absently flipped one of them open. There was my answer, staring me right in the face.

Chapter 32

It took me a minute to place the face. The maintenance man who'd been around Casa de Tranquilidad. He'd stepped into the yoga room, looking for Rita, the first day. I'd passed him in the corridor at least once, near Trudie's room. The unkempt blond hair and four-day beard growth were the same in the photo. It was a mug shot. The attached report showed an arrest four years earlier for trafficking in stolen merchandise.

I dialed Drake's cell phone and he picked up immediately.

"Leo Malone?" he said, once I'd described how I found the picture. "He's the mechanic who is probably behind our crash. We think he failed to safety wire that engine nut and then conned Manny Salazar into signing off the maintenance record. That mug shot comes from an arrest for dealing in stolen aircraft parts. He got a year probation and a fine."

"I think he's tied in with Rita's death."

"He knows David Ratwill. Ron and I saw them meeting."

A few more pieces fell into place.

I dialed the number for Detective Gallegos in Santa Fe.

"Before you even get started, Ms. Parker, I'll let you know that we weren't able to hold David Ratwill. Brought him last night, but the most we could charge him with was aggravated assault. He never took Dr. Casper off the resort grounds, so we can't really make a case for kidnapping. And Trudie Blanchard refuses to press any charges against him at all. She says they are in love and were just planning to go away together. Your whole story about him tying her up and leaving her in a closet—she won't confirm it."

I gritted my teeth, almost wishing I hadn't rescued her.

"He's already out on bond today and making threatening noises about pressing charges against you for shooting at him."

Not surprising.

I didn't give up. "I think he had an accomplice. Leo Malone. He's got a record. Malone is implicated in causing a helicopter crash a couple of years ago. It's also connected with David Ratwill."

There was a minute of silence, during which I could hear computer keys clicking in the background.

"Yeah, I got something here on Malone. Last known address is Albuquerque. That's out of our jurisdiction. I don't think I can do anything about him."

What about various departments working together? What about actually trying to solve this crime? I wanted to demand answers but felt on shaky ground still about the shooting incident.

He'd closed up by then anyway, and he ended the call by telling me there was nothing more he could do.

Chapter 33

My blood pressure spiked—I could feel it. Why did I let the detective get to me like that? I leaned back in the chair and stared up at the ceiling, letting my head hang back. Tried sitting upright and meditating for a couple of minutes but my mind was racing. Linda probably never would get me to be disciplined enough for this. Shirley had tried to teach us well. Why wasn't I getting it?

Shirley. A scene popped into my head. Standing in Shirley's office, a casual mention of Rita's personal belongings, a tote bag on the floor. She'd told me that the police left Rita's things with her, at the conference center.

Now that the conference was over, could I catch her in time?

I grabbed for the phone, fumbled it, shuffled through

papers until I found the number.

"Shirley?" My voice came out kind of squeaky when the female voice answered. It was Nicki but she put me through.

"Shirley, do you still happen to have Rita Ratwill's belongings?" I blurted out the question without even introducing myself, but I backtracked and tried for the niceties.

"I think so, Charlie," she said. "Let me check . . . um, wait a minute." I heard drawers and doors thunking. "Here it is. I'd put it away in my credenza."

"The police in Santa Fe don't seem to have enough evidence to get serious about an arrest, and I'd really like to look through Rita's things. Something in her tote bag might provide me some clues." The minute I mentioned the police, I wished I hadn't. She might decide to turn it over to them instead.

But she didn't seem to care about that.

"I'm leaving in about fifteen minutes to drive some of our people to the Albuquerque airport. I could meet you somewhere. But I don't have much leeway in time. A couple of the flights have tight connections."

"Which airline? I'll meet you near the check-in counters."

A little over an hour later I was sitting on a little ottoman-type bench near the entry doors when she came in. I watched her shepherd three people toward one airline's counter and a couple more to another. She had Rita's tote bag and purse over one arm. A quick greeting and she handed them over, glad to be rid of the extra weight.

Much as I wanted to dig right in, I drove all the way home and put the purse and tote on the dining table before opening either one. When I dumped the contents, the purse appeared to contain a woman's normal collection of junk—wallet, keys, lipstick, a hairbrush, two old shopping lists with the items crossed off, some breath mints, two ballpoint pens.

The tote bag contained her teaching materials, mainly cassette tapes. A sweater, headband, a spiral notebook. I spread the tapes across the table, a motley collection of home recordings mixed with professional ones. Most were labeled with Sanskrit-sounding words.

One tape was not labeled.

I found a tape player and popped it in.

Chapter 34

R ita's voice came through. A whisper, scared. Not the pushy dominatrix from our yoga classes.

"David's guy . . . that Leo . . . he's stalking me. I've seen him twice when I'm out shopping. Once I was in my car and saw him in a big white pickup truck. He drove right up behind me to freak me out." A loud sigh and long pause. When she spoke again the voice was ragged.

"He's really scaring me. I think he's going to kill me."

She paused for a full minute but didn't stop the tape. I heard whishy sounds, as if she were pulling a blanket around her. "In case he does get me, I think I better tell the whole story."

Again, a pause as she gathered her thoughts.

"David is moving money offshore. He put a lot of it

in my name, thinking he would avoid taxes. But he knew I wanted to leave him and thought he could get rid of me by sticking me in that place. While I was in there he did something else with the money. I never found the records—"

A sudden thump sounded on the tape and she shrieked.

"Oh, Cleo, what are you doing?" Her voice became tender and a cat's meow explained the interruption.

She spoke to the cat for a few moments before she seemed to remember the tape.

"Where was I? Oh yeah, David and the money. I don't know if that's the reason Leo is following me now. I heard something else . . ."

My interest perked up.

"After I got out of the hospital David insisted I work in his law office. He acted nice, made it sound like he really wanted us to be closer again. I think he just wanted to keep tabs on me, to make sure he knew where I was all the time."

I was still a little fuzzy on the time frame here, trying to remember how long Rita worked for David. But her voice pulled me back to the tape.

"One night I was there later than David thought. He'd told me to go home at five and start making dinner. But there was some extra filing . . . I'd gotten behind and it made him mad. So I stayed that night because I knew he had a conference call and wouldn't go home right away. While I was in the file room I heard the back door open and David went to greet someone. It was Leo, but I didn't know that at the time. I mean, I didn't know Leo.

"David didn't invite him in. They just stood by the back

door and talked. And I was just on the other side of the wall from them. I stayed really quiet."

The cat meowed again. I wished *it* would stay really quiet.

"Leo said some stuff about his job as a mechanic. Then something about a helicopter crash. I remember that because David answered him back like, 'yeah, it was a mistake, that's what you'll say.' Kind of wink-wink, nudge-nudge, if that makes sense. But Leo didn't like it. He said he better leave the state. He wanted to just get away. David said that Leo couldn't leave yet because there was still that other matter—that's what he said, that *other matter*... Then he said they'd talk about it tomorrow and he kind of shoved Leo out because the phone was starting to ring and it was that conference call." She sighed loudly on the tape.

"So, anyways, I just stood there like a statue and I heard the back door close and then I heard David talking on the speaker phone and once it seemed like he was busy with that, I went really quietly back to my desk and got my purse and keys and started to get the heck out of there . . . and then, oh god, this is so dumb . . . I bumped my desk and a coffee cup crashed on the floor, and then David called out but the people on the line were asking him what's wrong and so he didn't come after me— But he knew it was me, I know he did, and I know he figured out that I'd heard him talking to Leo. The money from that big chemical lawsuit is gone—he's moved it somewhere. He'll just disappear and, no one will ever know what he did. I'm scared. I don't know what to do . . ."

She must have gone home and packed her things. Made the tape as insurance. I picked up the cassette case again to see if there were any markings on it. A date, anything. But there wasn't. I tried to create a timeline of events but I couldn't be sure. I could guess that the Ratwills, once Rita was released from Peaceful Haven, had moved to Santa Fe—maybe as a place to hide awhile from California authorities—who knew? She'd worked in David's office for a few weeks or months until she overheard David's conversation with Leo, then clearly she felt that she had to get out.

But instead of going very far away, she'd stayed in town and just picked a new career—dumb move. Why hadn't she moved across the country, changed her name, really disappeared? Remembering Rita's flighty ways and disorganization I guessed that she just didn't plan that far ahead. Now we would probably never know. Her guess that David and Leo would try to get rid of her, though, seemed accurate. I couldn't prove who gave the actual push over the wall, but I knew one of them did.

Chapter 35

I knew the Santa Fe police weren't going to take the investigation any further than they'd already done. Why? In a town that size, you never knew. Maybe David's law firm wielded some influence, maybe the cops were satisfied with their accidental-death ruling and didn't want to put in the extra work. But Gallegos's statement that Leo Malone lived outside their jurisdiction was the real clincher. Case closed for them.

I tapped my pen on the dining table.

Well, if Santa Fe wouldn't work the case because Malone lived in Albuquerque, then I would get the Albuquerque police involved. I caught Ron at the office and got the direct phone number for Kent Taylor, the homicide detective who is really my one and only inside link at APD.

It took about twenty minutes but I laid out the whole story—Rita's fall, David and Leo both hanging around the resort, how a huge amount of money from the AceChem settlement had disappeared, the weird relationship that seemed to exist between Trudie Blanchard and David. I even told about the confrontation in the woods, although I glossed over the fact that I'd actually fired my gun. Told him what Gallegos had told me about closing the case.

He asked a few questions but otherwise didn't interrupt as I basically related everything that had happened during the last week, including the fact that David's law firm was trying very hard to get a huge settlement in the helicopter case. My opinion was that David couldn't resist one last big-money score, but that he was certainly taking a risk if he was hoping that Rita's death would be ruled accidental. With Santa Fe PD dropping their investigation he probably felt pretty safe now.

Over the phone I could hear Taylor hitting a few keys on a keyboard. "There's a note in the database that the police questioned you about firing a weapon, Charlie."

Uh-oh, the one area of shaky ground for me. "I don't think they found any evidence of that, except that Mr. Ratwill was somehow frightened into wetting his pants. I suppose he could pursue me in civil court if he wants that fact to become public."

Kent didn't seem to see the humor in that. "Well, if Santa Fe PD wants a signed statement from you, we'll call and you can come downtown."

I certainly didn't relish that idea—at all. I hung up, a little less sure of myself.

Deciding I'd done about all I could for the moment, I gathered Rita's belongings back into her purse and tote bag.

Maybe I could find someone at Casa de Tranquilidad who knew how to contact whoever should get her things.

I set the two bags in the guest room and headed to the kitchen.

There were still a ton of unanswered questions. Who really pushed Rita? What was David's connection with Leo—I mean, why did Leo show up at David's office to tell him about the helicopter's maintenance records? Was this before or after David's firm had taken that case?

And of course I had to ask myself—what was I going to make for dinner?

Since I'd been away for most of the week, and poor Drake had fended for himself, it kind of fell to me to be the provider tonight. Other than Elsa's bag of tomatoes, I wasn't seeing a lot of options in the fridge. Rummaging in the cabinets netted me a package of spaghetti and jar of sauce. A quick trip to the store and I could add a salad and some garlic bread and call it good. Drake would undoubtedly be able to add some extra things to a bottled sauce to make it truly fabulous, but that was a little beyond me at this moment. I grabbed my keys and wallet and convinced Rusty that he didn't really need to go along on the ten-minute trip.

There's a little market just a few blocks from the house, which is a lot more convenient than any of the huge chain supermarkets—a quicker trip and fewer parking hassles— so that's where I headed. I told myself to drop all thoughts of the investigation, including the nagging possibility that a lawyer like David Ratwill would most certainly be the type who would haul me into court in a heartbeat.

I let myself revel in the variety of fresh lettuces and I acted like a real connoisseur of fine produce as I checked for the very best cucumbers in the bin. Since I'm completely missing the gardening gene, this is about as close to the farmer instinct as I ever get. I chose my salad ingredients, grabbed a fresh baguette in the bakery section and headed back toward my Jeep.

The rest of it happened in a blur.

I'd barely clicked the remote door lock when I sensed movement behind me. A white van. An iron-like grip clamping my arms to my sides. My feet leaving the ground.

Chapter 36

Drake walked around the engine wreckage one more time then shut off his digital camera. He'd probably taken four dozen close-ups of the parts in question, with at least half of those focused on the place where the missing nut should be. Every conceivable angle, every properly wired bolt to show the contrast with the one improperly done. Would it be good enough evidence to convince the attorneys—who could guess? His head was beginning to pound.

He arrived home to find Rusty anxiously waiting by the front door, no sign of Charlie.

"Hey, boy." He rubbed the dog's ears. "Didn't you get your dinner yet?"

Keying on the important word, Rusty spun and headed

for the kitchen. His dish was empty but that was no surprise. This wasn't a critter who left spare food lying around. Drake supposed a little more wouldn't hurt so he scooped a few nuggets. Charlie could let him know whether to add more later.

Where was she anyway? A kettle of water sat on the stove, cold. With the package of spaghetti and an unopened jar of sauce on the countertop, it was pretty clear what her intentions were for their own dinner. Maybe she'd gone next door to borrow something to finish it out.

He walked into their bedroom, didn't see her, spent a couple of minutes washing his face and combing his hair, went back to the kitchen and pulled a beer from the fridge. Debated walking over to Elsa's house, but it looked dark over there. Settling in front of the TV sounded more appealing than getting hooked into female conversation at this moment. He headed toward the living room when the blinking light on the answering machine caught his attention and he set his beer down.

"Ms. Parker, this is Cindy at Hudson's Market? We wanted to let you know that a customer found your wallet out in the parking lot and turned it in. We'll have it at the customer service desk for you. Thanks."

Charlie's wallet in a parking lot? The hairs on his neck rose.

Chapter 37

I fought panic, trying desperately to think, to calmly rationalize my situation and decide what to do. But with duct tape wound around my ankles and wrists, and strips of it over my eyes and mouth leaving only my somewhat stuffy nostrils to grant me a scant amount of musty air, terror loomed right at the surface. I felt about a nano-second from completely losing it.

The one rational thought that I could conjure up was that I would probably lose all my eyelashes when that tape was ripped off. I nearly laughed at the sad realization that this was suddenly important to me, but I couldn't even grab enough air for a small chuckle to form.

Get a grip, Charlie. If nothing else, just take stock.

I was in the back of a white van—I knew that much.

There were two men. I could hear their voices, vaguely sensed both of them, although I'd not gotten a look at their faces.

Grabbed from behind and dragged into the vehicle, I'd barely had a chance to kick out before the shock of having my eyes taped, then my mouth. One of them sat on me and bound my ankles, adding another wrap at the knees, while the other taped my wrists and then looped that wrap around the one at my knees. I felt like a trussed bird waiting for the ax on the neck. All those sick news stories filled my head with lurid details of women whose bodies were found out on the mesas. Raped, murdered, buried in shallow graves. Hopelessness threatened to simply take over but, instead, the images just made me mad.

I'm not a victim type. I'm very careful, very aware of my surroundings. Always. I'd not been overburdened with bags nor was I daydreaming when they grabbed me. The horrifying thing was how fast it all happened. The squeal of the tires, the steely grip that disabled me. I forced myself to relax my muscles and pulled in all the air I could get. My head cleared a little.

The men's voices seemed far away. They were both up front, while I must be at the back of the van's cavernous interior. I scraped my face against rough carpeting, trying to catch the edges of the tape. A dozen or more firm brushes and I felt the tug of adhesive on carpet. The tape at my eyes was sticking to the floor so I rolled with it and got it peeled away from one eye. I was right—pulling out the lashes really did hurt like crazy.

Two solid blinks and I gained a little focus. My guess about the two men was correct. The larger man was driving—blondish or light brown hair haloed by the setting sun outside. We were heading west, and the steady thunk-thunk-thunk made me think of the sound of tires on a bridge. And if that were the case we were probably on I-40, crossing the Rio Grande. They were conversing but the noise level was too great for me to hear them.

I used the same carpet-rub maneuver to expose my mouth and sucked in deep breaths. Even the combination of carpet fibers, dust, and something like old motor oil that lingered in the air seemed like an elixir. I filled my lungs and exhaled, several times, feeling stronger immediately.

If only I could get the tape off my hands . . .

I put my proven method to work again, but we'd now left the evenly-paced speed of the interstate and I had a hard time not rolling side-to-side as the van took an exit ramp a little too fast, sped up for a brief time, then squealed the brakes for a traffic light. I lay very still, guessing that this would be the moment when one of them would look back to check on me.

I don't know whether they did. The light must have changed because we lurched into motion again. I pictured the layout of the city's west side. Coors Road was the most developed area, with many traffic signals and in the late afternoon, bumper to bumper traffic. The fact that we'd already stopped once made me think this is where we were.

The van turned, stopped, idled. Someone came up to the passenger's side and they talked through the window. I got a fuzzy impression of some kind of package being passed through, into the van. The third man walked away, we started moving again.

If they'd been smarter about getting rid of me they

would probably have driven farther west, out into more open space. Then again, I could be all wrong, I realized, as the vehicle picked up speed.

Chapter 38

"Ron, I need your help." He knew his voice sounded ragged but he couldn't seem to control that. He gave about a two-sentence synopsis, although for all he knew he might have babbled for minutes.

"Okay, Drake, I'm coming right over. She talked to Kent Taylor this afternoon. I'm going to call him on the way and see if he might know anything pertinent."

Drake paced the entire house. At his desk in the room he used for an office, he spotted the folder from his investigation, open to the mug shot of Leo Malone. He plucked the photo from the file, glanced around but didn't see much else that might be of use. It would be dark soon.

From the garage he grabbed two strong flashlights and a small toolbox that he kept on hand with basics. In the bedroom he yanked a sweatshirt from his side of the closet, then reached into Charlie's side and got one of hers too. She'd probably gone to the store wearing no more than jeans and a T-shirt on the warm autumn day. While he was at it, he picked up her favorite boots, some extra socks, a blanket that they sometimes added to the bed on cold winter nights. He stuffed it all into a duffle. Into his waistband he jammed his Colt .45, the pistol with which he was most accurate at the target range. Just in case.

Ron's Mustang roared up in the driveway. Why hadn't he noticed that Charlie's Jeep was gone when he first got home? He could have saved at least thirty minutes, maybe more, if he'd just been more alert.

Rusty waited at the door, wanting to go along. Drake debated. Would the dog actually be of help or would he simply get in the way?

The moment he opened the front door, though, Rusty pushed his way through and ran directly to Ron's car. Drake grabbed Charlie's jacket that hung on the rack by the door, slung the duffle over his shoulder and locked up after himself.

"Shall we take my truck? We might get off the roads."

"Sure." Ron opened the passenger door and gave Rusty a push toward the small back seat.

"What did Kent Taylor say?" Drake asked as he started the engine and put it in gear.

"Gave me some names. Leo Malone, David Ratwill. Is this somehow tied to our crash investigation?"

"I don't know. She mentioned that Ratwill was related to that yoga instructor who died out at the spa. She thought he might have had something to do with that."

"Yeah, she had me do some background work on several people at that place."

Drake had backed out of the driveway and realized that he didn't have a clue where to go first.

Ron filled in. "Let's start with the market where they found her wallet."

Five minutes later they pulled into the small parking lot that edged one side of the squarish cinderblock building. No windows faced the lot at all—they were all in the front, facing the street. At the small customer service desk they asked for the girl who had placed the call—Cindy.

"I didn't see anything myself," she said. "A customer came in with this wallet and said someone must have dropped it in the parking lot. Oh, and there were some keys." She reached into a drawer and pulled them out. They were definitely Charlie's and Drake felt his breath catch.

"Who was the customer? Would he or she still be here?" Ron asked.

"Oh, Mrs. Baca. She lives on the next street over. Usually walks here to do her shopping. She just picked up some bread and eggs and—"

"I don't want to be rude, but we don't need to know her whole list. We think my wife may have been kidnapped out there."

"Can we speak to Mrs. Baca?" Ron asked, his voice more normal than Drake could even hope for right now. "And how about anyone else who was in the store at the time—which other employees were here?"

Cindy finally seemed to grasp their rush. "I'm the assistant manager. Two cashiers are on duty." She nodded toward the busy checkout lanes. "The produce manager and butcher both go home earlier in the day."

"I doubt the cashiers would have seen anything outside," Ron said.

"You got that right. When you're checking out the customers you don't see anything but the groceries and the customer who's standing right in front of you. "Maybe Randy." She paged a young man, the only bag boy on the shift. He came forward, giving Drake and Ron a look, probably wondering if they were cops.

Once they assured him they were not going to hassle him, he opened up.

"Are you talking about the green Jeep that's been out there quite awhile? Where Mrs. Baca said she found the wallet?" He shuffled a little. "Well, the only thing I can think of was maybe an hour ago. I was pushing Mr. Guthrie's cart out for him and this white van just screamed out of the lot. It was near that green Jeep when I first saw it so I don't know if it's connected. But, man, that thing just peeled out and laid rubber."

"The van. That might be important, Randy. Was there anything painted on it? Signs, logos, business markings?"

The teen was shaking his head through all this.

"License plates. Did you notice at all?"

No flicker.

"New Mexico, or out of state? Can you picture anything in your mind?"

"New Mexico, I'm pretty sure. The old fashioned bright yellow ones with red letters. It made a left turn out of the lot, down at the far end, onto San Carlos street, so I got a good look at the side. No design or anything on it. It was just solid white, the kind without windows."

Drake was anxious to get moving.

"Oh, you know, there was one thing. It had two ladders on top of it. Like the cable guys have sometimes, or those installers for satellite TV or something."

"But no company logos."

"No sir, I'm really sure about that."

"The driver? Did you get a look?"

Randy scratched at his peach fuzz face and thought. "A man, seemed like a big guy. I don't know what he was wearing—I think a saw a red sleeve, like a windbreaker or something like that. And I *think* there was somebody else with him, in the passenger seat. I'm not really sure about that."

They thanked the kid and the manager and walked outside. Drake felt discouraged by so little information. "So, a plain white van with two ladders on top? Ladders that they could easily dump off anywhere. Maybe one person, maybe two."

Ron's cell phone rang and he snatched it from his jacket pocket. "Parker."

Drake watched anxiously as Ron um-hmm'd a few times then relayed what they'd just learned about the van.

He picked up the pace toward Drake's truck as he clicked off the call. "Kent Taylor called an APB. It's the closest thing to an amber alert they can do for an adult abductee. I gave him the info on the van—well, you heard that part. He already knew most of it. Ran registration checks for vehicles owned by our suspects and their employers. The FBO that Leo Malone works for owns a couple of white vans. They're thinking he may have borrowed one of them."

"And . . .? What are they actually *doing*?"

"He didn't say. Probably the best that they can."

"Let's get out to Double Eagle," Drake said. "We've got maybe an hour before it's pitch dark."

The trip to the far west side airport had probably never been driven so quickly. Still, with rush hour traffic and the distance they had to cover, Drake knew there would only be another thirty minutes of light—if they were lucky. He, Ron and the dog piled into the Jet Ranger and he cranked up.

"This may be a waste of time," he told Ron. "But I have to be doing *something.*"

Chapter 39

I didn't know how long we'd been driving, but it must be close to an hour by now. After the exit past the river, there had been a series of stops and turns, acceleration and then steady, highway driving for a long time. I could imagine that we might be back on Interstate 40 but really, I had to admit that I didn't have any real idea.

I continued to sneak blurry, one-eyed peeks toward the two men in front and, except for an occasional glance my way by the one in the passenger seat, they seemed pretty unconcerned about me. I guess they were thoroughly familiar with the wonders of duct tape and felt like I was pretty secure. I let them think that.

With my hands tied in front of me I could have wiggled enough to reach up and pulled off the rest of the strips covering my eyes and mouth, but that would definitely give away the fact that I was working my way loose. I'd rather they thought I was out of it.

Meanwhile, I rubbed at the wrist tape, picked at it, rubbed some more. I was making a little progress and from what I could tell by feel, they had only done a once-around loop there. It provided a glimmer of hope.

If only I had a sharp object. Unfortunately, I didn't have a single thing on me but my clothing—thank goodness I had that. My wallet and keys and the bag of groceries were no doubt strewn around the parking lot at the market. I latched onto the hope that someone would use that information to come looking for me, not to merely steal my identity. I used my one eye to scan the small portion of the van that I could see, but nothing presented a solution. So I continued to pick.

The van slowed noticeably. Oh shit. This is one case when the kid in the back does not want to get there any faster. I raised my head a little, trying to hear what the men were saying.

I caught one word—cops.

It wasn't the word they wanted, apparently, because the van suddenly whipped around, squealing and throwing me violently against the wheel well on the driver's side. I had a really bad feeling that we were headed into oncoming traffic.

<h1 align="center">Chapter 40</h1>

Drake was thankful that Ron had so willingly hopped aboard the helicopter with him, knowing that being airborne was not his brother-in-law's favorite state. However, being on the telephone was Ron's normal state, and he was handling it quite well. He'd gotten Kent Taylor to talk to someone in charge at APD who allowed them to use the police frequency, so they knew there were extra patrols around the city.

"Remind them that Leo Malone works in Gallup," he told Ron, who was currently working at getting APD to alert the state police to the situation as well.

From the radio chatter, Drake thought they were probably monitoring I-40 westbound, but mere hope wasn't enough. He'd set a heading to follow the interstate himself. If the white van had hit the freeway immediately and stayed—as he assumed they would—close to the speed limit, they couldn't be much farther than the town of Grants by now.

He kept the Jet Ranger about five hundred feet off the deck and scanned every vehicle.

Darkness was closing in fast.

Chapter 41

Oh. My. God. The van rocked dangerously. Squealing brakes and horns sounded outside. I waited for the impact that would surely kill me.

The van veered downward and I braced myself as well as possible to avoid rolling all the way to the front. I used the moment of noise and confusion to rip the last of the tape from my wrists, my eyes, my mouth. I was clawing for the ends of the pieces at my knees and ankles as we bounced across the dirt median and up the other side. This time I had no chance to stop myself from rolling out of control toward the back doors. A scream tried to form in my throat but I held it back. If those doors were to come open—I didn't want to picture the mass of Charlie-hamburger roadkill.

I kept picking at the tape ends, searching in the almost-complete darkness for a weakness that I could use to simply rip the stuff off my legs.

The van threatened to roll as it hit the upslope of the eastbound lanes. I gave up any pretense of remaining wrapped up and spread my arms to avoid slamming to the other side of the cargo space again. I was already going to be one big nasty bruise.

Up front there was a fair amount of cursing going on. The driver was clearly at the limit of his abilities and the passenger somehow thought that shouting his displeasure would change that.

I found a decent rip in the tape at my ankles and gave it a hard pull, savoring the sucking sound it made as it peeled away from my jeans. But the sound drew attention from the front. The passenger turned fully in his seat and stared at me.

It was David Ratwill.

Chapter 42

Almost calmly I told myself that I should have known who grabbed me. Ratwill and Leo Malone were really the only choice. All that self-talk about rape and abduction and identity theft seemed a little silly now. Clearly, the whole goal was murder.

That thought had roughly a tenth of a second to flit through my head before David barreled between the seats and came at me. He only failed to remember that a woman's strength lies in her hips and legs, and since mine were still tightly bound at the knees, I had a fairly good weapon right there. I kicked out and got him right in the face. His nose gushed blood, his eyes rolled back and he went down hard.

For good measure, I gave another solid kick to his left collarbone, but he was out cold—limp as a stuffed toy.

Leo managed to get the van somewhat under control and was standing on the horn to make other vehicles get out of our way. When David's dead weight landed with a crash Leo turned to look back at the ruckus.

Bad move.

The van went squirrely and began to shimmy hard. I rattled around in there a bit, and Leo's attention went right back to the road.

Red and blue lights began to flicker in the rearview mirrors.

I started to offer up a little thank-you prayer, but that turned out to be a little premature.

Leo regained control and floored it.

I found myself against the back doors again, grabbing around for anything that might save me from flying out the back if they came open. The van was completely utilitarian, unfinished on the inside, so there were some metal crossbars and struts along the sides. I ripped off my remaining duct tape and inched up the side of the cargo space gripping them whenever I could.

"You fool!" I screamed at Leo. "You'll never outrun them."

Doesn't this jerk watch TV?

He pulled a gun and aimed it over his right shoulder. That shut me up pretty quickly. I edged over to his side of the vehicle, figuring it would be harder for him to hit me at that kind of angle. Nudged David again but he was still limp as a rag. Beyond his body I got glimpses of a spare tire mounted to the side of the compartment, at the rear. And where there's a tire, there must be . . .

Yep, the tire iron was there, neatly fitted into a bracket.

I grabbed it and yanked.

I had no idea what I would do; clearly, whacking Leo from the back while we were moving at eighty-five miles an hour wasn't smart. I edged forward again, scooting my newfound weapon along the carpet with me.

Chapter 43

Drake stared out into the night. The last of the glow in the west was fading quickly. Ahead, the westbound stream of cars had slowed, brake lights flaring as drivers realized it.

"Man the spotlight," he called out to Ron, showing him the handle and switch. Ron tested it, getting the feel for aiming it.

"Something's going on. Looks like a half-dozen emergency vehicles, at least."

"I don't like it." He slowed airspeed as they caught up to the line of traffic.

"I think it's a roadblock."

Below them, a vehicle suddenly whipped out of the westbound lane, bumped its way across the median and climbed the embankment to the eastbound lanes.

"Shine the light! Is that our van?"

Ron worked the handle and finally spotlighted the one. Two ladders on top.

"What can we do?" he shouted toward Drake.

"Just keep the light steady. I'll hover right over it."

A couple of miles down the road he saw that two of the state cruisers had seen them. Lights blazing, they came after the van. The other traffic had pretty much come to a stop, cars pulling off to the sides everywhere.

"He's going close to ninety," Drake said. "I'm tracking him."

Over the radio he heard the pursuing officers order someone ahead to lay out the tire strips.

He held his breath. What would the strips do at this speed? What if the driver saw the strips in advance and went off the road? What would he do if they'd hurt Charlie?

Chapter 44

A bright light shone down on the van and I had the fleeting feeling that maybe heaven was calling me— one of those bright light in the tunnel things? Then I heard the overhead thrum of rotor blades and a huge feeling of relief rushed over me.

Unfortunately, Leo heard them too. He slowed down enough, barely, to take his eyes off the road for a second.

Pointing the gun at me he said, "I didn't think anything of bringing down one helicopter, you know. And pushing Rita over that wall wasn't too bad either. So don't think I won't shoot you and then take out your nosy 'expert witness' husband."

Threaten me all you want. But don't threaten to take away the guy who has made my life so happy.

Without hesitation I raised the tire iron and smacked his wrist. The pistol dropped behind the passenger seat and I snatched it up.

"It's time to stop the van, Leo."

Chapter 45

Linda Casper and I got together for lunch a week later. I'd spent the week babying my sore muscles and bruises, hiding my stiffness from her as best I could when we met up. I wondered again about the woman I'd run into at Casa de Tranquilidad, Samantha Sweet, whose brief touch had seemingly healed my head wound. I would have loved to see if the same magic worked on my current condition.

As we filled our plates at Soup R Salad's long salad bar, Linda asked how my interview with the police went. It took me a moment to shuffle everything in my mind and remember which interview she was talking about—there'd been so many. I'd watched through the glass as Leo Malone was interrogated, got to see his admission that he'd stalked Rita in Santa Fe at David's demand, blackmailed by David because of his involvement in the cause of Mike Walters' fatal helicopter crash. Gossip in the corridors at Casa de Tranquilidad had told him what he needed to know to track Rita's movements and catch her alone in the courtyard. In a maintenance uniform he'd blended in and gotten access to all parts of the spa and hotel. The police weren't convinced that Manny Salazar's death was suicide. Clearly, Malone saw Manny as a weak link, and may have chosen to eliminate him. That particular investigation was just beginning.

It was a confession of sorts, but realistically, if those two could have made me vanish before I had the chance to tell anyone else the whole story, they might have gotten away with everything—Rita's murder, Salazar's death, the helicopter crash, and skipping the country with the AceChem settlement money. Leo admitted that they came after me because I just wouldn't let it go.

Linda's question, I realized, pertained to the shots I'd fired at David Ratwill in the forest that final night in Santa Fe.

"I spoke to Gallegos on the phone. That was a real study in frustration."

David was still making noises about sticking some kind of civil rights violation on me, not to mention assault charges for what I did to him during the wild ride. I told the police the entire story about that, and they assure me that self defense allows a woman to do a lot against two armed abductors. That's reassuring.

Linda spoke up again. "Shirley has called me a couple of times and we've chatted. She's given me a couple of cookbooks on the vegetarian lifestyle and I'm adopting it."

"You are?" I smiled to take some of the utter surprise out of my voice. Linda's always been a girl who loved her burgers.

"Yep. I've lost six pounds already," she said, spreading her arms to show me her slimmer frame. "And my blood pressure's down a few points, too."

"Well, good for you." Although I couldn't see myself ever giving up Pedro's chicken enchiladas, I genuinely wished her luck.

"And have you heard anything about Trudie?" I asked.

"She's still locked away in the state mental hospital. Not much word from there, but one of the masseuses went up to visit her and said she just babbles about how much David loves her and how they're going to be together. That woman never did have much of a handle on reality, did she?"

Remembering the wild look in Trudie's eyes, I had to agree.

"Does Shirley say anything about Celeus Light's involvement in David's financial schemes?"

"Oh, no. He wouldn't be. He's way above all that. His seminars are more popular than ever. I've heard there was standing room only at his talk last week."

Oh boy. I stopped eating for a moment and reached across the table to touch her hand. "Linda, I don't want to step on your good spiritual intentions, but take my word for this. Celeus Light is not all he seems. There's a whole other side to the guy."

Something in her face closed.

"That's all I'm going to say. We learned some good things from his program. Just don't put all your faith in one person. Keep your eyes open."

She jabbed a chunk of lettuce and chewed it with vigor. Luckily, Linda isn't one to hold onto anger and her mood lightened considerably by the time we finished our meal and walked out to our cars. We hugged in the parking lot and she said, "Take care of yourself, girl. Lunch again on the eighteenth?"

"Yeah." I squeezed her hand and walked to my own vehicle.

At home, I found Drake organizing his desk. He looked as if a giant weight had come off his shoulders as he tucked his research documents into folders and stuck them away in a file box, labeled for delivery to Rick Valdez's office.

"Even though Mike Walters died in that crash, I'm glad we were able to clear him of any fault, " he said. "And I feel that the case being dismissed was the right thing. It wasn't the manufacturer's fault either. Leo will do jail time and he'll never get his mechanic's license back. That's about all the victims can expect."

"Didn't you say that all three men had life insurance?"

"Yeah. I know that doesn't replace a husband or a father, but neither does a million-dollar settlement. I just hope everyone is able to get on with their lives now."

"And us? Maybe we'll be able to put the worries behind us and get on with life too."

"Planning on it," he said. "Starting right now." He pulled me onto his lap and gave me a kiss that sent tingles clear to my toes.

More Charlie!

It's a terrible case of mistaken identity when a gang of bank robbers think that Charlie is a famous movie star. Disappointed with their take from the bank, they decide that a hefty ransom will be their ticket to riches. But what will happen when the real star steps forward? Charlie knows that only her wits will save her from this band of desperate men.
Get *Stardom Can Be Murder* now!

And . . . Connie is pleased to announce a new mystery series, featuring Samantha Sweet, the lady you met in this story, as the main character.
Sam breaks into houses for a living.
But she's really a baker with a magical touch, who invites you to her delightful pastry shop—
Sweet's Sweets.
Don't miss *Sweet Masterpiece*,
the debut book in this series!

Sign up for Connie's free email mystery newsletter and get announcements of new books, discount coupons, monthly prizes and the chance for some 'sweet' deals.

www.connieshelton.com

www.ingramcontent.com/pod-product-compliance
Lightning Source LLC
Chambersburg PA
CBHW071739190726
48292CB00003B/804